Praise for D. A. Mishani's Avraham Avraham series

THE MAN WHO WANTED TO KNOW

'Avraham is quiet, stubbornly impressive and the novel is full of insights into love and sex'   *The Times*

'Takes us into the hearts of these compassionately drawn characters. Sensitive, perceptive and quietly memorable'
                              Crime Club, Star Pick

'He writes in such a cool, one-paced style . . . Powerful insight . . . "Those Swedish and Danish cops, they're not real," Mishani seems to be saying. "My steady, plodding Israelis show what police work really is"'   *Jewish Chronicle*

A POSSIBILITY OF VIOLENCE

Winner of the Bernstein Prize
Shortlisted for the Sapir Prize

'Compelling . . . Morally complex and psychologically convincing, *A Possibility of Violence* is a terrifying and disturbing psychological drama'   *Sunday Herald*

'Definitely lives up to the promise of its excellent predecessor . . . Strong on police procedure and quotidian detail, with a refreshingly average and self-doubting protagonist, *A Possibility of Violence* is both tense and touching'
                              Laura Wilson, *Guardian*

'Mishani, with an almost frightening skill, succeeded to shatter the very intimate parts of my soul . . . This is such a difficult task to achieve for a detective story in general and for an Israeli one in particular, that I find it difficult to restrain the superlatives' *Time Out*

THE MISSING FILE

Winner of the Martin Beck Award
Shortlisted for the CWA International Dagger
Shortlisted for the Sapir Prize
Guardian Best Crime and Thrillers of the Year

'A wonderfully satisfying detective mystery, with a heart-breaking finale. A tense, gripping page-turner that I devoured in two days'

S.J. Watson, bestselling author of *Before I Go to Sleep*

'An assured debut, with a wholly unexpected resolution'
Guardian, best crime and thrillers of 2013

'Impressive! D.A. Mishani writes with profound originality and his main character is a quite remarkable man on the stage where detectives dance. Once again: impressive!'
Henning Mankell

'Marks the start of what could become a fine series of detective novels, centred on a striking detective – the lugubrious, self-doubting Inspector . . . Mishani's bittersweet story hums with humanity' *Daily Mail*

'A thoughtful character study of a good man deeply troubled by issues of innocence and guilt' *New York Times*

D. A. Mishani was born in Holon, in Tel Aviv, Israel in 1975. He has worked as the News Editor for Tel Aviv's leading daily newspaper, Haaretz, as the Editor-in-Chief of the Haaretz Book Review and as Editor of Israeli fiction and international crime fiction at Keter Books publishing house. He has taught at Tel Aviv University and at Cambridge. Now a full-time writer, he lives in Tel Aviv with his family.

The Missing File was a groundbreaking debut in its native Israel: a thriller that dealt not with national security but with crimes closer to the home. It was the first crime novel written in Hebrew to be shortlisted for the Sapir Prize, the Israeli Booker; the sequel, *A Possibility of Violence*, was the second. A French TV adaptation of the novels is currently being filmed, starring Gérard Depardieu as Inspector Avraham. Internationally, these first three books in the Avraham Avraham series have received unprecedented critical acclaim and been translated into eleven languages, publishing in fifteen countries.

THE MAN WHO WANTED TO KNOW

D. A. Mishani

Translated by
Todd Hasak-Lowy

riverrun

First published in Hebrew in Israel in 2015 by Achuzat Bayit
First published in Great Britain in 2016 by riverrun
This paperback edition published in 2017 by

riverrun

an imprint of

Quercus Editions Limited
Carmelite House
50 Victoria Embankment
London EC4Y 0DZ

An Hachette UK company

A CIP catalogue record for this book is available
from the British Library

Paperback ISBN 978 1 78429 6 933

10 9 8 7 6 5 4 3 2 1

Typeset by Jouve (UK), Milton Keynes
Printed and bound in Great Britain by Clays Ltd, St Ives plc

In memory of my father,
Mordechai Mishani
(10.4.1945–9.4.2013)

In Israel, weekends are Friday
and Saturday.

When half way through the journey of our life
I found that I was in a gloomy wood,
because the path which led aright was lost.
And ah, how hard it is to say just what
his wild and rough and stubborn woodland was,
the very thought of which renews my fear!
So bitter 't is, that death is little worse;
but of the good to treat which there I found,
I'll speak of what I else discovered there.

Dante Alighieri, *Inferno*

PROLOGUE

At the beginning of December a Boeing 737 landed at Ben Gurion Airport with a young woman onboard, her hair short and her eyes large and brown. Police Superintendent Avraham Avraham watched her from his hiding place while she passed through the glass doors and entered the arrivals hall, rolling a cart with three suitcases before her. Until the last moment he hadn't believed she would come, certain he'd be returning home alone. He looked at her from a distance for a moment longer before leaving his hiding place, and his eyes met her eyes, which had been searching for him among the crowd of greeters.

They had no great plans then for the future, except just living together for a few months. To discover each other again and only afterwards to think about what would come next. And they did indeed discover each other, slowly and cautiously, by casting the hidden glances of people used to watching. He learned that Marianka liked to shower early in the morning – and for a long time. When she eventually came out she would leave a small lake on the bathroom floor, with wet footprints leading to the bedroom. She found out that Avraham would sneak into the kitchen after dinner, when he thought she wasn't watching, in order to continue eating alone behind the closed door. Once their belongings were scattered around the apartment, Avraham tried to store the suitcases on top of the wardrobe in the bedroom, but since there wasn't enough space one case remained beside their bed for the entire winter.

Marianka asked to see his new office, and he took her there one Friday, in the morning, when the station was nearly empty. In contrast to his old room on the first floor, the office of the Head of the Investigations Division was spacious and looked out from the third floor on to Feichman Street, along which residential towers sprouted from the sand. He could look through the window at the grey morning skies or the cool evenings over the city where he was born. For the first time he was also able to light a cigarette in his office, but just then, of all times, he had given up smoking.

The winter was unpredictable, and once Avraham noticed how changes in the weather affected Marianka's moods he began reading the forecast each morning with trepidation. When the temperature dropped and rain fell she was happy. When the sky was clear and the air mild, almost warm, she told him about the snow in Brussels and was unable to hide from him the longing in her face and voice. This was actually the only thing that overshadowed his joy. During times of inactivity he would stand at the window in his office and wait for the rain for her.

At the end of February, when the news announced that the winter's last storm was approaching, they decided to take a day off to welcome it together. And they did just this, but a few hours after the start of the storm the murder occurred that changed their plans.

PART ONE: THE VICTIM

I

She saw the gun that night as she went up to persuade Kobi to come to bed or at least not sit outside in the cold. It was one o'clock in the morning and the weapon was lying on the table in the small utility room on the roof, but she didn't assign any importance to it because she was too hurt and exhausted and because she was afraid of so many other things. Besides, the gun wasn't a reason to be afraid; quite the opposite in fact. It was a source of security for her.

A few days later she recalled that night and understood. Everything could have happened differently had she watched Kobi more closely during those hours.

In the morning, when they were still in bed, it would have been impossible to know that this was how their last anniversary together would end.

Daniella and Noy woke up before them, scattered eleven balloons across the bedroom floor and jumped on their bed. When the girls went to get dressed and just the two of them remained under the covers, Mali drew close to him. She touched him from behind and whispered in his ear, 'Happy anniversary,' surprised when she felt his shoulders and back respond to her hands. His neck was warm from sleep and his cheeks unshaven. The storm's first rain could be heard through the window, and the girls had turned on the lights in the flat because the sky was dark. In the kitchen, a festive breakfast waited for them: orange juice the girls had squeezed themselves and croissants that they had bought the day before and warmed up. They were not allowed to boil water by themselves, so Mali made the coffee.

When they sat down at the table she saw that Kobi was tense, but she didn't say anything about the interview in front of the girls. She offered to iron his dark pants and white shirt, but he said that he'd do it himself before leaving, at noon. She didn't say anything else, not even when they were again alone in the bedroom, so that, if he didn't get the job, the disappointment wouldn't be too great, but when they said goodbye she kissed him on the lips and whispered in his ear, 'Good luck today.'

She took the girls to school and then had meetings until eleven.

In most cases only the husbands showed up, and even when the wives came they almost never said a word, but Mali tried to speak to them as well, like she always did, explaining to them too the differences between kinds of mortgages and the various payment possibilities. One of the men, whose wife's hair was covered with a kerchief, her face silent and pretty, stared right at her. He had a beard and his jacket, which he didn't remove, gave off a smell of mothballs and old, damp fabric. His wife rocked a blue buggy back and forth so that their baby wouldn't wake up. When he burst out crying she undid two buttons on her black dress and breastfed him in front of the two of them without shame.

Between eleven and twelve she didn't have any meetings, so she asked the branch manager for permission and went to buy Kobi a gift, even though they had agreed not to buy each other anything. She debated walking into town, but because of the storm she instead drove to the shopping centre. The streets were flooded and most of the traffic lights were out. And perhaps because of the unrelenting rain she decided to buy him an umbrella, to replace the one he had lost a few days earlier, and not a punching bag or a new button-down shirt for his interviews. At Zara the umbrellas were too expensive, but at For Men on the third floor she saw a black one with an elegant, wood-effect handle. The young salesgirl, whose fingernails were long and sharp and painted with shiny black nail polish, agreed to drop the price. She was so young, maybe still at school. Her hair was black and she wore black lipstick and had a piercing in her nose. When Mali entered she was reading a book, which she set face down on the counter.

After paying, Mali stared at her, maybe for too long, and when the salesgirl asked her, 'Is something wrong?' Mali just said, 'No, I'm sorry. Did you remove the sticker with the price?'

Kobi's interview was supposed to start at two, exactly when she finished her last meeting.

She imagined him sitting across from the interviewer, trying to mask his emotions. As always, he probably had no idea what to do with his hands. He'd spread them out on his knees and then rest them on the table, next to the pages of his CV, and then again under the table, in order to hide that his fingers were trembling. She didn't call

7

him before the interview, nor from the car on her way to pick up the girls. And since his car wasn't in the car park under their building she was sure he hadn't yet returned, but in the lift that took Mali and the girls to the seventh floor she could smell his aftershave. And the door wasn't locked like it was supposed to be.

She went into the bedroom and heard the water running in the bathroom. Their dog, Harry, was lying on the floor in a puddle of urine and didn't lift his head. And Kobi's keys had been tossed there next to him, along with the small satchel he took with him to meetings.

That wasn't a good sign.

It was only three o'clock and Mali had been sure he wouldn't be home.

The girls turned on the television in the living room and Mali cleaned up and made them something to eat. The water was still running by the time the pasta was cooked, so she knocked on the door and asked Kobi if he wanted to join them and from the shower he answered no. They started because the girls were hungry, and while they were eating they heard him leave the bathroom and close the door to the bedroom.

Mali went in. 'Is everything OK?' she asked, certain he was awake, even though he was lying on the bed with his eyes closed.

She was familiar with these mood swings of his and without even giving it much thought had been preparing herself since this morning. Had he been asked why he had changed jobs so many times in recent years, and instead of telling the truth had he evaded the question? She had pleaded with him to explain that it was her fault, but knew that he wouldn't.

Kobi didn't open his eyes, even though she stood there for a minute or two. The big picture from her second pregnancy hung above the bed, a bitter reminder, or like a memorial to the two of them.

Mali asked, 'You don't want to tell me how it went?'

That afternoon a barrage of hail slammed against the windows, after which silence fell. Mali helped Noy with her maths homework while Daniella continued watching TV.

At five Kobi came out of the bedroom with his sports bag for boxing, said he was taking her car and asked where her keys were. She asked him what had happened to his car and if he hadn't gone to his boxing class yesterday, but she didn't get an answer. When she reminded him they were going out that evening he didn't say a word either, and when she asked, 'Why'd you shower before boxing?' he looked at her as if she had said something awful.

She was tense all afternoon and evening and checked at least twice that she had locked the door behind him, looking out through the blinds in the living room to see if he had returned.

When she placed the wrapped umbrella on their bed for him to find, she again saw herself in the large photograph and wasn't sure if she'd tell him about the pregnancy tonight, although she had planned to. She had hesitated before agreeing to that photograph, but Kobi urged her to, saying that if they didn't take the picture she'd regret it, because this was going to be the last time she'd be pregnant. Over the years she learned not to hate the giant picture, in black and white, which showed her long, dark body with the swollen belly Kobi loved to caress, even in

9

public, and which she too had touched sometimes during the pregnancy, when she was alone. She hadn't liked the idea that guests would see her like this – perhaps she'd been embarrassed her father would see – but Kobi was actually quite excited about it. In the picture she could be seen from the side, her body turning a bit towards him, standing behind her, so that the difference in height between them wouldn't be so apparent. The two of them naked, and his arms simultaneously hiding and exposing her breasts. After what happened in Eilat she would have taken the picture down, but Kobi wanted to keep it up to remind the two of them of better days, and there were moments when she thought he was right, because when she looked at the giant photograph it brought her back to herself.

The rain started up again before dinner and its drumming on the windows and the roof intensified her restlessness. But the girls were quiet, as if they had noticed that she was struggling. Most of the time they kept themselves busy in the living room and their bedrooms. Only at six thirty did Daniella say that she was hungry, and Noy reminded Mali that she had promised they'd try on costumes for the festival of Purim.

She took down the dressing-up box from the wardrobe and Noy tried on the Elsa dress from *Frozen* that they bought her last year, but it was too small now. Daniella refused to try it on and said she wasn't going to dress up this year. Mali insisted she try it on because the dress had cost a fortune and this year she was hoping she would only have to buy one costume instead of two, but when she held it up in front of Daniella's small body she met her own eyes in the mirror and immediately averted her gaze.

There was no reason for all this to come back now, apart from, perhaps, her fear of Kobi's mood. And the pregnancy.

His boxing classes lasted between an hour and an hour and a half, so she thought he'd be back for dinner. At a quarter past seven she called to ask him to buy some pitta bread and hummus on his way home, but his phone was turned off. She tried him a few more times and in the end they ate without him and the girls went to bed at eight thirty. When the neighbour's daughter came up to babysit Mali told her that they had changed their minds about going out because she wasn't feeling well. She called Kobi again, and this time his phone was on but he didn't answer. And when she went up to the roof to see if it might be possible to hang out the washing, heavy rain clouds loomed and the wind shook the water tanks, so she decided not to for now and phoned her sister Gila. When Gila asked her if they weren't going out to celebrate, she explained that they hadn't managed to find a babysitter.

And Kobi returned around eleven, without an explanation or apology.

Just a year ago, on the day of their tenth anniversary, everything had been so different.

They left Daniella and Noy with her parents for the first time since Eilat and went to spend two nights at a B&B in the Golan Heights. Kobi had begun working for a company that provided security at building sites near the border and his mood was excellent. They planned to hike, like they used to before the girls were born, to spend a whole day walking along one of the rivers and another day at the Hula Nature Reserve, but the weather was awful so they barely left the B&B. Instead they watched DVDs and made love for the first time in several long weeks. They talked for hours in front of the fireplace. In the evening they went out on the deck wrapped in blankets, and Kobi spoke enthusiastically about taking a trip to his father's farm in Australia that summer and maybe even buying a flat now that they finally had two salaries again. When they called the girls to say goodnight it seemed to Mali that they were on their way to becoming a normal couple.

But all that had been last winter, and since then life had once more changed for the worse.

Kobi had been fired because his supervisor at the security company, who was ten years younger than him, had it in for him. He'd been sure he'd find other work, but after a few weeks she felt him sinking, avoiding her and the girls and his friends and barely leaving the house. Then he began going to boxing classes two or three times a week. He would return with his face beaten and bruises on his arms and stomach and would immediately shower and go to sleep. The sign of distress she recognized from back when they first met reappeared as well: when it seemed to him that no one was paying any attention he'd stretch his neck back and inhale deeply, as if he was unable to breathe.

She thought he'd go to bed without a word when he returned from boxing that night too, but he surprised her.

He turned on the television in the living room and sat

down on the sofa. Mali said, 'We were supposed to go out tonight,' and sat down next to him. A reality show of the sort that Kobi despised was on, but he insisted they didn't turn it off.

'Kobi, are you OK? You haven't talked to me since you came back from the interview.'

Without taking his eyes from the screen, he said to her, 'I'm sorry. I can't talk right now.'

'You can't tell me how it went?'

He didn't want to. He only said, 'I didn't get the job,' and when she asked, 'How do you know? They told you on the spot?' he nodded. And she didn't even know where the interview had taken place or with which company. After he was fired he decided not to interview for any more security positions and she had supported him. But in recent weeks he had stopped looking at all, so she had been so happy when he said he had an interview that she didn't even ask him where it was. And perhaps she really didn't look at him enough that night, because if she had she would have seen in his face more than despair.

Harry lay at his feet, his body still reeking of urine. 'I didn't wash him because I was afraid he'd get cold on the roof,' she said while Kobi continued staring at the screen.

'When are you going to take him to the vet? You can't let him keep suffering like this.'

'Maybe tomorrow.'

'The girls can't look at him, you know? They don't go near him. Like he's already dead.'

Was there some other way to reach him that Mali hadn't found? She could have told him about the pregnancy as she had planned, but she didn't want to talk about it like this.

'I spoke to Aviva today. She said her brother might have something for you. Do you remember him? He's started importing electric bikes.'

Kobi said, 'I'm not looking for work any more,' and Mali fell silent.

Did the late news on TV start then? She remembered that night's news very well. Homes and streets were flooded and there were power cuts across the country. Kobi got up from the sofa and sat down on the leather stool near the screen, as if her presence next to him was disturbing, and she too got up and left the room. When she returned he was watching a news programme on a different channel. On the TV screen two medical personnel assisted by a policeman could be seen rolling a stretcher with a body under a sheet.

'Where is it?' she asked him.

He inhaled as if it was difficult to breathe, because he hadn't noticed her coming back in. The body was put inside an ambulance, next to which stood two policemen wrapped in raincoats.

'Was that here? In Holon?' she asked, and he said, 'Yes, on the other side of town.'

'And did they say who it is?'

The report was nearing its end and she didn't manage to hear if the murderer had been caught or if the means of death was known, but she could tell that a woman lay under the white sheet. 'Can you turn that off? It scares me and I want us to talk,' she said quietly, and despite everything touched him on the shoulder. She didn't give up that night, because in moments like this one couldn't give

14

up. She went to their bedroom and returned with the umbrella, which was still lying on the bed. She said to him, 'Didn't you see what I bought you?'

But the umbrella didn't make him happy. Perhaps even the reverse. When he removed the wrapping paper he looked at it uneasily. 'To replace the one you lost,' she said. 'And it wasn't as expensive as it looks.'

He put the umbrella on the floor without thanking her, and it was this of all things that sent her over the edge. 'Are you seriously set on celebrating our anniversary like this?' she asked, and when he got up she almost screamed at him, 'Kobi, do you hear me at all? Do you hear that I'm talking to you? It's Mali from class. The war started.' He turned to her and his eyes flamed and it was then that she understood that something terrible had happened.

The two of them were around sixteen years old when they met. And the year was 1991. January. Ten years before they got married.

This was their first conversation, or at least the first they remembered, and sometimes – when they fought mainly – she would use it to pull him out of his silence.

Mali's father woke her at two in the morning and told her that George Bush was bombing Baghdad. She got dressed quickly and called Kobi. 'Kobi? It's Mali from class. The war started,' and he answered her in a sleepy voice and with the foreign accent he still had back then, 'Now? In the middle of the night?'

During the last few years she had sometimes tried to picture herself and him at that age without looking at old photos, but couldn't. Kobi was skinnier then and his body was soft, like the body of a boy. His chest and back were so smooth that she could caress him for hours. Mali knew nothing about him other than that he had come from a city called Perth without his parents and lived with his mother's relatives in Holon. He was an excellent basketball player and was exempted from English, because he spoke it much better than the teacher and corrected her mistakes, to the amusement of the other students, until she asked that he not come to class. There were rumours that his mother had killed herself in Australia but afterwards Mali learned that this was entirely untrue. Most of the boys in their class feared this boy who came from Australia, with jeans and Nikes and clear blue eyes that no one else had back then, so they made up stories about him. On the first day of school, when he introduced himself in class, he said that he had immigrated to Israel in order to volunteer to serve in an elite unit.

And it was completely by chance that they had met each other. A matter of fate or luck, like so many things that would happen afterwards.

She didn't think he could be interested in her, because no one else was then. Her body was too long and thin, she didn't get great marks, and she wasn't outgoing or daring either. She had been the school champion in sprinting and long-distance running for the last three years, but this wasn't something that drew the attention of the boys. But her last name was Ben-Asher, and Bengtson, Kobi, was the next name on the class contact list, and so she was supposed to call him in the event of a war breaking out. Three hours after the phone call, at five thirty in the morning, she and her father came by in the old Subaru pickup to give him a ride to the hospital. He was waiting for them downstairs, a Discman in his hand and white headphones on.

She was embarrassed by the truck, whose upholstery gave off the smell of sewage pipes, and maybe by her father too, who didn't speak English but nevertheless tried to talk with Kobi on the way.

'What will you do there?' her father asked, and Mali explained to him that they'd spray water on to those injured by the chemical weapons that Saddam Hussein would launch in the direction of Tel Aviv. And before he dropped them off across from the hospital he asked Kobi to keep her safe.

That was their first meeting, and who would have guessed then that years later they all would stand together under the chuppah?

A week later Kobi came to their house, and she was beside herself with excitement and embarrassment. Her father was late returning from synagogue, and while they were waiting for him her mother also tried speaking with Kobi in broken English. Gila was already fleeing from dinner on Friday nights, and this was a relief, because Mali had no doubt that if they were to meet, Kobi would fall in love with her twin sister, who had left school a year earlier and was already making money at work. Afterwards a siren went off, which of course happened when they were finally alone in her room, and they were forced to close themselves up with everyone else in the sealed room, which was her parents' cramped bedroom. She was filled with shame because her father's underwear was lying all over the floor.

The first time they slept together was also on a Friday night, a few months later.

Her parents took a trip with her younger siblings to relatives in Tiberias, and she invited Kobi to sleep over, even though her father didn't allow it. Mali didn't make a sound while they were doing it because she knew that Gila was listening to them through the wall, and she was indeed waiting for her by the door when Mali came out to wash her legs, still stunned by what had happened.

Mali continued waiting for him in their bedroom but Kobi didn't come. Since Eilat he never left her to fall asleep alone, not even when they fought. She lay in their bed and for a moment was able to see the boy with the headphones who waited for her and her father in the dark, his hands in his pockets. And perhaps that was why, at one in the morning, she tried one last time.

She went up to the roof and found him sitting on the white plastic chair in total darkness. This was her chance to tell him about the pregnancy, but she didn't. Something smothered and wild about his look and him sitting there in the cold frightened her. She caressed his head and his chest over the black polo shirt he was wearing. She whispered to him, 'Don't leave me alone in bed, Kobi. Please,' and also gave him every sign that if he came to bed they'd have sex. There was a deep cut on his neck that night, but that wasn't unusual; he always returned from boxing with injuries.

When she passed through the utility room on the way downstairs she saw the gun, which hadn't been there earlier when she'd gone to check the weather. She tried to fall asleep, placing her hands on her stomach, but then the face of the girl who sold her the umbrella at the shopping centre suddenly appeared in her head, and was immediately replaced by the covered body they had seen on TV. She opened her eyes in panic. The next image was the one that she had tried so hard to forget: the heavy hand coming towards her out of the darkness and crushing her throat.

2

Avraham identified the body straightaway, but didn't say so since he thought it best that as few people as possible knew, and also because of the silence. There were two patrolmen and some medical personnel standing in the kitchen awaiting instructions. One female officer stood by the entrance. And everyone who walked or spoke did so on the tips of their toes or in a whisper, as if not to wake the woman who lay on the rug in the living room.

When Avraham entered, one of the patrolmen pointed at the body, but he had already noticed her. She lay on her back, and only her right eye was open. On the rug under her were images of colourful birds. And perhaps he didn't tell anyone during those first hours that he knew who she was because of the shock he felt in the presence of her body. Ever since he had been appointed head of the district's investigations branch, Avraham knew that his first murder case would come, and yet when it began he wasn't certain he was ready.

The evening prior to this it had been announced on the news that the storm would start in the morning, and when Avraham woke up heavy rain could already be heard. He called the station and informed the investigations coordinator, Lital Levy, that he was taking a day off. Anyway that day he was supposed to be participating in a wholly unnecessary training session on cybercrime at National Police Headquarters. He made black coffee and brought the mugs to bed and they stayed under the blanket all morning, watching four episodes of *The Bridge* on his laptop.

Avraham's eyes slid closed.

His father entered the room, placed his hand on his forehead and declared that Avraham could stay in bed instead of going to school. When he heard the door slam, warm pleasure spread through his body because he understood that he was staying home alone. Should he get up right away? Grab another moment under the covers? They wouldn't be returning until the evening and he would have time to wander around the apartment like it was all his, make himself a giant breakfast . . . Marianka shook him gently when she heard from his breathing that he was asleep, and every time he opened his eyes the detectives on the screen discovered another body. He asked, 'What, they already have another murder?' and Marianka stroked his forehead. He had no chance of figuring out who the murderer was before that strange Danish detective Saga Norén did, not that he really cared.

That afternoon they took the car and drove to Tel Aviv. Avraham wrapped himself up in his ugly blue army parka that he last wore during the district's organized trip to Mt Hermon in winter 2007, and Marianka wore the wool jacket she had brought with her from Brussels. They parked in an almost empty lot by the beach and took advantage of a lull in the rain to sit on a wet bench facing the sea, which crashed on the rocks in front of them. No one else was on the promenade, other than an Arab couple with a baby. And Avraham's phone didn't ring once.

Most of the police in the district were busy clearing the roads, which were clogged up with rain, or evacuating flooded buildings or dealing with traffic accidents. This was what he too had done on days like this during his first years of service. Now he was head of investigations, thanks to solving an assault case that had occurred not far from their current spot on the promenade and to saving those two boys from death. There wasn't a chance he'd be required to stand at some junction in the pouring rain, directing traffic in place of a light that had failed.

When the rain started up again they took cover in the dolphinarium and afterwards had rice-and-bean soup in the market. And Marianka didn't speak longingly of the winters in her home town in Slovenia or in Brussels. When Avraham's phone rang for the first time, a little after four thirty, he didn't answer, and only when it rang for the third time did he realize it could be urgent. And maybe because he hadn't expected that this was what he'd hear, he didn't remember afterwards the exact words Lital Levy had used to inform him of what had happened. Did she tell him there had been a murder? Or only that a woman's body had been found in her home? She definitely didn't mention her name on the phone because, if she had, Avraham would have remembered it and wouldn't have been dumbfounded when he saw her face.

'Who's there?' he asked, and Levy said, 'No one. Just the patrolmen who closed off the scene. And Forensics are on their way, but everything's jammed up and it'll take them some time. Can you go?'

'It'll take me half an hour. If Ma'alul or Sharpstein come back, send one of them as well.'

Only when they'd finished the call did he remember that she hadn't given him the address, and he called her back, but the line was already busy.

Marianka suggested that he drop her off near the scene and that from there she'd get a cab, but he insisted on taking her home. They drove quickly and in silence. When they reached downtown everything still looked real and unreal at the same time, like it always does during a storm. Trees had fallen on the pavements and the streets were dotted with pools of water in which the evening lights flickered, as if Holon had transformed into Amsterdam or Venice. Avraham suddenly recalled that the first Maigret novel he had read took place from beginning to end in a rainstorm and that the clothes and shoes of the large French inspector were completely soaked throughout. Had that been a murder case? And would he know how to investigate a person's death? He couldn't remember how that case ended, but he did remember that he read the book when he was nineteen and in the army, one Saturday, when he was at the base taking an interrogation course. On Sokolov Street people walked bent forward as they struggled with the wind, and he drove peering out through a steamed-up windscreen, as if he was cutting through a cloud of fog. For a moment it seemed to him that he was still lying in bed, watching himself in a television series.

What already disturbed him even then was that the murder had occurred in one of the calmest neighbourhoods of Holon, where there were burglaries and stolen vehicles but almost no violent crime. And worse still was that Lital Levy hadn't mentioned anyone who had been arrested at the time of the incident or even any suspect who had escaped.

Two empty patrol cars and an ambulance were parked in front of 38 Krauze Street, and curious onlookers were gathered on the pavement behind police tape. Renovations were under way in the building on the corner, and in front of it stood a skip. The entrance to the building was closed, and Avraham stood waiting to be let in but eventually simply pushed on the doorknob and the door opened. He had time to prepare himself for what he was going to see since there was no lift and the flat was on the top floor.

The woman lying on the rug was named Leah Yeger. Her right eye, the open one, was green, but there was nothing to be learned by looking at it.

Avraham searched the pocket of his coat for his notepad, because he needed to write down his first impressions, but the notepad wasn't there; just a receipt for two cups of black coffee and a pretzel he had bought at a snack kiosk back on Mount Hermon in 2007. That wasn't a problem – he had a good memory and he didn't miss a thing. He asked that everyone leave the apartment except for one patrolman and the paramedic who had determined the time of death. His shoes were covered in plastic bags and there were gloves on his hands. And no one was allowed to approach the living room until the forensics team arrived.

In the meantime Avraham saw everything. He saw the hand marks on her neck and also the red ends of her ears and the swollen tongue lolling sideways out from her mouth. She lay on the rug, among blue, red and yellow birds, some of which held their beaks open as if they were trying to call for help. His eyes slipped away from the body and were drawn to the half-full mug of coffee and the tray of biscuits on the table in the kitchen. And to the car keys in a bowl on the sideboard. The television was on with no sound.

He took off his coat and placed it folded up on the floor by the entrance.

There was no doubt that the living room was the scene of the murder: a framed drawing of two women sitting in a yellow field had fallen off the wall, apparently during a struggle, and next to it, on the rug, was a broken lamp. The patrolman who remained in the flat, an officer whose face Avraham recognized but whose name he didn't know, said, 'Luckily, there wasn't a fire,' and Avraham suddenly remembered that he hadn't asked him who found Yeger. And only then did he discover that her daughter was still in the bedroom.

'She's here now? By herself?' he asked.

'Not by herself. There's an officer and a paramedic with her.'

Once, at times like this, he would have gone down to the street and smoked a cigarette to buy some time to think and perhaps call Ilana Lis. But at the beginning of winter he had quit smoking, because Marianka had begged him to and because his fortieth birthday was approaching. Only occasionally did he still try lighting the pipe Marianka had bought him in Brussels, but now the pipe was at the office. And he could not call Ilana Lis. So he returned to the kitchen and found a sheet of paper and a pen and nevertheless wrote down a few words the paramedic said about what was already clear to Avraham because he could see it for himself: Yeger apparently *died from strangulation. After a struggle.* The temperature of her body indicated that until approximately two or three hours earlier she had still been alive.

Her hands were closed. When they opened them at the Institute for Pathology he hoped they'd find something between her fingers, other than the slit marks left by her fingernails in her palms when she clutched them, and perhaps a few slices of skin that she had peeled off her own neck when she tried to free herself from the hands choking her. This was, then, his biggest hope.

And though he hadn't yet expressed it to himself in words, he did already feel that something was off about the scene. *Too clean, perhaps?* As if *someone had straightened up the scene after the murder? Or maybe before?* And he also felt that something else, other than her handbag and keys, had been taken from the flat.

At around six he called Ma'alul to verify when he'd arrive, and when Eliyahu said that they were delayed on their way back from the training session in Jerusalem because of an accident involving two buses, he no longer had any choice and so went into the bedroom to conduct the first round of questioning with the daughter himself. She sat on the bed and Avraham brought a chair into the room and sat across from her, very close, because the room was small. The paramedic was asked to leave but the female patrol officer, who called the daughter Orit, remained and held her hand throughout their conversation.

He began by saying, 'I offer my condolences,' and then he introduced himself and added, 'Please tell me how this happened,' regretting his flawed phrasing, even though she understood what he meant.

'She was supposed to pick up my daughter from nursery,' she said. 'This is her usual day because I don't have anything set up for her in the afternoon.'

'When did she pick your daughter up?'

'Nursery ends at three thirty. But she didn't get her. She didn't go.'

Her eyes, like the eyes of her mother, were green. The next day he discovered she was only thirty-three, and was divorced, but at the time of the interview he'd have put her at about forty.

'How did you know she didn't go?' Avraham asked, and she said, 'They called to say that my daughter was still there. I called my mother's mobile and tried her at home, but she didn't answer. I thought maybe that she was stuck in the rain.'

'And when did you speak with your mother before then?'

'At around one.'

'And she didn't say she wasn't going to pick your daughter up? Do you know if she was here in the flat when you spoke?'

Orit nodded. And then added, 'I think so.'

'Was anyone with her when she spoke with you?'

'Who could have been with her?'

'I don't know.'

'No. I don't think anyone was.'

'And did she sound OK? Like she normally does?'

'Yes. If I'd thought something wasn't OK, I would have . . .'

She stopped and Avraham didn't go on right away so that she wouldn't burst into tears.

'So when did you come to check what had happened?' he asked after a while.

'I went to the nursery and afterwards came here because I had to go back to work and I wanted to leave my daughter here. We heard the TV from outside.'

'Do you work in the area?'

'In a clothes shop in town.'

'And where is the nursery located?'

'Not very far away.'

He explained to her that he was asking these questions because he was trying to figure out the exact sequence of events.

'I arrived at four fifteen. And that's when I called the police.'

'And do you recall if the door was open or closed?'

'Closed. But I have a key.'

Now she did burst into tears, because in her imagination she saw the moment when the door opened. And it was actually because of this that this time Avraham didn't wait for her to stop crying and immediately asked her, 'When you opened the door, did you happen to notice if it was locked?'

She hesitated before saying to him, 'I don't remember anything. I think I turned the key.'

'And you're certain there was no one in the flat other than your mother?'

She collapsed against the officer sitting next to her and didn't answer his question. He should have just continued the investigation later, at the station, but instead of restraining himself he asked, 'Where is your daughter now?'

'She saw everything. She asked me, "Why is Grandma on the floor?" but she understood. I pushed her out and shut the door, but not before she'd seen.'

The time was 19.10 and there were now two television crews on the pavement outside the building. And Avraham was still the only detective at the scene. All the rooms other than the living room were undisturbed and there were no signs of burglary or a search. Despite this he asked Orit if there was a safe in the flat or if her mother kept large amounts of cash on her, and the daughter said not that she knew of. But her handbag could not be found anywhere: not in the bedroom and not in one of the cupboards in the kitchen, where she generally kept it when at home. As Avraham had assumed, because they weren't in the lock or in the bowl in the living room, next to the keys to the car, the keys to the flat had been taken. Before this, during the conversation in the bedroom, he had already written a note to himself: *Murderer locked the door behind him?* He extended the walk-through and asked her more questions, some of which he had already asked, only because he didn't want to leave her alone. And suddenly he remembered that Leah Yeger had a son as well, so he asked, 'You're not an only child, correct?' and she nodded and asked him, 'Has anyone informed my brother?'

Only once Ma'alul arrived, his uniform as wet as if he had walked from Jerusalem, was Avraham able to collect the neighbours' statements. Most of the tenants were of no help to him because they weren't home in the afternoons and mainly wanted to know if it was safe to remain in the building. In one of the flats he met a young couple who were packing baby clothes and nappies into a large bag because the wife insisted that they go and sleep at her mother's. Their twins had been in throughout the day with the nanny, and they gave him her phone number. In fact, only one of the neighbours shared any information of value with him. He lived on the second floor, directly under Yeger, and said that at around two, while he was resting in his bedroom, he had heard a noise from the flat above. 'Something fell,' he said, 'or was dragged.' There were shouts as well, but he wasn't sure who shouted because his hearing wasn't very sharp. It lasted two or three minutes; of this the man was certain.

Avraham asked him, 'What lasted?'

And the neighbour said, 'The noise. There were sounds of a struggle coming from up there.' Yeger was a quiet neighbour and she usually rested in the afternoon hours, like the neighbour himself. So he opened the door and walked up half a flight of stairs, only then it got quiet and he decided not to knock on the door. But his afternoon nap had already been disturbed so he didn't go back to bed, and a few minutes later he heard footsteps and through the spy-hole saw a policeman going down the stairs. He thought that someone must have called him because of the noise and that the policeman had looked into the matter, so he didn't call the police himself.

While Avraham was gathering a statement from the neighbour, District Commander Benny Saban phoned, and Avraham apologized to the old man and went outside to take the call. Saban had been at the training session at the National Headquarters and was supposed to drop by the crime scene on his way back, but his wife had bought theatre tickets and the heavy traffic was forcing him to go straight home. He asked Avraham, 'So what do you have to tell me?'

And Avraham said, 'Not a thing for now.'

'But what does it look like? Domestic violence? A burglary?'

Apparently, it wasn't a matter of domestic violence because Yeger was a widow and, according to her daughter, she didn't have ties to any men. So was there any chance that this was a break-in gone bad, in the middle of the day, when all that was taken was a handbag and maybe a set of keys, and in the rest of the rooms perfect order prevailed?

'In short, Avi, do we need to involve Central Unit or should the investigation remain with us?'

That was the first time he told anyone. He had to report it to Saban, and this also was a reason to keep the case in the district and not to drag it over to the Central Investigation Unit. He said quietly, 'The case has to stay with us because she's one of our rape victims,' but Saban either didn't understand or didn't hear.

'What did you say?' he asked.

'The woman who was murdered here. Her name is Yeger. She has been assaulted in the past. And we dealt with the case.'

For a moment there was silence on the other end of the line.

'You said she was raped?'

'Yes.'

'And we caught the rapist?'

The rapist had been arrested on the day that Yeger filed her complaint and had already been charged and convicted.

'And now it was a rape again? Who did it to her this time?'

Did Saban think that the case had already been solved?

'I don't know,' Avraham said, 'but according to the findings at the scene I don't think she was sexually assaulted. We found her dressed. But we'll wait for the post mortem to find out.'

Before hanging up he told Saban that, apparently, there had been a policeman in the building a short time after the murder, but Saban only asked if it was nevertheless necessary for him to come to the scene, and Avraham told him that they'd manage. He immediately returned to the neighbour's flat.

On his sheet of paper, which was becoming more and more filled up with short sentences in his rounded, childish handwriting, he had written: *Aharon Pranji, neighbour from the flat below: heard a noise around 2 p.m., something falling or furniture being dragged, sounds of a struggle.* A long blue line connected the last sentence to the word *struggle*, which appeared at the top of the sheet, in the things he had listed earlier from the mouth of the paramedic. Under the last sentence he wrote: *Was a policeman there minutes after the murder?*

'Explain this point to me one more time, please,' Avra-ham said. 'A few minutes after you heard the noises, even though you didn't call the police, you saw a policeman on the stairwell?'

'Yes. Like I told you. Ten or fifteen minutes afterwards.'

'Do you know if someone else called the police?'

In the questioning he had conducted so far, no neigh-bour had said that they had called them.

'That's what I assumed. That someone else called the police. And that the policeman checked and saw that everything was OK. That's why I didn't call.'

'The man who went down the stairs was wearing a uniform, you're sure of this?'

'Yes.'

'And it wasn't someone who lives in the building?'

'No policeman lives here. I'd know. I've lived here forty-five years now.'

'Do you remember if anyone else came down the stairs before or after him?'

The neighbour couldn't know this. He hadn't been look-ing through the spyhole the entire time. He also admitted that he fell asleep a while afterwards and woke up when he heard Leah Yeger's daughter screaming. But he did watch the policeman out of a window when he left the building and saw that the man did not get into a car.

In the kitchen where they sat there was a smell of cooked chicken. Pranji offered him tea and Avraham declined, but then he suddenly felt thirsty and asked for a glass of water. The last line that he wrote before leaving was: *A policeman on foot, didn't get into a car. Need to clarify: maybe he left the other flat on the top floor?*

As always, Avraham was relieved by Eliyahu Ma'alul's presence. He returned to the scene and told Ma'alul that Saban had called and that he wouldn't be coming tonight, and Eliyahu looked at him with his deep-set eyes, which reminded Avraham of his father's eyes, and smiled. He asked Avraham if there was anything useful in the neighbours' statements, and Avraham said, 'We might know the time of the murder. The neighbour from the apartment below says that he heard sounds of a struggle going on up here around two. And it's also possible that there was an earlier call to the police. Before the daughter arrived. The neighbour saw a policeman coming down the stairs a few minutes after two.'

Without saying so explicitly, both of them considered the same disastrous possibility at that moment: was a patrolman called to the building, who then politely knocked on Yeger's door, and when he didn't get a response simply left? Of course, there was another possibility as well, but for now they didn't even want think about that. 'That policeman needs to be found,' Ma'alul said. 'I'll ask who it was at the switchboard and at the station. And you should go home now. You've been by yourself here for a few hours now, haven't you?'

Did something in Avraham's eyes give away how he felt? He reached for his pocket, but there were no cigarettes there, and when Ma'alul asked him, 'Was the body still here when you arrived?' he just nodded and suddenly

34

saw again the open green eye and was filled with regret for not touching Yeger's forehead when he had entered the flat, as if, had he done things differently, she would still be alive. He tried avoiding Ma'alul's gaze and asked him where the daughter was, and Ma'alul told him that she had left.

'Alone? Without an escort?'

'What escort, Avi? Her ex-husband came to take her, and I OK'd it. There's no reason to for her to be here, right?'

Her brother, on the other hand, had been informed of his mother's death and was on his way to the scene. Avraham wanted to wait for him, but Ma'alul told him, 'Get out of here already. Everything will be all right. He lives in the north and won't be here for an hour. I'll speak with him. And you'll rest. In any case, there's nothing else to do here and you have another long day ahead of you.'

This was true but, all the same, Avraham lingered at the scene for a few more minutes, as if he was having difficulty saying goodbye or feared that if he left he'd miss something. But that evening he didn't discover anything else there that he had failed to discover at first glance. In the other apartment on that floor a sixteen-year-old boy wearing a red sweatshirt opened the door for him. His parents weren't home but neither of them was a police officer and it wasn't possible that a policeman had paid them a visit that afternoon because they were at work and he was at school. And only when Sharpstein arrived did Avraham call him and Ma'alul to the kitchen, to tell the two of them that Yeger had previously been a rape victim. Ma'alul's dark face turned pale. Like Saban, Ma'alul asked if the rapist had been caught, and Avraham said that he had been and that he was still serving time in prison. Then he asked them to come to an early staff meeting the following morning, and when he got into his car he remembered that he'd left his coat at the scene.

He didn't turn on the engine and sat in the car without doing a thing. The street was empty, even though the wind had died down and the rain now fell in a light drizzle. Ma'alul called to ask if the blue army coat at the scene was his, and then promised to take it with him and give it back to Avraham the next day.

Suddenly, it was clear to him that he was not watching himself on a television show but rather was in the city where he was born and had lived almost his entire life, on Krauze Street, outside a building numbered 38 on whose third floor a woman he knew had been murdered. At the beginning of his first murder case.

When he entered the station to pick up copies of the documents from Yeger's rape case he asked David Ezra, the desk sergeant, if the policeman called to 38 Krauze Street this afternoon had been identified. Ezra told him, 'Not yet, Avi. Not yet. Eliyahu asked me to check and I'm trying to figure it out for you, but, c'mon, give me some time. Do you know what it's like here today with this storm?'

Avraham hurried to put the folder in the study without Marianka seeing it, but on the way from the station he had managed to glance through it.

Leah Yeger had been raped in 2012. The detective who received her complaint, escorted her to room 4 at Wolfson Hospital and dealt with the case was Esty Vahaba. It was a straightforward case because Yeger knew the rapist and turned to the police just a few hours after she was assaulted. He was charged and sentenced to only four and half years, due to his age and other mitigating circumstances, but he couldn't have harmed her today because he was still in jail.

Someone else killed Leah Yeger. Someone else violently attacked her and then took her handbag and the keys to her flat and locked the door behind him.

Had he surprised her when he knocked on her door, or had she known he was coming and been waiting for him? And was he still in the flat when the policeman . . . Avraham hadn't thought about this possibility before now, and it alarmed him. He didn't say a word to Marianka about the rape when she asked him what had happened. Only that a sixty-year-old woman had been found dead in her home.

'Her husband did it?' she asked, and he shook his head. 'Her husband's dead.'

'So you don't know who killed her?'

'No.'

'And you're in charge of the case?'

'Yes.'

'How are you feeling?'

He felt terrible.

The morning they had spent together, first in bed and then at the seashore, was distant now, as if it had happened months ago. He changed into tracksuit bottoms and a T-shirt and got into bed without eating dinner or even watching the reports about the murder on the late-night news. Marianka lay next to him in the dark, but fell asleep long after him. Of all the things he saw at the scene, strangely it was the colourful birds that wouldn't let go of him.

'Do you have a lead?' Marianka asked him before he drifted off, and for some reason Avraham immediately said, 'Yes,' without knowing what lead he was referring to.

3

The second sign was given to her the next day in the form of a phone call from Harry, but she didn't understand this one as she should have either. She was feeling hurt by Kobi having ignored her on their anniversary and especially by the fact that he had let her sleep alone for the first time, and on the one day when she was revisited by the fear of the heavy hand.

When Harry called she was waiting for Gila in the café. A man with glasses, wearing a white sweater and a scarf, sat two tables away from her and looked at her over a newspaper. When she was searching for the phone in the pocket of her coat she was sure that it was Kobi, because ever since leaving the house she had been waiting for him to call. But an international number appeared on the screen, and she knew immediately that it was Harry, and debated whether or not to answer. She feared that, with him of all people, she wouldn't be able to control herself and that the anger would erupt.

She had tried not to think about what had happened yesterday, but all morning her fury with Kobi had grown more and more intense. Had he stayed alone on the roof all night? When she woke, a little after six, he wasn't next to her. She had a feeling he wasn't home, and when she passed through the apartment she discovered that she was right. On the roof, next to the white plastic chair, she saw his empty coffee mug: 'The Best Dad in the World'. She didn't look for the gun, but it was possible that it had no longer been on the table in the utility room when she passed through on her way downstairs. The door to the entrance again wasn't locked.

She didn't know if she should look for him. And she didn't call him, because he hadn't answered her even once yesterday. Before waking the girls she had a shower, and when she was getting dressed in the bedroom she heard the door to the flat opening. A moment earlier, when she stood facing the large mirror and watched herself buttoning her shirt, she again had the sensation that she was looking at another woman, like yesterday, and she closed the wardrobe door. Kobi was in the kitchen. He was standing at the table reading the paper.

For a moment she had a glimmer of hope: perhaps during the night he had decided it was premature to give up and was searching for work in the small ads? She couldn't think of another reason, since Kobi had never before gone down to buy a paper so early. When she stopped behind him and said, 'Good morning,' without touching him, she saw that he was reading an article about the murder that had occurred in Holon. And that her *good morning* had frightened him. He folded up the newspaper and left the kitchen with it, after giving her a dry greeting in return. She didn't generally read newspapers at home either, but on the table in the kitchen there was a copy of *Israel Today* and she opened it. The first few pages had only articles about the storm damage and pictures of flooded streets and snow in the Golan Heights. The article about the murder appeared on page sixteen, and in the centre of it there was a picture of an old woman. Her name was Leah Yeger, and it seemed to Mali that she had encountered the name before, but she didn't recognize the face that peered out at her.

The woman was sixty years old and had been murdered in her apartment on Krauze Street in the afternoon. *Her daughter found the body when she came to visit.* And a gag order had been placed on the remaining details of the investigation.

Mali prepared coffee just for herself and bowls of cornflakes for the girls. Kobi was pretending to be asleep, and when she entered the bedroom again she behaved as if he wasn't there. The girls didn't ask about him; the fact that there were days when they had no father wasn't worthy of comment. Before they set off she nevertheless said loudly, 'You remember that I'm working this afternoon and that you're picking up today?' without checking that he was awake.

Afterwards there were the errands.

This was her free morning, and she was forced to begin it at the post office. She queued for more than twenty minutes to pay their property tax and the water and electricity bills, which as always during the winter months had gone up despite efforts to cut back. In front of her in the queue was a secretary from a law firm who was sending dozens of registered letters. The storm had weakened, but from time to time rain continued to fall. Before ten, when the shops at the shopping centre opened, she had planned to go to Electronics to check prices on a tumble dryer, but had second thoughts at the last moment, because soon warmer days would be coming and it would be possible to manage without. The nausea didn't go away, and Mali hoped that it was tied to the pregnancy and not to the fear. She put off the call to the doctor.

Even on regular days most of the errands fell to her, but at times like this the load was unbearable. Kobi didn't take the girls to nursery or to school and didn't pick them up, even though he was at home most of the time. He grew quiet and disappeared, and even when he spoke it wasn't to offer her help. The clothes piled up in the laundry basket, the dishes in the sink, the fridge was empty within a couple days after shopping. And the flat transformed from a place of refuge into a hostile environment. Kobi almost never went out, except for boxing, and his silent presence paralysed everyone: her, the girls. They all moved more slowly, spoke quietly. Even the dog was dying without making a sound.

'Mali, is that you? I can barely hear you.'

When she heard Harry Bengtson's voice she immediately felt that she was going to burst into tears, and she choked them back as she straightened herself in the chair and took a sachet of brown sugar from the copper dish. She said to him in English, 'I hear you, Harry. Can you hear me? I'm not at home. I'm in a café.' The waitress placed a mug with a latte before her and signalled to ask if she wanted something to eat, and Mali shook her head. She assumed that Harry had called in order to wish them a belated *mazal tov* on their anniversary, but this was a strange assumption since he hadn't done that before and it

42

was possible that he didn't know when it fell. It seemed to her that he was a bit drunk, as he had been more than once when calling. 'Is everything OK with Jacob?' he asked her in English. He still called Kobi by his birth name. 'I'm trying to get a hold of him but can't. His damn phone is always turned off. Why the hell does he have a phone if it's off all the time?'

His voice was coarse and deep and hadn't changed at all over the years. The first time they met she didn't understand a single word he said.

'Yes, he's OK,' Mali answered. 'It could be that the battery died. Did you try calling him at home?' She didn't know the last time Kobi had spoken with his father or what he had told him, but she was sure that he wouldn't have told him a thing. Not about the firings and not about the loans and definitely not about the failed job interview. A few years ago she had discovered that most of the things Kobi told his father about their lives were complete lies, even though Harry could have helped them if he had known the truth. Kobi had decided not to mention Eilat to him either, and she had no reason to object to this. She heard him ask, 'Do you know why he tried calling me yesterday? I didn't hear the phone and he left me a strange message. He said something about . . . Were you with him when he called me, Mali? Are you there?'

She lowered her voice because the man with the glasses was still staring at her, without hiding behind the newspaper now. She said, 'I'm here, Harry. I'm in a café. And I wasn't with him when he called. He didn't say what he wanted?' She did think it strange that Kobi had called his father yesterday. They spoke on the phone three or four times a year, no more. Even when they had gone to visit him for the first time, Kobi hadn't let him know that he was bringing Mali with him.

Harry was silent, as if he hadn't heard her, and because she was scared that he'd hang up before managing to tell her what Kobi had said, she raised her voice when she asked him again, 'Harry? He didn't tell you what he wanted?' And he said, 'Mali, I'm still here.'

It was a short time after they had met again. The spontaneous trip to Australia that changed their lives.

They broke up when they were in the army since it was hard keeping in touch long distance and because Mali wanted to go out with other people. In the first months of their relationship at school, she was in love with Kobi, but his isolation already scared her back then. Gila received a draft exemption, worked in Tel Aviv and switched boyfriends every two weeks. And the fact that Mali was stationed at an intelligence base in Shomron, full of men, created non-stop friction between her and Kobi. They mainly spent the weekend breaks arguing. He interrogated her about her relationships with the commanding officers and about the people she shared a room with. When he called the base and she wasn't in the office he got furious, even once she'd explained that she had gone out for a run. She hesitated for weeks before telling him that she wanted to break up – and she knew why. Kobi simply refused to accept it. He continued to call and wrote long letters. One Shabbat when she remained at the base he even went to visit her parents and asked them to convince her to give him another chance. But then he suddenly broke off contact, and for years they didn't see one another, not even by chance. Mali heard stories about him from friends they had in common, and sometimes he called on her birthday or the holidays and they held a polite conversation without revealing to each other what was really happening in their lives, in order not to cause any pain. And she was strict about not calling him, even when she wanted to, so as not to give him any hope.

When they met one morning, by chance, in the queue at a health clinic – she was there because she had the flu, and he was having some tests – she didn't think that they'd start going out again, because she had just gone through a painful break-up with a guy she'd met during her studies at a business college and whom everyone thought she would marry. Kobi suggested that they meet up for a drink and she agreed, and two days later they went to see a film. She was already a bank clerk and still lived with her parents, and Kobi was renting a studio apartment close by. She told him openly how she had discovered that her ex-boyfriend was cheating on her, but didn't mention his name. Kobi said he was about to start working for the Mossad, having been accepted on to a training course for agents, and that he first planned to travel to see his father in Australia for a few weeks, and suddenly asked her if she wanted to join him.

How many times had she thought about that moment since then?

At the time she wasn't sure it was a good idea, but because of the break-up and since she'd never done the gap-year trip that everyone went on after the army, in the end she said yes. Yet it wasn't only this but something in him as well – or perhaps in them, actually. When they sat next to each other in the dark of the cinema and his leg accidently touched her thigh, she recalled his soft, smooth body and the careful movements of his hands on her skin. She decided she would be spontaneous, at least once in her life, and her parents supported her decision, perhaps because they feared she would wind up alone. Even her father didn't oppose her travelling with Kobi and only asked if she'd be sharing a room with him.

Harry Bengtson wasn't waiting for them in Melbourne, nor at the airport in Perth after the connecting flight.

What she knew about him before they met was that he was a professor of botany, and thus she was surprised when she saw him. He was sixty years old then, maybe sixty-one. A large, tanned man with a white beard and a red bandana wrapped around his head, who waited shirtless for them in his yard, watering the plants and feeding his two giant black dogs, Cerberus and Orthrus. No suit and no glasses. Only his clear eyes were Kobi's eyes exactly.

On their first day there he drank half a bottle of whisky after finishing a bottle of red wine during the meal, and despite this wasn't drunk when he took them around the farm, which was located in the heart of a valley the two of them called Valley of the Giants, and a forest with the tallest trees she had ever seen in her life. Afterwards, when they sat in the yard and Kobi went in to shower, Harry admitted that he hadn't known that Jacob would be bringing a girlfriend and asked her how long they'd been going out. She told him that they met in high school and broke up and met again just a few weeks ago, out of the blue. When Harry asked her, 'Did you two come to tell me you're getting married?' she laughed, because this hadn't occurred to her until that very moment. She said to him, 'For now, no,' and Harry's face was serious when he said, 'Fantastic. So do you think something could happen between us, or am I too old for you?'

It was so different from her parents' house and the life she had known until then. Not only the large house and the barking of the dogs at night and the dense forests she ran through each morning, but also Harry Bengtson – so different from her father, who was short and quiet and wouldn't ever think of saying things like that. Harry staring directly at her was embarrassing, but she tried to smile, and Harry himself smiled and said, 'I'm kidding. I wouldn't do a thing like that to him, even though I love dark women. I've caused Jacob enough harm. And it appears to me that he feels good around you.'

Kobi returned, and Harry became silent, then rose from his seat and wrapped his arms around his son. 'How long haven't I seen you, boy?' he asked, and it seemed to her that Kobi blushed and flinched while at the same time a smile of joy lit up his face as he was embraced by his father.

Mali didn't stop looking at the two of them during the four weeks they spent in Australia. In his father's presence Kobi was shy and restrained, and Mali imagined that this was exactly how he had been as a five- or eight- or ten-year-old boy, before he became a teen and decided to go to Israel by himself. Next to his father his shyness stuck out, as well as his gentleness. Hesitation struck when he stretched out his hand to caress her one evening, when just the two of them were in the hammock in the yard, as if after all these years he was asking permission. She moved her head closer to his hand because she was waiting for his touch. Something in Kobi's body, in contrast to the bodies of other men who had touched her, was always close by and right and simple. And she saw that he had changed since high school, that he had lost self-confidence and walked like someone who was afraid to fall; but she thought this would help him not to get hurt. They barely spoke about his father, but it seemed to her that Kobi admired Harry even as he feared him. During the week, Harry stayed in a small flat by the university, and Mali and Kobi rented a car and travelled, so they didn't spend much time with him, but from the conversations she did have with Harry it became clear to her that he knew almost nothing about his son. Kobi hadn't told him what he did dare to tell her when they met again: that his dream of being accepted into an elite unit had vanished when he fell during testing, and that he hadn't got into an officers' course. After being released from the army he began study-ing business management 'in order to make the first million before the age of twenty-five', but he had been kicked off the course because he was accused, unjustly, of cheating on a test.

They spoke about his mother only once, when Mali saw her picture for the first time, hanging up in his child-hood room. Kobi told her that she had always spoken Hebrew with him, since he was a baby, mainly so she wouldn't forget the language herself, and that she was a poet and had hoped to teach literature at one of the col-leges in Perth. But she never found work before dying of a cancer that wasn't diagnosed in time. Mali recalled the stories that had been told about Kobi when he had arrived in Holon, about how his mother went crazy and killed herself after his father put her into a mental institution. She asked Kobi if he had left Australia because his mother died, and he said no, that he had left because he couldn't stand the women who replaced her in his father's bed. 'But I also wanted to be a commando, remember? And I had heard that the most beautiful women in the world are in Israel.'

Inexplicably, it was when they returned from Australia that it became clear to her that at some point they'd get married.

And since then they had seen Harry Bengtson a total of three times.

Two years after the visit to the farm he appeared at their wedding, even though he had announced that there was no chance he'd come. He brought with him an Aboriginal woman, about their age, by the name of Lawanda, who was stocky and tall and didn't speak a word the entire time she was in Israel. Three years after this he called one evening and said that he would be arriving the next week in order to see the granddaughter who had been born to him. And the last time was four years ago, when they travelled with the girls and spent the summer with him. She did know that since Harry had had a heart attack, Kobi had been calling him more, but she hadn't known that he had called him yesterday. Nor what message he had left.

Her sister Gila still hadn't arrived at the café, and the man with the glasses had left his table, but his scarf was still on the chair where he had been sitting. Mali again said to Harry, 'I'm not at home right now, but did you try calling him there? I think he's at home,' and Harry coughed and asked, 'Are you sure he's OK? Because on the phone he didn't sound so good to me.'

Mali said, 'I don't know what you mean, Harry. What did he actually say in his message?'And then for the first time she heard about Kobi's plan to leave.

'He said something about coming for a visit. Next week, or even before then. Do you know anything about this, Mali? And why don't you all come?'

She didn't answer immediately. She tried to remember if Kobi had spoken about a trip to Australia. They couldn't travel together because she hadn't requested leave from work and the girls didn't have a break from school until Passover, and in any case they didn't have enough money for the plane tickets. And ever since Eilat he didn't leave her alone in the flat for even one night. She said, 'I don't think we can come, Harry. Maybe he meant that we'll come in the summer?'

But Harry was adamant. 'He said next week. Do you think he'll come? And he cried, Mali. Do you know why he was crying?'

The crying that she had been choking back since yesterday morning rose in her throat, but she succeeded in controlling it. She rested the phone for a moment on her knees so that Harry wouldn't hear. Then she said, 'Harry, I can't hear you properly. I'll go back home and call you from there, OK?' And he said, 'Don't forget, Mali, OK? I'm worried about him.' This was the first time she'd heard Harry speak about his son like that.

She hadn't intended to return home before work or to try to speak with Kobi, but after the conversation with Harry she didn't have much choice. She cut short the coffee with Gila as much as she could without giving away that something was up, and even while Gila was talking she thought only about what Harry had said. And she couldn't say anything to her about the pregnancy either.

She had nothing to be ashamed of, but nevertheless she suddenly filled up with shame about their lives and about what she would say to her sister if she dared to reveal anything. She just wanted to return home and ask Kobi if he really intended to leave her alone with the girls and travel to Australia, and she wanted to hit him, if she could, or to sit him down across from her and not let him go anywhere until he told her what had come over him. She knew that he wouldn't call; she was always the one forced to back down, since Kobi simply didn't know how to stop fighting. This was his problem at the places he worked as well. Small sources of tension, which other people could undo or ignore, Kobi turned into bitter wars. If it seemed to him that someone had wronged him, he was unable to forgive them.

Gila had placed a new bag on the table, and before even ordering coffee had told her about the man who had kept her from sleeping last night. He was six years younger than her, a lawyer, and they had met when she showed him a flat in a new luxury development in Tel Aviv, by the sea. Afterwards she asked Mali, like always, as if trying to provoke her, 'How are you for money? Has he found work yet?' And when Mali answered, 'Not yet', she said, 'Can you tell me what he's waiting for?'

But these sentences didn't distance her from Kobi but rather brought her closer to him. Maybe because despite everything she understood what had come over him and how humiliating the interviews were for him and how much scorn he had to absorb, and she also knew that she had a part in this. When she told Gila she had to run, she already wanted to go home, not only so she could ask him about Australia but also so she could hug him and tell him about the nausea and the fact that the fear was returning and that yesterday, before she fell asleep, she felt the heavy hand that comes from the darkness; but when she got home all that was forgotten.

The door again wasn't locked.

Kobi stood in the living room among clothes and objects that he had removed from the sideboard and from the cupboard by the entrance. The doors to the girls' rooms, which she had tidied that morning, were open, and there too she saw toys thrown about and clothes and books on the beds and on the floor. And his look scared her, just like last night, when he had turned around to face her. Harry came out from the bedroom and looked at her and then came up to her with slow steps and lay down on the floor. Kobi said quietly, 'I can't find the umbrella. Do you know where it is?'

He was wearing the same black polo shirt as the day before, and his hands were shaking. 'It's there, under the sofa,' she said to him. 'You left it there after I gave it to you yesterday. And are you going to clear up all this mess?' Kobi looked in the direction she was pointing in and said, 'Not that one. The old umbrella.'

She looked at him in fear, not understanding. He had moved the cupboard in the living room, and the armchairs from their places, and rolled up the rug. The stool had been overturned and was far from its place near the television, as if he had sent it flying with a kick. 'You said that you lost it and that you don't remember where, no?' She tried to control her voice. 'That's why I bought you a new one.'

And, anyway, the rain had stopped.

Kobi's eyes continued to search for the umbrella as he mumbled, as if to himself, 'I don't remember where I forgot it. You sure you haven't seen it anywhere?' She stood there another moment and then went down in the lift and got in the car and did not try to stop the crying; and even if she had tried, she wouldn't have succeeded.

4

He hadn't slept long, but when Avraham woke up at five fifteen he was ready. The shock that had seized him for a moment at the sight of the body had vanished, and in its place was a desire to be at the station, working. There were no new messages on his mobile but he nevertheless hoped that when he arrived at his office findings from the forensics lab would be waiting for him, perhaps because of a dream that he'd had in which Ilana Lis informed him over the phone that fingerprints the murderer had left on a plate in the kitchen had been identified – but the call was cut off before she could tell Avraham his name.

Marianka got up with him, even though she didn't have to. While they ate breakfast Avraham studied the newspapers and the sad lines of text passed before his eyes as he expected: *Body of Sixty-year-old Woman Found in Holon*, *Leah Murdered in Her Home* and, of course, *Police Have No Leads*. Leah Yeger's murder joined four others that had taken place since the start of winter and still hadn't been solved, and a wave of investigations that had been opened against senior police officers, all under suspicion of sexually harassing female officers. The joke at the station was that the only thing less pleasant these days than being a female officer in the Israeli police was being a male one. In all the papers Yeger's face could be seen in the passport photo provided by the family, while only at him did a different face peer out, one beaten and lifeless.

Avraham prepared rolls with cream cheese and a thin slice of tomato and made black coffee for the two of them. When Marianka asked him what was in the paper, he spun them around on the table as if she could read the Hebrew. While drinking his first cup of coffee the need for a cigarette was intense, and he took another roll for himself instead. In recent weeks he had gained ten pounds; not because he had quit smoking but rather due to the fact that since Marianka had arrived he ate two dinners each evening – the one they ate together and the one he had alone afterwards, when he snuck back into the kitchen. They sat at the table for a few more minutes in uncharacteristic silence, as if it had crawled into their flat from the scene where the body was found.

The meeting of the Special Investigations Team which had been scheduled for that morning began at seven thirty exactly, and this was the only thing on the first day of the investigation that took place as planned, and as he had hoped. Avraham arrived early and thought Ma'alul would be late as usual, but Eliyahu entered the conference room next, his dark, bald pate and the hair around his temples wet, as if he had just come out of the shower. Commander Eyal Sharpstein, Investigations Coordinator Lital Levy and Sergeant Esty Vahaba, who had been the officer in charge of Leah Yeger's rape case and who had been temporarily added to the team, also joined the meeting. Major General Benny Saban was supposed to arrive at some point but had been held up at Tel Aviv district headquarters.

When the members of the team entered the room, Avraham tried to forget that this was the first time he was running a Special Investigations Team meeting about a murder case. In the past he had taken part in investigations of deaths occurring in unnatural circumstances, but Ilana Lis usually headed them up. She too would always arrive early and wait in the conference room for everyone. Like him now, she had sat at the head of the table back then, rectangular glasses resting on the end of her nose and her eyes on the pages spread out before her, waiting patiently for everyone to get coffee and grab their seat. During those briefings Avraham had sat where Eliyahu Ma'alul was now. Always with a blue pen in hand and an open notebook. Waiting for Ilana to begin speaking. But Ilana was now on sick leave, in and out of hospital for cancer treatment, and Avraham was by himself, Head of the Investigations Division, and the responsibility fell on his shoulders only.

'As you know,' he opened the meeting, 'yesterday at four o'clock the body of Leah Yeger, resident of Holon, sixty years old, was found in a third-floor flat at 38 Krauze Street. She was discovered by her daughter. At present we don't know much about what happened to her, but I hope that this will change when findings from the forensics lab arrive. I want us to visit her apartment again, with one of her family members, or with more of them, but at present it appears that only a set of house keys and a handbag were taken from the scene. They have not been found. On the other hand, there are no signs of a break-in and her car wasn't stolen, even though the keys were at the scene. We have no eye-witnesses to the murder, but it appears we have a witness who heard something, a neighbour who lives on the floor below. Around two p.m. the witness heard sounds of a struggle from the flat above, and his testimony correlates with the time of death as determined by the paramedic, and his view that Leah Yeger was murdered by strangulation, after a struggle and having been struck on her head. And as I said, it's highly likely that we'll have good DNA findings and it appears we'll be receiving them today. According to a conversation I had this morning with the lab, there are samples under the nails and between the fingers of the victim that can be used. In any event, the state of the scene and the circumstances of death indicate an unplanned murder, perhaps the result of an argument that deteriorated into violence. An additional detail, which I ask you to keep secret even within the station, so that it doesn't accidentally leak out, is that Leah Yeger was the victim of a rape we investigated in 2012, for which the attacker is still serving time. In the meantime we have a gag order on this. Initial evidence is that yesterday she was not sexually assaulted.'

He looked at Esty Vahaba while he said these things. She had dealt with the rape investigation, and Avraham's glance explained her presence in the room. Sitting next to Ma'alul, she looked to Avraham like his daughter, and perhaps therefore he felt an immediate closeness to her, as if they were siblings. Like himself and Eliyahu, Vahaba was short, and her eyes were dark and very serious. Her facial expression barely changed, even when Avraham turned to her, and if she was disconcerted at finding herself there, she hid it well. The only things Avraham knew about her was that she wasn't married, that she lived with her parents and supported them, and that both of them were deaf.

Avraham paused for a moment, lifted his head from the papers and one by one examined the faces of those present in the room, as Ilana always did. Sharpstein wasn't listening to him, or so it seemed. His eyes were glued to the screen of his phone. The previous day too, when Sharpstein had arrived at the scene, he had done everything he could to avoid a conversation with Avraham and spoke to Ma'alul most of the time. Avraham had seen him before he went home, walking around with his hands in his pockets and examining the window and door hinges, as if he was debating whether to buy the apartment. It was clear to everyone that Sharpstein had not got over Benny Saban's decision to appoint Avraham and not him head of the division. A short time after the appointment he had requested a transfer to the Fraud Investigation Unit or some other national unit, but in the meantime he was forced to continue working in full cooperation with Avraham. It was impossible, however, to force him to hide his resentment.

'During this initial stage of our investigation,' Avraham continued, 'and until findings from the lab are received, I think we have at least two scenarios that we need to work on. The first is a break-in gone sour, or in any case a random act of violence. The second is that there's some connection between the murder and the rape.'

Ma'alul interrupted, saying, 'Avi, I would like to say something in this context. May I?'

Avraham signalled with his hand that he should go on. Sharpstein continued looking at his phone.

'Last night,' said Ma'alul, 'after you left the scene, Yeger's son arrived. I questioned him on the spot, and he conveyed to me information that seems to me to be of some importance. According to his statement, and Esty can elaborate on this in a moment, family members of the convicted rapist have not come to terms with the results of the trial. They harassed Yeger in the lead-up to the trial, demanding that she drop the charge; and after the conviction the situation worsened and they threatened to harm her in revenge. After the reading of the verdict there was even a skirmish between the two families in the court car park.'

Avraham looked at him dumbfounded, and Eliyahu identified the question in his eyes and smiled as he added, 'Wait, wait, Avi, that's not the end. And I didn't update you because it was late and I assumed you'd be sleeping. The man who was convicted is called David Danon and his son, who threatened the victim, is called Ami. He's the owner of a construction company and resides in Rishon. I contacted him immediately and he denied that the family had threatened Yeger, but it was clear that he felt they had an account to settle with her; I have no doubt about this. He claims that there was no rape and that the sexual relations between Yeger and his father were consensual. From his perspective, his father shouldn't have spent even a day sitting in jail. In any case, the son has an alibi for yesterday, and the alibi has been checked and confirmed. Ami was in a business meeting with clients. He's willing to take a lie-detector test and will be coming to the station this afternoon.'

Most of the details about Leah Yeger's rape that Esty Vahaba later delivered were known to Avraham from reading copies of the documents he had taken home the previous night, and he tried to listen to her and not brood on the treachery of Ma'alul, who for a few hours had hidden from him a possible direction for the investigation.

David Danon, who was convicted of rape, had been Leah Yeger's husband's business partner. They jointly owned a taxi and operated it themselves or through hired drivers. After Yeger died from a heart attack, Danon asked to buy Leah out of the partnership, but she refused because it was her main source of income. A few months after she became a widow, they met in her flat to talk business, and it was then that she was assaulted. She filed a complaint that same night, underwent medical tests at Wolfson Hospital and the findings were unambiguous. Despite this, Danon argued that the sexual relations had been consensual and that this wasn't the first time they had had sex. According to his argument, there was a romantic connection between them that had begun when Yeger's husband was still alive. He was arrested and brought before a judge the next day. The case was relatively simple, and Danon was convicted, primarily on the basis of the medical test and Yeger's testimony, and sentenced to four and a half years in prison. His family, as Ma'alul had said, refused to accept the conviction. Vahaba said that they had even engaged a private investigation company to gather incriminating evidence about Yeger.

Avraham's gaze passed from Ma'alul's face to Leah Yeger's in the picture that he had asked Lital Levy to put up on the board, next to the photographs of the scene. The picture that was taken when she was still alive. He hadn't played any part in the rape investigation, but he had met Yeger at the station and was familiar with the incident from discussions at division meetings, and he wondered if the picture had been taken before the rape or after. Yeger looked directly at the camera, and her expression was serious, but with a shadow of a smile. The facial expression of someone who grew up in the days when photographs were something you prepared yourself for, he thought. When this photograph was taken, was her husband still alive? Did things start to go wrong from the moment he died? First her husband's heart attack, and a short time after this she's assaulted by his partner. And accused by the rapist of having an affair with him before the death of her husband. And now the murder. Yeger herself apparently opened the door, perhaps to a person she knew, and was then attacked and strangled. And if her husband was still alive, none of this would have happened. David Danon wouldn't have dared to attack her, and the man who entered her home yesterday perhaps wouldn't have found her alone. But what were the chances that she would have set up a meeting with or opened the door to one of Danon's family members?

Vahaba's diction was quiet and matter of fact, and when she finished reviewing the rape file he said to her, 'Thank you, Esty. You'll work on this angle with Eliyahu. Call the rapist's family members in for questioning, as well as the private investigators they hired. And if there's DNA from the scene today, we'll soon know if it belongs to a relative of his, without even asking for samples from them, because Danon's DNA is in the database, right? Also, order Yeger's call log for the last month and check whether she received any calls from them, OK?'

He asked Sharpstein to call in Leah Yeger's son and

daughter and gather additional statements from them, and at the same time to work on the hypothesis that Yeger had been murdered during a break-in or burglary. He looked at everyone but was referring mainly to Sharpstein when he said, 'I don't know if you noticed, but renovations are under way in two buildings on the street. This means that there are workers in the area and this must be explored as well. Check who the workers are and if any have criminal or terrorist backgrounds, and also if any among them has been absent since yesterday afternoon. Other than this, we have to find her handbag. And before you leave, go over the pictures from the scene, OK? Perhaps you'll spot something you didn't see before.'

This was an investigation procedure he had learned from Ilana Lis, and it seemed to him that only Sharpstein noticed it. To examine photographs from the scene a day or two later with fresh eyes. To present them to police who weren't involved in the investigation and hadn't seen the scene before. Maybe someone would notice a detail that no one had yet registered.

Sharpstein and Lital Levy were getting up to leave when Avraham said, 'Just one more thing,' and Levy sat back down in her seat. 'We received a report that we haven't yet managed to verify regarding a police officer who was in the building a short time after the murder,' he added. 'We're finding out if the testimony is correct and, if so, who the officer is and if he arrived at the building as a result of someone contacting the switchboard. I request that you don't discuss this testimony with anyone not currently in this room before we understand what's going on.'

He thought that the meeting would end with this, but Sharpstein suddenly asked him, 'How old is your witness do you know?' Avraham didn't understand his question at first. He didn't recall the exact age of the neighbour from the second floor, or his name, and the pages on which he had written his notes at the scene were on the table in his office. 'He told this story to me too,' Sharpstein continued. 'He grabbed me on the stairs yesterday when I got there. He's seventy-plus. And had just woken up when the whole thing happened.'

Vahaba didn't understand what Sharpstein was getting at either and asked him, 'So what?' but Sharpstein turned directly to Avraham as he continued. 'Did you maybe clarify with him if he usually wears glasses?' he asked, 'and if so, did he manage to put them on before he saw the policeman through the hole in the door for less than half a second?'

Vahaba and Lital Levy looked at Avraham, but he didn't answer. He hadn't asked the neighbour a thing about glasses. And he didn't remember if the man had been wearing glasses when he questioned him yesterday.

As Saban was busy at the Tel Aviv district headquarters, his meeting with Avraham was postponed until the afternoon.

Avraham returned to his office and for a few minutes merely stared at the building site visible from his window and the cars passing by on Feichman Street, waiting for the phone to ring. He studied the photos from the rape file again and examined David Danon's face, and since the phone didn't ring he eventually called the forensics lab at

National Police Headquarters, but they still didn't have any news regarding the samples taken from the body and from various items in the apartment. He asked the reason for the delay, and the clerk said, 'Are you serious? Do you think this is the only case we're working on here?'

Other files were sitting on his desk as well, cases at various stages of progress, but he couldn't bring himself to open any of them. He tried to recall whether the neighbour from the second floor had been wearing glasses during their conversation. The investigation was being conducted without him at the lab in Jerusalem and in interview rooms on the two floors below and he was doing nothing concrete, and he wondered if this was how a division commander should direct a murder investigation; if, in fact, Ilana Lis would direct it in this way. The first stage in solving a case is selecting the investigators correctly, she had always told him, but he wanted to question Leah Yeger's daughter again himself and speak to her son, whom he still hadn't seen, and sit in the interview room facing the rapist's relatives. Mainly, he wanted to return to the murder scene, even though he still didn't know what he was looking for. And in the meantime he restrained himself and didn't call Ilana. When the chemotherapy treatments began she had informed him that she was not willing to have anyone other than her family members accompany her through the process, and when Avraham tried to understand why, she said to him, 'Because I don't want anyone seeing or even hearing me in the state I'm going to be in. Not even you.'

The wooden pipe that Marianka had bought him in Brussels was in a drawer, and he took it out and held it unlit in his mouth. After he had decided to give up cigarettes he had tried to use it a few times when he was alone in the office, but it kept going out and he finally gave up, but every so often he would bite it between his teeth to help him to relax. Later he went down to the cafeteria and bought himself a cheese sandwich and ate it in his office while reading the brief reports that Sharpstein had sent from the interviews with Leah Yeger's son and daughter, which were in his inbox when he returned.

The son claimed that he hadn't been in contact with his mother for a few months, and thus couldn't say a thing about her life, whether she had relationships or if she was involved in disputes of any sort. *According to the witness*, Sharpstein wrote, *he had no conflicts with his mother, including conflicts over the inheritance or any other financial matter.* He was thirty-six years old and was employed as a caretaker of a secondary school in the north. *Yesterday afternoon he was serving army reserve duty and he there received the message about his mother.* When Sharpstein asked him when the last time he spoke or met with his mother was, the son claimed he hadn't spoken to her in months and didn't remember the exact date on which they last had a conversation. Afterwards he was asked if in his opinion anyone wanted to harm his mother, and he said there's no doubt that it's *one of the rapist's relatives.* The daughter, by contrast, had a close connection with her mother. They met up a few times a week and spoke on the phone at least once a day. Despite this, she didn't know of any disputes her mother was involved in and claimed that to the best of her knowledge no one wanted to harm her.

Avraham read the reports twice and then tried to get

Sharpstein on the phone, without success. What bothered him was the disconnect between the fact that the son hadn't spoken to his mother for a long time and his conviction that he knew who had attacked her. And there was another thing, which he wrote in pen at the bottom of the report in order to remind himself to ask Sharpstein: *How is it that her son wasn't in contact with her despite the rape she went through?*

Ma'alul had tried to call him twice since the morning meeting, but in the end they met in the cafeteria, accidentally. Avraham had gone down to eat lunch before two, even though he wasn't hungry, and Ma'alul entered the room a few minutes later and sat down next to him. Ma'alul ordered himself a large cheese pastry with an egg, and even before taking a bite of it asked Avraham if he could try the cooked chicken and potatoes that were left on his plate, as they were making him nauseous. He asked Avraham, 'Has Sharpstein seen her kids already?' And Avraham nodded. And only when Ma'alul continued as if nothing had happened and asked, 'And did you meet with Saban? Is he interested in the case at all?' did Avraham say to him what he'd wanted to say during the meeting.

'You should have updated me yesterday about the rapist's son. It's a shame you waited until the meeting this morning.'

Ma'alul set down his fork. He asked him, 'Why? It was late and I knew we were going to meet first thing this morning,' and Avraham said to him, 'Because I needed to know yesterday, not discover it at the meeting like everyone else.'

Ma'alul returned the plate with the chicken to Avraham and wiped his mouth with a napkin. It seemed to Avraham that he was hurt when he said quietly, 'Avi, what's up? I understand that there's a lot of pressure on you, but you do know you're not working alone, right? That you have people to rely on? You know very well that I can't immediately report every single thing that comes up, and I definitely don't think that I need to report every single thing *to you*. Did I try to hide something from you?'

His deep-set eyes searched for Avraham's gaze and didn't find it. Avraham was remembering the dream in which Ilana had hidden the name of the murderer from him and thought that perhaps it was because of this that he wanted to call her so badly, when Ma'alul continued, saying, 'Please conduct this investigation with peace of mind and with the team, Avi. And do me a favour, let's not start dealing in bullshit, OK? This isn't the first case for any of us, and it isn't the first time we're working together either. So let's work openly, like we usually do.'

But it was his first murder case! Perhaps there was little difference between an investigation like this and any another investigation. Nevertheless, there was a difference, because in most of the cases he investigated the victims could speak, and even if they didn't know everything or hid details, he relied on the fact that he'd succeed in reading between the lines and the lies, and he couldn't ask Leah Yeger a thing, despite the open eye and gaping mouth that had been frozen as if in the middle of a breath or an effort to tell him something.

Ma'alul waited for his answer and Avraham pushed the plate back in his direction and tried to appease him when he asked, 'When did you work until?' And was stunned when Ma'alul responded that he had been at the scene until two in the morning and even then hadn't gone home, but instead slept at the station so as not to be late to the meeting. 'And it was nice,' he said. 'Do you know how long it's been since I've slept here? I felt thirty years younger.'

It was strange, how each of them was responding to the case differently. Ma'alul was right when he said that Avraham was dealing in bullshit. He waited all day for a call from the lab that didn't come, for a meeting with Benny Saban that was postponed again and again, and it wouldn't be until the following day, when he was back in his office questioning Diana Goldin, that he would feel that he had actually started to investigate the case.

When his meeting with Saban finally started, a little after four, Avraham was still thinking about the conversation with Ma'alul. Saban blinked at him from behind his wide desk when he said, 'You understand that it will be a disaster if we don't solve this case quickly?' And Avraham nodded. 'Did you see the articles in *Yediot* and *Haaretz* today? They're coming down hard on the police commissioner because of the unsolved murders and the inquiries into the police officers' sexual-harassment cases. You understand that this is an investigation that he'll take personally, right, Avi?'

Avraham said to Saban quietly, 'We'll solve it.' Saban interrupted to add, 'And the worst is that damn rape, Avi. That this woman was raped and now she's been murdered. Do you think there's a connection?'

Avraham still had nothing to share with Saban, but he said

that there were good findings at the scene and then he told him about the threats from the rapist's family. If it became clear that this was the angle, then there was a chance to solve it quickly: David Danon's DNA was in the police database, and if a relative of his had assaulted Leah Yeger they'd know it within twenty-four hours at the most. Also, they'd know if Leah Yeger had been assaulted by one of her own family members. Saban asked if these were the main angles of the investigation, and Avraham answered that for now, yes, but he wasn't exclud-ing the possibility that she had been killed during a burglary gone wrong. Sharpstein had spent the afternoon going over burglary cases in the area and was trying to obtain a list of labourers working at local building sites, and intel-ligence agents were out searching addicts and dealers in stolen property for the contents of Yeger's bag, primarily her credit cards and mobile phone. If the burglar was a known criminal, it was reasonable to assume that his identifying marks would be in the police database too.

'Do you think it could be her son?' Saban suddenly asked, and Avraham said, 'Don't know.' Something in what the son had said to Sharpstein bothered him, but without having met him personally he couldn't say what. And he again thought about the fact that the son was the one who had so confidently directed them to the rapist's family members.

Without a doubt, Leah Yeger wouldn't have hesitated to open the door for her son.

Avraham didn't say any of this aloud, but Saban said to him, 'So let's exhaust these angles for now. That's what's most available to us, no? And let's extend the gag order until we have a suspect in hand. I don't want any detail of the investigation to leak out, and especially not the fact that Yeger was raped and that afterwards threats were made to her. Do you realize how we'd look?'

Avraham had just stood up to leave his office when Saban recalled what he had told him yesterday during the phone call at the scene, and asked him, 'And what about the policeman who was there? Do you know anything about him yet?'

And Avraham had to respond, 'Not yet.'

'You still haven't managed to identify him?'

'According to the log, there was no prior call to the switchboard, and no police officer was sent to the building before the daughter got in touch at four thirty. The eyewitness might be mistaken.'

'And if he wasn't mistaken?'

If he wasn't mistaken, Avraham explained, then Leah Yeger's murderer might not be a relative of David Danon or her son but a policeman instead. And another possibility was that during the murder, or a short time after it, someone contacted the switchboard and a patrol officer was sent to the scene of the incident, and someone was now trying to hide this and had even erased the call from the log.

Saban was astounded by this idea even more than by the possibility that Leah Yeger had been murdered by a police officer. 'Why would someone do a thing like that?' he asked, and Avraham said, 'If someone contacted the switchboard and a policeman went to the scene, knocked on the door and then turned around and left without doing a thing, while the murderer was inside the flat and Yeger was maybe still alive, he has good reason to hide it.'

Saban didn't want to think about this at all. He closed his eyes for a moment and then rose and closed the door.

'Let's hope that that isn't what happened, Avi. Or that your witness is mistaken,' he said quietly when he returned to sit down. Then he asked Avraham to put his mobile on the table. 'This entire conversation is off the record, Avi. From my perspective, it didn't take place – not this part of it – is that clear? You did not inform me that a policeman may have been there, and I know nothing about it, do you understand?'

It took Avraham a while to understand what Saban was telling him, because while he was speaking Avraham was thinking about something else. He saw in his imagination the patrol officer going up to the flat and knocking, and on the other side of the door he could picture Leah Yeger struggling with a man who was attacking her, trying to call for help. A man who was, perhaps, her son. 'If a policeman was there during the time she was murdered, the entire district is in deep trouble,' Saban continued. 'And even if that turns out to be true, no one's saying that we have to concentrate on that now, correct? For the time being, that's a marginal detail in the investigation, and our task is to find the murderer and not the policeman who perhaps screwed up. Are you with me, Avi? Do you agree with me?'

Only in the evening, when Avraham had returned home and reconstructed the conversation for Marianka, did he understand that Saban had hinted to him that if indeed prior contact had been made with the switchboard and the log erased, it was better for neither of them to look into the matter. It was possible to accuse the neighbour of making a mistake and, as for the existence of the police-man who came down the stairs and disappeared, if there was such a person, there was no other evidence.

'Do you really think that this is what he asked of you?' Marianka asked, and Avraham said, 'Yes.'

'And what did you answer?'

'That for now we have other angles to investigate any-way. But that I'll investigate this case as I know how.'

'And what did he say?'

'Nothing. What could he say?'

When they sat down at the table in the kitchen to eat dinner he wanted to talk about her, about her day at work, but Marianka insisted on discussing the case, and he tried to tell her about it, again omitting any mention of the rape. They ate pasta with tomato sauce and drank red wine, and Avraham told her about the findings that were supposed to arrive from the lab in Jerusalem and about the keys and the handbag that hadn't yet been found, about the ques-tioning of the construction workers in the area and about Sharpstein's conversation with Leah Yeger's son, but he didn't tell her about David Danon and his family's threats.

While he was speaking, was there a glimmer of longing or sadness in her eyes because she had given up her posi-tion with the Brussels police; or did it just seem so to him? He wanted to spare her the sadness and therefore, when she asked to see them, he said that he didn't have photo-graphs of the scene with him. She touched his hand when she said, 'You look worried, but it sounds to me that up to now you've done everything you should, no?' And he said, 'Could be.'

'And you haven't started smoking again, right?'

All this was so different from the flat he had always returned to at the end of a workday before Marianka had arrived.

Now there was a working radiator in the living room, and when he opened the door he entered lit and heated rooms, and for the first time in a while he had someone to talk to. So why was it that every time he stuck the key into the keyhole he was sure she wouldn't be there? And why, even though she was, did he act as if he was alone? Marianka suggested that they continue watching *The Bridge*, but the last thing he wanted to see were detectives who knew everything. He washed the dishes, and when he heard her turn on the television in the living room he closed the kitchen door and made himself an extra sandwich. Afterwards, he returned to the living room and sat down next to her, and a little while before he surrendered to the heat coming off the radiator and fell asleep on the sofa, in his clothes, he did ask her about her day at work, and she started to tell him, but his eyes went on closing.

By the time she asked, 'Do you remember that next week my parents are coming to visit us?' he could no longer hear.

5

That afternoon, while she was at work, Mali succeeded in hiding her tension and functioned as always. She stayed at the bank until six thirty, and on the way home went to her parents to pick up the girls. They had just eaten dinner and her mother laid an extra place on the table and served her rice-and-bean soup. This was the dinner they had often eaten in her childhood, in the winter, when her father returned from work, at five thirty or six, and perhaps because of that Mali would have liked to remain there. Perhaps it was also the pregnancy that made her want someone to take care of her so she could stop taking care of everyone for a moment. When she had left the flat it had been in disarray, with Kobi wandering around the living room looking for his umbrella, and she would have to clear all that up when they got back.

Her mother, as always, didn't notice. She talked about her winter migraines and the water stain the rain had made on the ceiling. Only her father looked at Mali while she ate. From time to time he placed his hand on Daniella's fair hair, and when she had finished eating he helped her wipe her mouth with a napkin. And even though Mali had asked her mother to do homework with Noy, she discovered that the books hadn't been opened and that

Noy hadn't prepared for a maths test, and this of all things caused her to feel that she was losing control and that her family was disintegrating.

Kobi hadn't called since she left him at noon. And Mali hadn't stopped thinking about the conversation with Harry and about Kobi's plan to leave her with the girls and travel to Australia. Would anything have changed if she had dared to speak to her father that evening? But what could she have said in front of the girls? That this time the collapse was too frightening? That Kobi was falling and that they were falling along with him?

Afterwards, back at the flat, she found a note on the dining-room table, written on the back of an electricity-bill envelope. And even though it was two lines long and didn't say much, it gave Mali a bit of hope, because in it Kobi finally spoke. *I'll be back in the morning. Sorry about everything. Tomorrow I'll explain to you what's happened.*

The flat wasn't in the state she had expected, and Mali saw that Kobi had tried tidying it up, especially the girls' rooms. But Daniella, who never missed a thing, asked her, 'Why did someone make a mess for me?' And Mali said, 'I started to rearrange the wardrobes, but I didn't manage to finish before work.' In their bedroom there were clothes and bedding scattered on the floor, but her clothes, which Kobi had removed from the wardrobe, had been placed on the bed as if he had started to fold them and then given up. The umbrella that she had bought wasn't discarded on the floor in the living room. He had stood it up next to their bed as if he wanted Mali to see. Their luggage was in its place in the utility room on the roof, and when she saw it she was almost certain that Kobi hadn't been packing for a trip when she had surprised him earlier.

She got Daniella into bed without a shower, but it took her some time to fall asleep, and while Mali sat on her bed and caressed her thin arm they talked about Purim, and this conversation Mali wouldn't ever forget. Daniella asked if she had to dress up and Mali said that she didn't and then asked, 'But why don't you want to? Because we didn't buy you a new costume? All your friends at nursery will be dressing up,' and Daniella turned over in her bed and said to her, 'Not because of that. Because I'm scared,' and a few days later, when Mali recalled her answer, it gave her the chills. That evening of all times no calming sounds came from outside: not the neighbours' conversations and not the distant noise of buses from the boulevard. Mali tried to smile when she asked, 'Of what, my sweetie? Of costumes?' And Daniella was silent and after some time said, 'Of princesses, Mum.'

Afterwards, Mali helped Noy with her homework in the living room, despite the late hour, and the maths exercises calmed her down because they caused her to think about other things. Maybe she and Kobi weren't yet disintegrating? Was it just another temporary setback? They'd had difficult periods since Eilat and, actually, there had been some even before then. They had never spoken of a separation, but two years ago Mali did suggest to Kobi that they go to therapy; only this wasn't a practical suggestion because there were things neither of them could say.

When Noy asked to go to sleep, Mali ceased trying to extend the evening. She took her to bed and when Noy asked her, 'Where's Dad?' she said that he'd be back in a bit because she was certain of this, despite his note. And until around midnight she was still hoping. She continued tidying up the house and tried Kobi once on his phone and then went up to the roof, as if there was a chance that he was hiding from her there. Harry lay in the utility room and next to him was a small puddle of vomit, and she filled the bowl with water and opened the door for him in order to air the room, but he didn't want to leave.

Only at midnight did she remove the key from the key-hole before getting changed in the lit bedroom.

This was a fundamental rule that Kobi was forbidden to break: it didn't matter what was happening between them, he didn't leave her to sleep alone. She lay in bed and tried thinking about the conversation with Daniella and the pregnancy that she still hadn't told anyone about, just not about the heavy hand. The fear was with her in the room, even with the lights and the phone. She felt it there and didn't close her eyes. She opened a window despite the cold wind, but the street was still silent and the fear didn't leave her. And her mistake was that she wanted to call Gila, because when she looked at the clock she saw that the time was almost one thirty. *The same time.* And then Mali could no longer control the fear, and it returned and placed its hand on her throat.

Eilat had been her first trip alone since the girls had been born, and she hadn't been sure she wanted to go. Kobi had encouraged her, because all the branch managers were supposed to participate, and on the Thursday and Friday mornings professional-development sessions were being held for mortgage advisors and there'd even be an informal discussion with the board members. An opportunity not to be missed, he said. And he and the girls would have a good time.

On Thursday morning she the other managers took off from Tel Aviv airfield and before ten were in their rooms at the Royal Club Hotel on the beach. She was lucky because she got room 723, with a balcony looking out on to the sea.

The first day was long and ended with a dinner in the hotel's dining room, after which she went out with her close friend Aviva and a few friends from other branches to a pub on the beach called Zorro. After this, when she was asked about it, she didn't remember if there had been a man at the pub who was staring at her. During the lectures that day and the next morning she sat in one of the last rows in the conference hall, next to Eran Amrami from the Jerusalem branch, who had worked with her at the Holon branch until two years ago. At the end of the second day, before Shabbat began, a celebratory meal was held in the events hall. Prizes were awarded to outstanding employees and speeches were given by board members. Those who observed the Sabbath went up to their rooms, and everyone else continued to the dance party in the hotel's disco, which was also open to outside visitors. They were given vouchers for drinks at the bar, and Mali drank two glasses of white wine. When she was asked at the police station if she had felt that someone had been looking at her during the party, she didn't know what to answer. Most of the people at the disco were bank employees, some of whom she knew well and some hardly at all, but there were others there as well, tourists perhaps, though at that weekend at the beginning of March the hotel wasn't full. And there were also waiters and maids and caretakers, men and women, but she didn't remember anyone in particular, and everyone was questioned. During the police investigation it came out that a Swiss tourist, a forty-three-year-old man, who was staying at the hotel, had left suddenly in the early hours of the morning, and the police asked her to look at the pictures of him that had been recorded on security camera, but she couldn't say if that was him because the cameras were old and the pictures blurry. There were no cameras in the hotel hallways, in order to maintain the guests' privacy, but the lobby and car park had CCTV, and Mali spent hours looking at tapes, to no avail. At the entrance to the hotel there was, of course, a security guard, but because the restaurants and the disco were open to visitors it was impossible really to know who was coming and going.

Mali had gone up to her room some time before one in the morning. They knew this from text messages, and also from Aviva's testimony.

Was he already in the room? Had he entered it when she was at the disco and lain in wait for her in the bathroom? Or maybe he'd been on the small balcony, hiding behind the heavy purple curtain? She didn't check whether the door to the balcony was locked before she lay down to sleep, and the female detective from the Eilat police who took her statement had thought that this was because she was drunk, but back then she simply wasn't a person who checked if doors were locked.

Perhaps you said something inviting to someone that you didn't intend to say? You met someone at the club and it may be that you don't remember. How can you be sure that you went up to the room alone, or that you didn't arrange to meet someone in the room if you were drunk?

But she hadn't been drunk, not to that extent, and this was evident from the text messages that she had sent to Kobi before settling down to sleep: *I wasn't outstanding this year. No employee of the year award and no bonus. Are you already sleeping?* Kobi had replied immediately: *There's no such thing, to me you're always outstanding. We miss you. I'm watching a movie in bed.* She turned on the television to see what he was watching.

Did you go to the bathroom before you fell asleep? But you didn't wash your face? You went to bed without removing your make-up? The policewoman had asked her so many questions. And the next day there were indeed traces of make-up on her face.

On the television was an episode of *Friends* that she'd seen countless times, and she had watched it as she got into bed, in warm pyjama bottoms and a long-sleeved shirt, not in the clothes that she'd worn to the party. And a short time after this she fell asleep, apparently, because the next thing she remembered was the hand.

It came from out of the darkness and crushed her throat.

Did she wake up a moment before she felt the weight of his hand on her neck and then the second hand on her mouth only because it cut the air off, or because of its smell? The smell she remembered. A smell of beer and a smell of a body she didn't know and a smell of sweaty cotton and a smell of soap. Mali recounted it to the detective, but the woman lost patience and said that the smell wouldn't help, that they needed a description of the man's facial features or physical build, but she couldn't supply one because it had been dark and the assailant had worn a ski mask over his face. He wore jeans, of this Mali was certain, and it seemed to her that his left shoulder was lower, or drooping, as if he had a curvature in his back. By his weight she felt that he was thin and narrow.

The other questions they asked her Mali didn't understand either. Not the questions about her family or about her relationship with Kobi or why he wasn't with her in the hotel, and not the question about whether or not the rapist had been violent. At the hospital they clearly saw signs of the ties around her elbows and ankles, and there was also the small cut he made on her neck, at the very beginning, with a knife that seemed to her to have been a regular knife, for cutting vegetables, maybe not in order to injure her but rather so she'd understand that she was in life-threatening danger. When the policewoman insisted on asking again if he had been violent throughout the time of the rape, Mali didn't know what to say to her. He hadn't removed the knife from her neck for even a second, but there were moments in which he hadn't been violent, or at least not *only* violent, perhaps mainly the moments in which she closed her eyes. The time at which everything occurred was known as well because, right at the beginning, she heard another ding from her phone, another text, which she only afterwards saw had come from Kobi: *The movie's over. Are you asleep?*

It was sent at 1.44 and she remembered that immediately after she heard the ding she again tried to plead with the assailant to stop; she didn't succeed because of the cloth that he had wrapped around her mouth, but, nevertheless,

she kept trying to say to him, 'Stop. Please stop. I'm beg-
ging you. I have two little girls. I have two little girls. I
have two little girls . . .'

Was he able to understand her at all? For some reason,
she had thought about her father and Gila and especially
about the girls, but not about Kobi. 'I have two little girls'
was a sentence she grasped on to like a drowning person
to a lifebelt. She imagined her father looking at her and
herself running quickly when everything was over, running like she used to, in school, for miles without stopping.
And there was also a moment when she saw Kobi in the
room, and he was smiling at her as if he was trying to
calm her. But when she wanted to call to him for help, he
disappeared.

In the end the assailant removed the ropes that he had
tied around her hands and legs, as well as the scarf that
covered her mouth. He again placed his hand over her
mouth as he said to her through the ski mask, in English,
'I'm coming back. If you try to scream, I'll murder you,'
and she heard him enter the bathroom and the tap running. She couldn't see a thing from the bed because the
door to the bathroom was in the hallway, right next to the
entrance to the room, and because it was dark. So she
waited. The television was still on, because she remembered that she heard an advert. The policewoman didn't
understand why Mali didn't scream at that moment or
flee from the room, and Mali tried to explain to her
that she didn't know he was no longer there. She didn't
hear the door to the room closing because of the television and the running water and, only after a long time,
perhaps an hour, did she dare to get up.

The bathroom was empty, and the tap was on.

The first thing she thought to do was to call Kobi. Her phone was still next to the bed. But she first took off her pyjamas, put on the clothes that she had worn that evening and went out into the illuminated hallway. Fighting the impulse to run, she walked slowly the length of the hallway and went down a floor in the lift, which was where she saw for the first time in the mirror her face and the cut bleeding on her neck.

It wasn't her.

It was almost three when she knocked on Aviva's door, room 606.

The next morning Kobi was already there and she remembered him standing in the doorway at the hospital. She hadn't cried at all until then, but when he hugged her, without saying a word, the sobs burst forth, wild and uncontrollable, and Kobi held her in his arms until the policewoman and the doctor entered the room and asked him to leave. He refused and demanded to stay with her, even when the policewoman insisted, and only when Mali asked him to go did he agree.

Mali got out of bed because it was clear she wouldn't be able to fall asleep. And walking relaxed her somehow. Her hands and legs weren't tied together. And the living-room lights were on. She peeked through the blinds at the street. No traffic. Only parked cars. Her mobile phone was clenched in her fist. Suddenly, she thought about his car. She hadn't seen it since yesterday, and where could he have gone without it? Her anger at Kobi came and went, but it was mixed up with a desire for him to return so that

83

she wouldn't be alone. She checked that the front door was locked before entering the girls' rooms. Their windows were shuttered, and from the stairwell too there was only silence.

Would it have been different if her attacker had been caught? During the first few weeks Mali didn't want to know a thing about the investigation. She didn't recognize herself, like at that first instant in the mirror in the lift. She didn't understand who this woman was who couldn't overcome the panic attacks that froze her in unexpected moments or couldn't choke back the uncontrollable outbursts of crying. And in moments of silence she thought only about the girls, about what they were seeing.

Kobi was wonderful then, better even than she could have hoped. She was still on leave from work and they were eating lunch at home when he informed her that he had quit his job. It wasn't a perfect job – he had never expected that he would be a security guard at clubs and building sites – but the pay was reasonable and the work in shifts left him two, sometimes three, free mornings a week, during which he could look for another job, or maybe even return to college. When she asked him not to be in a rush to leave, he revealed to her that he had demanded not to do any more evening shifts, but that the man in charge of scheduling wasn't willing to oblige. They had got into a row that almost ended in blows, and in the end Kobi had left. He hadn't told the man why he didn't want to work evenings, of course, because he hadn't told anyone what had happened to her in Eilat. Not even friends. And certainly not the girls. Mali hadn't known what to say to them when she returned from Eilat, but

Kobi was adamant that they couldn't tell them a thing, and in the end they went with the story that Mummy was sick with the flu and needed to rest, and Daniella and Noy stayed another two days with Mali's parents. She still didn't feel that she was back to herself when they returned home, and in those first weeks she had crying and panic attacks that she couldn't control and hated herself for this, and Kobi took the care of their daughters entirely by himself. And despite her efforts to hide it, it seemed to Mali that Daniella, who was less than three at the time, picked up on something. She stopped crying, as if she had matured all at once, and also cuddled up with Mali much more and invented the affection game that the two of them had played ever since: Mali would lie on the sofa in the living room, usually in the afternoon, pretending to be asleep, and Daniella would stroke her hair for a long time, speak in a whisper and sing lullabies to her, as if her mother was the baby daughter.

At the bank they knew everything, because of the circumstances of the assault and the extended leave Mali took, but no one said a word, other than Aviva. And Mali never spoke to her parents about what had happened either; she could speak about it only with Gila. Contact with the Eilat police dwindled, and every time Kobi called them to find out if there was anything new, they told him that the investigation was ongoing. Only in May, two months after the rape, did she consider for the first time that the assailant was still free, and this set her trembling. So they began sleeping with the lights on and locking the door even when they were at home. In July she was urgently called to Eilat to participate in a line-up, even though she repeated to them that she hadn't seen the attacker's face, and among the black men who were paraded before her at the station she didn't see any with a drooping left shoulder. Because he had spoken in English, the police were certain that the assailant was a foreign worker or an illegal refugee or perhaps the Swiss tourist, but she thought that the English could have also been a ploy and the detective agreed that this was a possibility. They tried reassuring her, telling her that her room in the hotel had been chosen at random because there was easy access to its balcony from the emergency staircase, and that fingerprints as well as two cigarette butts had been found on it, the assailant apparently having waited there for some time. And only a year and a half after the rape did a different detective from the Eilat police call her and admit that the investigation was stuck. Then they were inclined to think that the assailant was the Swiss tourist and they managed to locate the cab driver who had taken him from Eilat to Ben Gurion Airport, and the driver said that the passenger didn't utter a word during the four-hour trip. But the man was questioned by the Swiss police and denied any connection to the attack and said that he had returned to Switzerland because he had received a message that his mother was sick, and the Swiss police believed him and refused to investigate further. The pictures of the Swiss man that the detective emailed her to look at again didn't help: he was wearing jeans in them, but his face could barely be seen and no deformity in his body was detectable. Most terrible of all was that a year and a half later she was no longer certain that she remembered things well, not the clothes that her attacker had been wearing, and not even his smell, which she had thought would never leave her. Only the face of the woman she had seen in the mirror remained.

She saw it in the mirror almost every morning.

Despite this, in her thoughts, over the course of a few weeks, it was the Swiss tourist who had followed her that evening, at the party in the hotel and perhaps even before then. She was unable to free herself from him, as if even having untied her hands and legs from the ropes and removed the scarf from her mouth, she was still there, bound hand and foot to that bed. When she attended a meeting of a support group for rape victims, on the advice of the police, she was jealous that the other women there knew who had attacked them, and she never went again. No one cast any doubt as to whether she had been raped, but the fact that the rapist had never been found, and had taken with him the ropes and the scarf, made it seem as if the rape, even in her eyes, was less real, and also prolonged it endlessly. So she too stopped searching for the Swiss tourist and began searching for the attacker among the bank employees and among the clients who came for a meeting and among the men who sat next to her at the café or looked at her from their cars at a traffic light. And only during the last year had it seemed to her that the ropes around her hands and feet were no longer so tight. And when she looked in the mirror she sometimes saw in it again something of what had once been her face.

Mali succeeded in falling asleep that night only in Daniella's room, in the pullout bed.

She went in there after tucking Noy in and sat down on the bed that Daniella used for her dolls, and Daniella turned to her in her sleep, reached her hand out to her hair and a short time after this Mali fell asleep. Her sleep was deep, apparently, because she didn't hear the key turning in the lock nor the door opening, and she woke up only when she felt Kobi next to her.

He sat on the bed and looked at her. She asked him, 'What are you doing here?' as if this was no longer his home, and he said, 'I just got back.'

'Where were you?'

He didn't give her an answer to this question, not that night and in fact not afterwards either. They left the room so as not to wake Daniella and sat facing each other on the living-room sofa. She said to him, 'You left me alone all night. How could you do that to me?' From outside came a faint morning light and the sounds of a dustcart at work in the street. On Kobi's clothes was the smell of alcohol and cigarette smoke, and his eyes were red. She asked him, 'What happened to you?' and when Kobi said, 'Mali, I need help,' she responded immediately, 'Help with what? Help going to Australia? Do you need money for a plane ticket?'

Kobi didn't understand what she was talking about, and when she said, 'I spoke to your dad this morning,' he fell silent.

'What's happened to you?' she said again. 'Tell me what happened now. Don't you see you're torturing me? I can't live like this any longer, Kobi. I didn't do anything to you, right? I didn't do anything to you.'

He looked lost and hopeless to her. But what he told her

she couldn't have anticipated. And even in retrospect she thought there was no way she could have known that he was lying. He said, 'Mali, the police are looking for me,' and she looked at his red eyes.

In fact, the collapse was much greater than she had thought.

6

The news from the forensics lab arrived at the beginning of the second day of the investigation, when Avraham was on his way to the funeral. Rain wasn't falling and the car window was open, and when the telephone rang Avraham closed it and lowered the volume on the radio. 'Do you want the good news first or the bad news?' Lital Levy asked him, and he answered, 'You've known me long enough, no?'

The good news was that from the traces of skin and blood that were found under Leah Yeger's nails and between her fingers they had succeeded in producing a good sample of DNA. The bad news was that the DNA wasn't in the database, nor did it belong to a relative of the rapist David Danon. Avraham asked her about Leah Yeger's son, because from the moment he had opened his eyes that morning, the statement the son had given to Sharpstein at the station the day before had been on his mind. 'Did they check if it could belong to a relative of hers?' he asked, and she replied, 'Of whose? Do you mean of the victim? Don't think they did. But they certainly could. You want me to ask?'

It was usually like that. As Ilana always said: the second day of the investigation is the key day.

On the first day every angle is possible and every testimony or finding that is added to the case can become the start of a new investigatory lead. On the second day the possibilities dwindle because a few suspects have already been cleared and avenues of investigation that appeared reasonable the day before are ruled out, and also, new testimony and findings merge with stories that have already started developing, filling them in with details and granting them force.

On the same morning, while Avraham was on his way to the cemetery, Detective Eyal Sharpstein was busy gathering statements from foremen who worked on the street overseeing renovations, and later on he dropped in to question one of the workers, a resident of an Arab village in the north by the name of Adnan Gon, who had been absent from work on the day of the murder and the next day as well, and had been questioned in the past on suspicion of vehicle theft and aiding break-ins. Ma'alul and Esty Vahaba summoned the private investigator the Danon family had hired to find incriminating evidence against Leah Yeger. And Avraham was the only official representative of the Israeli police at the funeral, where for the most part he kept his eyes on Yeger's son. He arrived early and waited among those gathered in the courtyard of the funeral home, at the Salvation Gate. The morning was warmer than on previous days, almost spring-like. Avraham squeezed the daughter's hands when he saw her and told her that he was sorry for her loss, but he didn't approach the son and watched him from a distance while he greeted the mourners. His wife and children stood next to him. What surprised Avraham, when he understood that he had identified her son, were his proportions, which Sharpstein hadn't described in the interview report.

Erez Yeger was a broad, tall man, over six foot two, and his hands were those of a giant.

A little after ten the undertakers rolled the corpse on a stretcher to the funeral yard, and the small crowd gathered around it in a silent circle. Under the sheets the body looked so small to Avraham, as if it was the body of a child. He was surprised when Leah Yeger's children chose not to speak in her memory, and only an older woman, a friend apparently, spoke at length about the lovely years of her life, the years of raising the children and the shared trips abroad, before the suffering she had known in recent years. 'Now you're going to Yossi, who you loved so,' she said at the end of her speech, 'and at least you'll no longer have to miss him.'

The friend didn't mention in her speech that Yeger had been murdered; it was as if she had died of natural causes. Nor was the rape mentioned, except by implication, when her friend spoke about 'the bad years'. Nevertheless, it seemed to Avraham that all around him things were being whispered about the murder and that the mourners were staring at him. And for some reason the police photographer, who had been instructed to document the crowd of mourners, mainly photographed Avraham.

Afterwards, the short procession marched behind the stretcher through the paths of old and new graves to the burial site. In the distance Chinese workers were crawling inside giant beehive-like structures that were being erected to house the dead that were yet to come. And it grew hotter and hotter.

Because there were few men in the crowd, Avraham too picked up a shovel and helped to fill in the hole into which Leah Yeger had been lowered. And when the rabbi began saying the prayer of the orphans for the dead, the *Kaddish*, he found himself mumbling the opening sentences together with him: *Yitgadal veyitkadash shemei raba, be'almah divrah chirutei*, and then he suddenly bit his lips and stopped, because he was not an orphan.

After the body was interred, Leah Yeger's son threw himself on to her grave, and Avraham waited until his wife and other mourners lifted him up and carried him to a nearby water fountain and rinsed his face, before he rose and placed a small stone on the narrow mound of dirt. Among the people who helped lay her to rest, Avraham was the only one who knew almost nothing about her, and despite this he was supposed to try to understand the circumstances of her death, and he attempted to recall her face as he had seen it in the picture pinned up in the investigations room, and not the beaten face with the gaping mouth that he saw at the scene.

The contrast between the testimony of Leah Yeger's son during questioning, when he said he wasn't in contact with his mother, and his behaviour at the cemetery, bothered him. And when the son bent down and collapsed on the mound of dirt, almost in the position in which Avraham had found his mother in her flat, he thought how little he looked like his mother. Perhaps he looked like his father.

Leah Yeger, daughter of Hannah and Moshe Kantor, was buried next to her husband, Joseph Yeger, who was born in 1951 and died three years ago, before his time.

Avraham couldn't remember if he had seen his photograph in her flat.

Leah Yeger's phone log was waiting for Avraham in his office when he arrived, along with the information that the assailant's DNA indicated that there were no family ties between him and the victim. On the log there were no calls from Ami Danon or from the other numbers given by the rapist's relatives, but two details shocked him. The day before the murder a lengthy telephone call took place between Leah Yeger and her son, in contradiction to what the son had said to Sharpstein in his statement. According to the log, Yeger called her son in the morning, and he didn't answer. A brief time after this the son called her and their conversation lasted approximately seventeen minutes. The second number was the last one on the list and it surprised Avraham even more: on the day of the murder and at the presumed time of the crime, two o'clock, a call was made from the telephone line in Leah Yeger's flat to the emergency services The attempt was made from the flat's landline, but the call was disconnected before it was answered.

Avraham circled the son's telephone number with a blue pen, and immediately dialled the switchboard to clarify how they dealt with calls that were cut off before they were answered. 'Do you call back if the call is disconnected?' he asked the operator, but she didn't understand his question. 'The number shows up for you on some sort of screen, no? Can you see which number called?' He asked again, and the operator explained that she personally didn't return calls that were disconnected unless

94

several attempts had been made. 'Do you know how many kids call and hang up?' she asked. But, apparently, someone did get back to Leah Yeger, even though the additional call didn't appear in the log, because a policeman was sent to her house. He asked Lital Levy to check that there wasn't an additional call that was mistakenly dropped from the list and also to find out who was operating the switchboard at the time of the crime. He debated whether or not at that moment to call Erez Yeger in for additional questioning. According to the DNA, he wasn't the man who attacked his mother, so why did he lie to Sharpstein in his statement, saying that he hadn't spoken to her for months?

When Eliyahu Ma'alul entered his room Avraham was still puzzling over those two phone calls. Their conversation of the previous day had been forgotten, at least by Avraham, but Ma'alul remained standing while informing him about the statement of the private investigator hired by the Danon family. He said it was hard for him to believe that the investigator was involved in the murder or knew anything about it. According to him, the family had employed him only during the trial, and he had sworn to Ma'alul that he hadn't tapped Yeger's phone or illegally obtained any document or evidence. 'So what did he do? What exactly did they pay him for?' Avraham asked, and Ma'alul said, 'Mainly, he followed her. And photographed her. But nothing came of it. They had been hoping to get evidence that she was meeting with men and to base their defence on the fact that, therefore, the sexual relations had been consensual. And he hasn't been in contact with any-one from the family since the end of the trial.'

Avraham told Ma'alul about the findings sent from the lab in Jerusalem and Leah Yeger's phone call with her son, which Erez Yeger had hidden from Sharpstein, and Ma'alul thought that they needed to summon the son to the station immediately, despite the funeral, and asked Avraham if, in Sharpstein's eyes, the son was a suspect in the murder, but Avraham didn't know. He didn't tell him in his office about the phone call from the flat to the switchboard, but instead waited until they had left the building. He sat down on the steps to the station.

'I thought you quit smoking,' Ma'alul said to him, and still didn't look him in the eyes, as he always used to, and when Avraham said, 'I did,' Ma'alul asked, 'So why are we here?'

The reason was Benny Saban and the policeman who went down the stairs and disappeared.

Avraham told Ma'alul about the conversation with Saban and his request that Avraham not focus on the neighbour's testimony regarding the policeman. Now, when the list of Leah Yeger's calls included an attempt to contact emergency services, it was no longer possible to ignore it.

Ma'alul's large eyes opened wide while he listened to him. And when Avraham had finished speaking he told him in a whisper, 'Don't you even dare think of doing that, Avi. I won't let you, do you hear? What, are you crazy? We'll investigate it like all the other leads. And definitely now. If they got back to her from the switchboard and someone was sent there and didn't do what had to be done, we'll report that exactly like we're supposed to. And if you're scared of Saban, let me do it; I'll take that on myself, OK?

It'll be on me. I can't believe you're even considering this. And Benny Saban can go to hell.'

The conversation with Ma'alul encouraged Avraham because he felt that Ma'alul had forgiven him, but when he returned to his room he nevertheless picked up the phone to call Ilana Lis. But he had second thoughts and hung up. Sharpstein then called, to update him on the statements he had taken from workers at the building sites near the scene, and Avraham told him that Erez Yeger had lied to him during questioning. Only while they were talking did Avraham understand that if the son was involved in the murder, then it was possible to understand the disconnected call as well: had he injured his mother during an argument and then got frightened, dialled immediately himself and then changed his mind and fled? Maybe *she* had called when it seemed to her that the argument between them was liable to deteriorate into violence, but hung up in order not to put her son at risk? But, in any case, there was unambiguous evidence from the lab determining that Erez Yeger could not have been the assailant.

Avraham spread out the pictures taken at the scene, as well as his notes, and he read the sentence he had written in pen while taking the statement from Leah Yeger's daughter: *Murderer locked the door behind him?*

Why in fact had he written that? Perhaps because he thought that locking the door indicated that the murderer hadn't fled in a panic. He had stuck around. For a few minutes even. Tried to revive his mother and digest what had occurred. Had he dialled with the intention of turning himself in? But hung up when it occurred to him that he could disguise the murder as a burglary? He would have known where her wallet was, and that was why the scene was so orderly. He hadn't needed to search. He had locked the door behind him, because any delay in the discovery of the body would enable him to get further away from the place. Avraham read the question he had written again and again, and then added additional questions next to it, to some of which it seemed to him there were now answers:

Why did she open the door for the assailant?

Was she waiting for him? Did she know that he was coming?

Why didn't he take anything other than the handbag and keys?

Exactly when and how did he leave?

Exactly as he had done in the hours after the murder, he imagined Leah Yeger drinking coffee in the kitchen when the knocking came at the door. She set the mug down and got up from her seat. She walked slowly in the direction of the door, a distance of five or six steps, and Avraham opened the desk drawer, took out the pipe that Marianka had bought him and chewed the end of the mouthpiece. The door to Leah Yeger's flat opened in his imagination, and he thought that he was able to see the man of large proportions who stood on the other side.

He called Erez Yeger straightaway, but the phone was answered by a woman. She said that her husband was out driving, but when Avraham identified himself she added,

'Just a moment,' and a short time later the voice of Erez Yeger could be heard. Avraham asked him to come to the station immediately, and when the son asked him why, he merely said, 'For further questioning.'

'We're already in Haifa. It's urgent? People are coming to our house to offer their condolences.'

He wanted to see him right now and to gather testimony from him personally, but perhaps there was some logic in putting it off. He barely knew anything about the son, other than that he was a school caretaker, and postponing the interview for a few hours would enable him to research additional details and verify his alibi and perhaps even clarify with the sister the reason for the dispute between her mother and her brother. 'Can you come first thing tomorrow morning?' Avraham asked, and when Erez said, 'Yes, but can you tell me what's so pressing? Are there developments in the case?' he didn't answer.

The cafeteria was almost entirely empty when Avraham ate a late lunch there, alone. Only Efrayim Bachar, from the traffic division, was there, sitting at the other end of the large room, talking loudly on the phone to his daughter while chewing on toothpicks. He nodded a hello to Avraham.

Avraham ordered a salad and two sandwiches and ate quickly, and in his head the thoughts about the son and the phone call to the police mingled together. If he was feeling more energetic, for the first time since the start of the investigation, this was because he was no longer just waiting in his office. Again he thought about Benny Saban. During his years in the police Avraham had seen officers turn a blind eye to details of evidence more than once, but never before had he been explicitly asked to ignore testimony. And in these moments it seemed to Avraham that the neighbour's statement was telling a story that was simply impossible to deny: a policeman who was now trying to conceal his identity had gone to Leah Yeger's flat a few minutes after two, even though, according to the records, no patrol was sent to the building before four thirty. Avraham was determined to report the conversation to Ilana, although she wasn't on active duty.

On his way back to his office Avraham stopped at Lital Levy's desk to ask if there was anything new. She said there wasn't, and then looked down and handed him a sheet of paper. 'I forgot to give you this before. A list of people who were looking for you two days ago, when you were off,' she said, and he asked, 'When was I off?' before he remembered. He glanced at the paper on the way to his office and meant to put it on the stack of files on top of his desk when he saw the name Diana Goldin and next to it a telephone number. He went back to Lital Levy to confirm that he had read the name correctly.

'Do you know who took the call?' he asked, and Levy said, 'I did.'

'And did she say why she was calling?'

'She asked to speak to you, and when I told her you were off she said it wasn't important. Do you know who she is?'

He called the phone number that was written there but didn't get an answer and so he left Diana Goldin a message. Ilana Lis, on the other hand, picked up straight away, and his voice shook when he said to her, 'Hi, Ilana, how are you? It's Avi.'

She recognized his voice and he thought that she sounded happy to hear from him, despite her instructions. After all, for years, even when she left the station and transferred to Tel Aviv district headquarters, they had spoken on the phone almost every day, updating one another on their investigations. He didn't think Ilana would be able to disconnect from police work after twenty years in investigative departments. He didn't know if she was at her home or in the hospital, but he was too embarrassed to ask. When she was first diagnosed he had done some checking on the internet and to his delight discovered that she wouldn't be hospitalized for long weeks but rather just for each of a series of intensive treatments, between which she could recover at home. When he asked her again, 'How are you?' since she hadn't answered him, she only said, 'Couldn't be better, Avi. And you?' And he got down to business to cover up his awkwardness. 'I need your help with something,' he said. 'May I visit you when you're home and feeling OK?'

'It can't wait?' Ilana asked, and he said, 'It can wait a few days. But no more.'

'On the condition that we don't talk about any cases, as I asked. If it's something like that, then let's pass.'

'It not exactly that, Ilana. It's something else,' he said, and it wasn't a lie, because he did think that they'd speak only about Saban's request.

Diana Goldin tried to phone back while he was on the call with Ilana, and when the conversation ended, his phone rang again. He couldn't imagine why she'd been looking for him and, even once she explained, it took him time to understand. He said to her, 'Diana? Thanks for getting back to me. Police Superintendent Avraham. I had a day off and saw that you were asking for me, is that right?'

Diana said that it wasn't anything important. She wanted to return to the policeman who had been at her place a few days earlier the umbrella he had forgotten, and because she didn't remember his name and didn't have his phone number, she called the station and asked to speak to Avraham. When he asked her, 'When was the officer with you?' she said it had been a few days ago. Last Thursday. 'And in regards to what matter was he with you? Did you call for him?' Avraham asked, not expecting that his question would frighten her.

'What do you mean, "what matter"?' she asked quietly. 'With regard to the rape. What other matter could it be?'

He didn't want to worry her more than he already had and so he said he'd get back to her right away. He asked Lital Levy to find out who the policeman who had been sent to her home was. The idea that there was a connection between the two incidents, between the two policemen, occurred to him only when Diana Goldin's rape file was brought to his room and he studied it, but even then, when the idea expressed itself for the first time for an instant, he dismissed it immediately. There was a different killer in his thoughts during those hours, and there was a simple explanation for the policeman who had been observed at the crime scene. And only when he sat across from Diana Goldin and took her statement did he sense that perhaps he had been mistaken in hurrying to rule the connection out.

He rose from his seat and welcomed Diana Goldin warmly

when she entered his office, an hour later. Her hair was gathered in a ponytail and her face was small and beautiful, as he remembered. There was anxiety in her gaze, and he thought that perhaps he shouldn't have insisted that she come to the station straightaway. But Lital Levy told him that, according to her checks no police officer had been sent to Diana Goldin's home in recent days, and Avraham didn't want to wait. Studying the rape file before Diana arrived, he couldn't help but think about Leah Yeger.

Diana Goldin was assaulted in September 2012.

She was raped in her flat by an actor who was then her business partner at a small theatre that put on plays for children. She was thirty-two years old and resided in Bat Yam, and Avraham was the detective who investigated the case, over many hours. He was present at the confrontation between Diana and her attacker in the interview room on the second floor, when the actor continued to deny what Diana said. She had turned to the police a few weeks after the attack and, therefore, they didn't have good physical evidence, but Avraham believed her – and so did the court.

He asked Diana, 'How are you?' and when she immediately said, 'Can you explain what's going on?' he didn't answer. He hoped to calm her down by asking if she was still acting, and she told him that she had established a new theatre company for children's plays in Hebrew and Russian and that she performed them by herself, with puppets, mainly at nursery schools and libraries. About Michael Lan, the actor convicted of her assault, she didn't know anything other than that he was still serving his sentence. Avraham hadn't yet decided what exactly he would say to her, but Diana asked immediately, 'What, he wasn't a policeman?' and he asked her, 'Do you remember when he was there?'

'Almost a week ago. Two days ago I noticed that he'd left the umbrella at my place, and then I called you because I didn't have his phone number. He was there last Thursday.'

'And can you explain to me why he came to visit you?'

He had called her a few days beforehand, she said. Introduced himself as a detective in the investigations department of the Ayalon district and asked to see her. They agreed to meet on Thursday morning because she had a performance in the evening, and he said that he'd call the day before to confirm that it would take place and that he hadn't been forced to cancel because of other, more urgent matters. He suggested that they meet at the station, but said that he could also come to her home so that she wouldn't have to visit a place about which she must have unpleasant memories, and she agreed because it was more convenient.

'He didn't explain why he wanted to talk to you?' Avraham asked, and Diana said, 'Of course he did. Otherwise I wouldn't have met up with him.' According to what the policeman had said, Michael Lan had appealed his conviction and, prior to its coming to court, where she would probably be called to testify, the policeman had been appointed to interview her.

When Avraham looked at Diana he recalled that the thing that had surprised him when he first met her was that, despite the assault, there was something smiling in her face, almost clownish, as if even when she wasn't standing on a stage in front of children she remained a performer. But now she wasn't smiling. According to the inquiries

Lital Levy had made, Michael Lan had not appealed. And the main detail that Avraham was trying to understand in Diana's story was whether the policeman who had interviewed her knew the name and details of the rapist.

'That's what he called him from the beginning – Michael?' he asked, but Diana didn't remember. Then she added, 'Maybe not. I don't think so. Maybe he called him "the rapist" at the beginning.'

'And he knew your address?'

'He asked if the address had changed, and I said no. The second time he called, a day before the meeting, on Wednesday, he asked if the address was the same address, and I think I gave it to him.'

She said the last sentence quietly. Avraham poured her a glass of water, and she asked him, 'Why aren't you admitting that he wasn't from the police?' And Avraham answered, 'Because I don't know. It's reasonable to assume that he was from the police, but I'm trying to clarify on whose behalf he was sent.'

Diana covered her face with her hands. When she removed them she said, 'But what does that mean? Explain to me who he is,' and Avraham continued trying to calm her down. 'As I told you, I don't know,' he said. 'The police are a large organization with many departments and divisions, and one department doesn't always know what the others are doing. This happens a lot, I can assure you. It could very well be that he was a policeman who was sent to you to complete an investigation, but for now we haven't managed to find out on whose behalf. Can you describe him to me? What did he look like? That could help.'

The policeman was around Avraham's height, perhaps a bit taller, stocky, and his hair was light. Diana called the uniform he wore 'regular': dark pants and a light blue shirt, with a pin in the shape of the police logo and epaulettes. She didn't notice if he had a rank, nor did she remember his name, maybe because he didn't tell it to her, and she suddenly thought that she hadn't even asked him his name, and again she covered up her face and folded in on herself.

'Why would someone do a thing like that?' she asked, and Avraham saw that she was suffering not only because she understood what had happened but also because she was angry at herself for not being more cautious, and so he again said to her, 'Diana, I'll say to you once more that it could be that the man was a police officer on an assignment. Do you understand me? And even if he wasn't, you had no way of knowing that he wasn't sent by who he said he was,' and she interrupted him and again said, 'But I didn't even ask him his name. Don't you get it?'

Avraham waited for her to uncover her face. What he didn't reveal to her throughout their entire conversation, other than that he already knew that Michael Lan hadn't appealed, was that if someone had been sent to her to complete the details of the investigation it would have been a policewoman – not a policeman.

'Do you remember how much time he spent with you?' he asked, and Diana said that he had stayed for a long time. Maybe two hours.

'Why?'

'Because he wanted to know everything. You understand? Every detail. From the beginning.'

'What, for instance? What kinds of questions did he ask you? Can you tell me exactly how the conversation proceeded?'

The man had wanted to know how long she had known Michael Lan and what kind of connection there had been between them before the assault. And if she had a boyfriend at the time of the rape. And then he asked about what had happened that day, when they returned from a performance at the city library. How she invited Michael up to discuss their next project, and how they had too much vodka and got a little drunk, and how Michael suddenly asked her to dance and she agreed for some reason, even though his request seemed strange to her, and how when she felt him get hard up against her she asked him to stop and freed herself from his embrace and turned off the music. Michael had a girlfriend, whom Diana knew well and liked, and when he clung to her in order to continue dancing despite the silence, she grabbed the phone and told him that if he didn't stop she would call her. And the policeman also asked her about the clothes she had been wearing that evening, and whether Michael had torn them or if she had got undressed herself, and about what happened afterwards on the sofa in the living room and what she said to him during the assault and what Michael said to her when everything was over. And he recorded everything, from the very beginning.

'How do you mean, "recorded"?'

'On his phone. He showed me that he was turning the app on.'

'And while he was listening?'

'What about while he was listening?'

'What did he do?'

'Nothing,' she said. 'He looked at me. Sometimes he checked that the device was working, and also wrote in a notebook he had.'

'Did you get the impression that he was familiar with the details of your case?'

'He asked me to describe everything as if I was telling it for the first time, so I don't know. Maybe not. He said that it was necessary for the investigation.'

'And did he say anything about himself that you re-member? Something about the station he worked at? About his exact role with the police?'

Diana was unable to recall.

'And at no point did he try to harm you?'

'By hitting me? No.'

'You didn't feel threatened during the conversation?'

'Not at all.'

'You were at home alone while he was with you?'

'Who else would be there? I live alone.'

'And you don't remember any other details that could help us to identify him?'

'Other than what I told you? No. It might be that he spoke with an accent.'

'A Russian accent?'

'Not Russian, actually. English, maybe.'

'And did you feel that he was trying to get you to say something specific? That he was trying to force some-thing out of you?'

Avraham had no other questions, but Diana didn't want their conversation to end, perhaps because she was scared to leave the station and be alone. The piece of paper with the questions that Avraham had written that morning was sitting on the table in his room – *Why did she open the door for the assailant? Was she waiting for him? Did she know that he was coming?* – but now he was no longer as sure of the answers. And despite this, at the brief meeting that the investigation team held towards evening, Avraham avoided mentioning the conversation with Diana Goldin, because he wasn't yet convinced that the connection between the two incidents was anything but coincidental.

He walked Diana out of his room and asked Lital Levy to escort her to the computer unit so they could draw up a facial composite of the policeman, even if it turned out later that there was no need. Before they said goodbye she asked him, 'You don't want the umbrella?' and Avraham took it from her hand and looked at it. She had been holding it on her knees throughout their entire conversation, and he hadn't even remembered that it was the reason she had called.

7

For the next few days Mali was sure that Kobi had told her everything that morning, before the girls woke up, and in his way he had indeed tried. The woman he had spoken about and the circumstances of the injury were different, but there was a seed of truth in what he told her, as if he nevertheless wanted her to understand.

At a quarter to eight Mali called the bank and informed them that she'd be absent from work. She waited for Kobi to take Daniella and Noy to nursery and school in her car. At the point at which she tried to catch a cab on Ben Gurion Boulevard, she still wasn't certain that this was the right thing to do and hoped that when she returned she would succeed in convincing Kobi to consult someone, perhaps even a lawyer. She had suggested that they do this together when he told her what had happened, but Kobi wasn't ready to listen. 'What would a lawyer tell me? Just to turn myself in to the police,' he said. 'And there's no way I'm doing that.'

The taxi driver had the news playing on the radio but he also kept asking her questions. He asked if she was going to work and where she worked, and her answers were confused. He wasn't from Holon and was in the city after dropping off a previous customer, and she had to direct him to the centre. When she got off at the corner of Jabotinsky Street and Krauze and started walking down the latter, Mali saw that the cab remained in the spot where it had stopped, and she turned down one of the smaller side streets and waited until it disappeared. And she didn't see the car in the place where Kobi said it would be. She crossed the street and made her way back, and only then spotted the old blue Toyota Corolla on the other side of Krauze and crossed over again. She didn't waste time examining the car, but instead opened the driver's door with the naturalness of someone leaving for work. The car didn't start straightaway, and Mali placed her bag on the seat next to her and tried again. It had ignition problems and had sat there for days without moving, most of the time in the rain, and she had to try again, patiently and without getting stressed. The SUV parked in front of her was empty, and there was almost no traffic on the street. And no one paid her any attention while she tried to start the Corolla, again and again, until the purring of the engine could be heard.

Mali wasn't used to driving a large car. She turned right on Sokolov and left at Shenkar, and only when she reached Feichman Street did she realize that she was about to pass the police station, the same station she'd find herself inside a week later – but little did she know that then. The night without Kobi and the memory of Eilat had brought back the fear, and it didn't leave her throughout that entire day. The Swiss tourist was again lying in wait for her in the darkness and she didn't know where. But her anger at Kobi had dissipated after he had revealed to her that the police were looking for him and asked for her help. The danger of the collapse was palpable, but it wasn't taking place within him or within her; rather, there was an external threat against the two of them, a threat that they had to fight, and she tensed up inside in order to protect him. Or them.

A traffic patrol car pulled out of the car park and drove along behind her. At a red light the cars waited next to each other, and Mali didn't look to the right so that the cops wouldn't see her face. Her phone rang in her bag, but only once she arrived home did she look, to see that it was her sister Gila, who seemed to have picked up on how much Mali was in need of help. When the light changed she accelerated too quickly, but the police car turned right. Of all the things Kobi had asked of her, the hardest was not revealing his story to anyone. She knew what Gila would say, could hear her voice even without them speaking, but nevertheless she wanted to tell her. It wasn't until she had parked the car in the car park under their building that she dared to examine it, but without wanting to linger and without bending down towards the bumper she couldn't see any signs of damage or scraping. Under the front windscreen wiper there was a ticket and a few leaflets that the rain had turned into papier mâché, and she tossed them into the bin in the stairwell on her way to the lift. Her phone was ringing again.

She didn't answer Gila all day, because she didn't know what to tell her. She couldn't say that on Monday, on his way back from a job interview, Kobi had hit a pedestrian who had charged into the street without looking. That had been their anniversary. The day when a storm had raged. The roads were slippery and the visibility was poor, and Kobi had been driving quickly, thinking about the failed interview when the woman came out into the street from between two parked cars. He didn't notice her in time to stop, and merely swerved to the left a little, but despite this felt himself strike her and heard the body hit the car.

Mali's heart had beaten rapidly as she listened to him early that morning, when he had come back. Everything that had frightened her in recent days took on a different meaning. She had no reason to doubt that he was telling her the truth, because the accident provided an explanation for everything. For the way he had been when he returned from the interview, the way he watched the news that same night and read the newspapers the next day, the message he left his father about the trip to Australia, in which it seemed to Harry that he had cried. Even the gun that had been lying on the table in the utility room, though they hadn't discussed that.

The papers had featured nothing about a hit-and-run in Holon, and this was a relief to them both. Kobi didn't even know if the woman was hurt or how severe her injuries were because he had fled the scene without slowing down and only saw her lying on the ground in the car's rear-view mirror. Mali googled 'woman injured in accident in Holon', but didn't pull up any results from the previous week, just more and more items about the murder of the old woman. For a second she thought about calling the hospital and asking if a woman hit by a car in town had been brought to A & E on Monday and what condition she was in, but she didn't call that day. Nevertheless, she couldn't stop thinking about her. Was she still hospitalized? And from the moment she imagined the woman on the street, for some strange reason it was the girl with the black hair and the black nails who had sold her the umbrella at the shopping centre.

Kobi had continued driving, without knowing where but not in the direction of their flat, because he feared that some driver would have seen the accident and would follow him, and so he decided to park the Toyota right where he was and continue home on foot or by cab. When Mali asked him, 'Why didn't you stop?' he just said, 'I was afraid. I fled without thinking.' If someone had taken down his number plate and the police came asking, he would say that the car had been stolen. But because two days had passed since the accident and no policeman had yet arrived he thought they were safe, and asked Mali to retrieve the car because he didn't want to return to the place where he had abandoned it in a panic.

The second thing that Kobi had asked of her was to say, if anyone asked, that they had been together on Monday afternoon. He knew that this would be hard for her because she was terrible at lying, but he said that there was almost no chance she'd need to. Every moment that passed since the accident minimized the possibility that they'd track him down, or that the injury to the woman was severe. And if, despite this, the police came, Mali would need to say that their car had been stolen the day before and that he had waited for her outside her work and that they had gone together to pick up the girls from nursery and school. They hadn't yet reported the theft simply because they hadn't got around to it.

When Mali got home Kobi seemed calmer. He said, 'Was it there?' and asked if she had noticed anything unusual around the car, and Mali shook her head. 'There aren't any scratches or dents on it either,' she said.

In his eyes and in the way he wandered around the flat she saw that he wasn't yet entirely at ease, but as the hours went on the tension passed to her. He prepared lunch for them both while she again searched for news about the accident, careful not to let him see. Gila called her almost every hour, leaving messages asking her to call back, but Mali still didn't answer. When they sat down to eat Kobi tried to talk about other things.

'Did the girls say anything about me not being home?' he asked, but when she asked him suddenly, 'Why did you decide to tell me?' he fell silent. Afterwards, he said, 'I didn't know what to do. And I didn't have anyone else to tell. Would you rather I hadn't said anything?'

But he had, nevertheless, called his dad first. And had planned to travel to see him without her knowledge. 'Did you seriously plan to flee to Australia?' she asked him, and Kobi said, 'On the first day I did, yes. I didn't know what to do.' He didn't mention it, and she didn't ask, but she thought that since the accident there had certainly also been moments when he had considered suicide. Chills went through her when she saw him again in her imagination, sitting alone on the roof, that same night, weighing the gun in his hand.

'And now? Do you still plan to go?'

'No. I don't think it's necessary now.'

What she should have done was encourage him to go. Or told him about the pregnancy during those hours when they were alone in the flat together. Before Eilat they had spoken about having another child, but after that it wasn't possible, and from a financial perspective as well it was hard to think how they'd cope with another baby. The fear she had felt last night and the adrenalin that had flowed in her body this morning changed into a deep, hollow sadness. She told him that she wanted a nap before Daniella and Noy returned home, and she turned off her mobile, because Gila kept calling. Before she drifted off she thought that she was doing exactly what he had been doing for the last few days: hiding, concealing. As if she had caught it from him. Her sleep was long and deep, and Kobi went instead of her to get the girls, and that was good, because she was too tense, and even when they returned she tried to avoid them, and Kobi sat with the two of them in the living room and watched television.

Shortly before sunset, when Mali went up to the roof to hang up the washing, she looked at the water heaters and television aerials spread out before her. She thought about what Kobi had said to her at noon: *I didn't have anyone else.*

She still felt that they needed to consult with a lawyer, or at least with one of their friends, but after Eilat she didn't want to speak to anyone else either. There were days when she couldn't get up in the morning. When she tried to get dressed or put on make-up it was as if she was dressing a doll or another woman, and only when she looked at Kobi did she remember that she was still Mali Bengtson and that she had two girls and a home and a job. Once, she asked Kobi how he could do it, how he hadn't despaired and given up on her, and that was one of the few times he had spoken to her about his mother. During her illness his father was almost never home, so Kobi took care of her all by himself. 'Harry escaped because he couldn't see her suffer,' he said, 'but I had nowhere to escape to. And besides, she had no one else in Australia. He would come home once or twice a week from the university to confirm that she hadn't yet died, and you could smell his lovers on him.'

Evening descended and it was chilly on the roof, though it was no longer rainy but almost spring-like.

Mali remembered the photograph of Kobi's dead mother which she had seen in his room, and she too got mixed up in her imagination with the woman lying in the road after the Toyota had hit her. If it weren't for the storm, would the accident have happened? The woman wouldn't have been hurrying to get out of the rain and rushed to cross the street, and even if she had sprung out from between parked cars, Kobi would have noticed her in time.

If only the storm had arrived a day sooner or a day later. Or if Kobi's interview had gone differently. If they had been just a bit luckier.

She never had any luck, but she didn't expect anything else for herself. It was Kobi's life that was supposed to look different. Her job was OK and she was grateful for the patience they had showed towards her at the bank, after

Eilat. She was used to their rented flat too, even though it wasn't a home. When they had moved there they had decided not to invest any money in it because they were hoping to save for a place of their own, and the walls remained mostly naked. They didn't buy new furniture either, using what they had brought from the previous flat and what the owner's son had left behind. Mali had got used to walking around her apartment as if it was some-one else's, but Kobi never stopped dreaming about the place they'd one day buy. And Gila didn't stop asking her when they were finally moving to a real home.

Daniella called to her from below, but Mali wasn't yet ready to go downstairs. And she kept her phone turned off.

There was something similar about Kobi and Gila, and perhaps that was why they didn't get along, she suddenly thought. Like Gila, Kobi too had once been confident that life would give him everything he wanted. He and Mali were officially a couple again when they returned from Australia, and he started the course at Mossad and would return from there full of stories. She had never seen him as happy as he was during that period. He talked about tracing exercises and bursting into houses and sim-ulated assassinations of random women and men in the street, and he was certain that he'd finish with distinction and be accepted, thanks to his English and his Australian passport. When he stopped talking about the course, almost at once, she thought that it was because he wasn't allowed to, and only a few weeks later did she learn, almost by accident, that he had been thrown out. He hid this from her for around two months, pretending that he was heading out to training each morning, and it was only when he started working as a security guard at the shopping centre that he was forced to admit it, because he was worried that someone would see him and tell her. This was temporary work, and when they got married, almost a year later, he warned her that they'd need to travel because he was trying to get work as a security officer at Israeli embassies abroad, but that never happened either.

Gila was already divorced by then, not yet twenty-five and already with a three year-old son and swearing that she'd never marry again. She thought that Kobi was keeping Mali shut up at home, away from her friends, but in a weird way her conversations with her sister actually brought Mali closer to Kobi, because it seemed to her that the main problem Gila had with him was that he didn't earn enough money and wasn't successful, like the men she went out with.

And after Eilat her sister was forced to admit that Kobi took care of her like no one else would have.

When Mali came down from the roof the three of them were on the sofa in the living room, and this was to be the last time she saw them together like that. Daniella sat next to him and Noy lay on his other side, her head on his knees. He asked if he should make dinner for everyone, and the girls asked for hot chocolate. Harry lay at their feet, his head on his front paws, and even though he wasn't moving, it looked as if even he had another chance.

After the girls had gone to bed Mali checked that the door was locked and the lights were on and got into bed early, despite her afternoon nap. Kobi followed a short time afterwards, closed the door and switched off the bedside lamp. When he lowered the straps of her nightgown and caressed her neck, she closed her eyes, but his fingers were unable to wake and excite her as they sometimes could. She both felt and didn't feel his hands on her arms and on her thighs while they had sex. And despite the darkness, suddenly there was no fear in her, just sadness. Was it just because of the woman who lay in the street in the rain waiting for help? Or did she already understand some of what was likely to happen? She turned the lamp back on and was trying to fall asleep when Kobi asked, 'What are you thinking about?' and Mali said to him with her eyes closed, 'Her.'

'Who?'

She was even thinking about going to the shop where she had bought him the umbrella to confirm that the woman lying in the street wasn't the girl with the black hair. Did cars pull up next to her after Kobi had fled, and did their drivers get out to help her? Maybe she managed to call an ambulance herself, or did one of the passers-by phone for her instead?

And there were two other things Mali thought about without telling Kobi. When she had asked him that morning where the accident took place, Kobi had hesitated before answering, and she didn't understand why. If he had told her the name of the street, it would have been easier to search for news and to find out what had happened to the woman. The second thing was the umbrella he was looking for. The accident provided an explanation for what had become of their anniversary, his watching the news and reading the newspapers and the message he left for Harry. But it didn't explain the umbrella.

Kobi said to her, 'If you're worried about the police, you can relax,' and she asked him, 'How can you be so sure?' even though she hadn't been thinking about this. She didn't look at him when he said, 'Because two days have passed. If they haven't turned up by now, they won't. And I did everything that needed to be done.'

When she fell asleep she still hadn't known she would do this, but the next morning, from the phone at the bank, she called Wolfson Hospital and asked whether on Monday a young woman had been admitted who had been injured in a car accident in Holon.

The nurse who answered transferred her to A & E, and when she asked who she was, Mali said, without having planned to in advance, 'I saw the accident and wanted to know how she was.' The receptionist asked Mali to wait a moment before saying to her, 'Look, I'm not finding anything here, but can you give me a name and phone number and we'll get back to you if we find anything?' And Mali almost hung up but then said, for some reason, 'My name is Michal Ben-Asher,' but gave her real telephone number. From that moment on, she waited for them to phone her back, but eventually it was somebody else who called.

8

Only at the end of the third day of the investigation was the team told about the testimony of Diana Goldin, about the policeman who had visited her. Until then Avraham kept this new lead to himself and breached a few more standards of police protocol, guided by an inner certainty that grew stronger as that third day progressed. In the evening, after a second visit to the scene, he summoned the members of the team for an urgent meeting and announced to them that he had in his possession the end of a thread leading to the killer.

The previous night, he had stayed awake until almost two. He drank black coffee on his porch, ate too many dry biscuits and thought only about the policeman who had gone down the stairs and disappeared. The main thing he was unable to understand was *why* the policeman had questioned Diana Goldin and recorded their conversation. And why he hadn't tried to attack her, even though they were alone. Diana had told him that the policeman requested that she tell him everything, *as if I was telling it for the first time*, and that was probably the key. Despite the growing certainty that the policeman had questioned her on his own initiative, the first thing Avraham asked Lital Levy to do when he arrived at the office in the morning was to check again with all the district department heads whether a policeman had been sent to Diana Goldin with the task of completing an investigation.

Sharpstein didn't understand why Avraham insisted on being present at the questioning of Erez Yeger early that morning, but in retrospect this was the right decision. Three days had passed since the murder, and Avraham had decided it was time for him to stop observing the investigation from the window of his office on the third floor. It was Thursday; the weekend started tomorrow, and after that was the short holiday he had requested because of Marianka's parents' visit, so he had to tell the team about the new lead that day, so that they would be able to continue working on it in his absence. All their other leads had gone nowhere: Ma'alul and Esty Vahaba had exhausted the investigation into the rapist's family and were convinced that none of them had been involved in the murder. And the worker Sharpstein had detained for twenty-four hours, Adnan Gon, had a solid alibi. He hadn't been at work on the day of the murder because of the storm. And even though, a day ago, Avraham had pictured Leah Yeger's son at his mother's front door, now he was certain that Erez Yeger wasn't the person who had attacked her, and not only because of the DNA evidence, which determined that Leah Yeger's assailant wasn't a relative.

When Avraham entered the second-floor interview room with Sharpstein, he saw the son up close for the first time. Erez Yeger was pacing back and forth in the room; he was ungainly and very tall. He wore a thick, checked sweater, which, without his knowing had become a part of the interrogation plan. He watched the two policemen as they took their places across from him. Sharpstein spread out the summary of his investigation from two days earlier on the table, and when he stretched his fingers over it he seemed to Avraham nervous, perhaps because Erez Yeger had lied to him during the previous interrogation and perhaps because of Avraham's presence in the interview room.

'Do you know why we brought you back here?' Sharpstein opened. Avraham sat off to the side and examined Yeger's facial expression.

'You said there were developments in the investigation.'

Sharpstein looked at the papers laid out before him and not at Erez Yeger as he nodded. 'There are definitely some developments,' he said. 'Important developments, even. Do you want to know what the developments are?'

Sharpstein smiled, as if to himself, and turned the gold ring on his finger, and Erez Yeger looked at Avraham. Did he recognize his face from the funeral? Avraham hadn't said a thing since he entered the room, not even his name or rank.

'Soon I'll tell you about the developments, but first there's something I want to clarify with you,' Sharpstein continued. 'During our previous meeting you told me that there hadn't been any communication between you and your mother in recent months. Can you confirm this statement?'

'Yes.'

'And you continue to claim that there was no communication between you?'

Yeger's face reddened, but he only nodded. Why was he lying? In his experience, Avraham had learned that most of those questioned don't lie because they believe they'll succeed in deceiving the investigators, but rather because they're ashamed of what they're hiding.

'Go ahead and explain to me why there wasn't any communication between you. Can you do that?' Sharpstein asked, and Yeger answered, 'I told you already. I didn't want to have anything to do with her.'

'Correct. That's what you said. And that satisfied me during the first round of questioning. But now, following the important developments, your answer doesn't satisfy me. I would like you, please, to elaborate on your reasons.' Yeger didn't respond, and when Sharpstein said, 'Should I write that you refuse to elaborate on the reasons for the conflict between you?' the son answered sharply, 'There was no conflict between us.' He again looked at Avraham, who signalled to him with his hand to turn his attention back to Sharpstein.

'What was it? Money? A dispute over your father's inheritance?'

'I said that there was no conflict between us.'

Sharpstein had told Lital Levy to turn the radiators in the room to full power, and Yeger was already sweating inside his jumper. His face and palms were damp. When he asked for some air, Sharpstein explained to him that the window didn't open.

But Erez Yeger wasn't the man who had sat opposite his mother at the kitchen table and afterwards strangled her and left her body on the rug, and only at that moment did Avraham suddenly understand why he was certain of this. If it had been him, the scene would not have been so orderly. Leah Yeger had arranged her flat for an *official meeting*, not for a meeting with her son. And it wasn't possible that she had told no one about this meeting. First thing that morning, Avraham had phoned Leah's daughter and asked her if she was sure that her mother hadn't told her that she was due to be questioned again by the police about the rape, and the daughter had said that she didn't know anything about it. But maybe the son had known? Avraham wanted to ask him about this immediately, but Sharpstein continued laying his trap around Yeger. And he hadn't been informed about Avraham's new lead.

'So what if you told me that there wasn't a conflict?' Sharpstein replied quietly. 'You also said that your last conversation had been a long time ago. Isn't that right?'

Yeger wiped the sweat from his forehead and looked at Avraham when he answered Sharpstein's question. 'That's what I said. Yes.'

'You're kidding me, right?'

'No.'

'What do you think, Avi? That he's winding us up?'

Sharpstein rose suddenly from his seat, and Yeger followed him with his gaze as he approached him. He erupted once he was bent over Yeger, his mouth right above his head, and it was impossible to know if this was a real outburst or a part of Sharpstein's interrogation plan. 'Do I look retarded to you, Erez? Or maybe the policeman sitting here next to me looks retarded? You're lying to me! As if I don't have a record of your mother's phone calls. As if I don't know the last time you two talked.'

Yeger again looked at Avraham, to figure out whether the things Sharpstein were saying were correct. And then, of all times, just as Yeger walked into the trap that

Sharpstein had set for him, Avraham showed him a way out. He said, 'Erez, we're asking you if you spoke to your mother not because we suspect that you were involved in her murder but rather because we want to know if she told you that she was expecting to be questioned by the police.' And Yeger said, 'I don't know what you're talking about.'

Sharpstein turned and looked at Avraham, and in his eyes then there was still only confusion. Avraham knew that he'd disrupted Sharpstein's interrogation plan and that he should have prepared him, but only at that moment had he understood what he wanted to hear from the son. 'I mean, questioned about the rape she went through,' Avraham continued. 'According to the phone log, you spoke to your mother on Sunday, twenty-four hours before the murder. And why you're lying doesn't concern me, only whether she informed you during your conversation that a policeman was due to come to question her the next day.'

'She didn't say anything to me about that,' Yeger said. And then added, 'Because I didn't speak to her.'

Sharpstein didn't relent. He remained where he was standing, over Yeger, and said to him, 'Let's go back to the phone conversation. Explain to me why you're hiding it. And try to stop lying.' But Avraham continued asking questions as if he was the only detective in the room, and Yeger spoke only to him.

'So tell me something else, Erez,' he said. 'If your mother was to set up a meeting or make an appointment with a doctor, where would she write a reminder for herself about such a meeting?'

'I don't know. What do you two want from me? I told you from the beginning that I haven't been in contact with my mother.'

'We examined her computer and saw that she didn't keep an electronic diary. But she would have had some other calendar or diary, no? Older people write things like this in a set place, because they tend to forget.'

This was the moment that Avraham was waiting for. Yeger was silent and then said, 'She had a calendar, I think. In the kitchen. She used to write dates of birthdays and other things there, but I don't know if she still has it.' Avraham tried to recall if he had seen a calendar at the scene.

'Are you sure she kept it in the kitchen?' he asked, and Yeger said, 'I think so. That's where it used to be.'

Sharpstein left the interview room, slamming the door behind him, but Avraham kept asking questions.

'Other than this calendar, she didn't have another place, a diary, perhaps?'

If Leah Yeger kept a diary it was possible it was in the handbag that was stolen, but it was also possible that it was somewhere else.

'I don't know if she had a diary. I think she did. Maybe my sister knows.'

'And do you have any idea where she kept her diary? Did she usually have it in a handbag?'

'Don't know.'

'So try to remember.'

'But I told you, I don't know. Have you asked my sister?'

Shortly after this, when he was in the car on his way back to the scene, Avraham called Orit Yeger, and she confirmed that her mother had a calendar in the kitchen on which she wrote reminders for meetings and events. She last remembered having seen it two weeks before, and even wrote a reminder in there herself about her daughter's Purim party. Her mother also had a diary, with phone numbers and addresses, but Orit Yeger didn't know where that could be, or whether it was likely that it was in the handbag that was taken from the scene.

Before he opened the door to Leah's flat Avraham put gloves on his hands, and as he turned on the light he noticed that the calendar was not hanging on the wall in the kitchen. The door hadn't been opened for two days, and the warm air was stale. Nothing had been moved in the rooms, and the visions came back to Avraham: the birds on the rug, the lamp, the drawing of the two women in the field, the table set for a meeting. Leah Yeger waiting for a knock at the door, but the man who stood there wasn't her son but a policeman instead. And now he understood that he didn't need to see her body in his mind any more in order to understand her death, as he had sensed, but to think instead about Leah Yeger's life in this apartment before she heard the knock at the door.

She didn't tell her son about the policeman who had contacted her to arrange another round of questioning, because relations between them had been severed. And she didn't mention it to her daughter either. Did she include anyone else in her life? On the fridge in the kitchen was a picture of her with her daughter and granddaughter, and next to it an old picture of her son with a tall man who he supposed was his father.

But her son didn't visit her, for reasons he was hiding.

Nor did his children, her grandchildren. Once a week she picked up her granddaughter from nursery and brought her back here, and on Fridays she would go to her daughter's for dinner, but the rest of the time she was forced to live alone in the flat where she was raped, the flat where her husband had died of a heart attack. Was this the reason she had agreed to meet with the policeman? That, other than him, no one wanted to listen?

Avraham sat down for a moment on the chair in the kitchen. How much time had passed before Leah Yeger realized that something wasn't right? In the living room, next to the television, there was a cordless phone, but Leah Yeger wouldn't have used it because the policeman would have noticed, so Avraham walked the length of the hallway. He peeked into the bedroom and then continued to the office, and there he saw it. On the desk was an old telephone whose cord wasn't plugged into the socket on the wall. He immediately called Orit Yeger and asked her if the telephone in the office was normally connected, and she asked, 'What telephone?' and then said yes.

'Do you know if your mother ever used that phone in the office? Was it kept plugged in?'

In contrast to his first visit to the scene, Avraham now knew exactly what to look for, and this time he wasn't alone there, because Leah Yeger was guiding him. Next to the phone, under a pile of documents, he found the diary she had apparently hidden. In the square for the day when the murder occurred – *Monday, 23rd February* – only a time was written, in tiny handwriting, with a red pen: *2 p.m.*

This wasn't much, but it was all Avraham needed. He was back at the station within less than five minutes and asked Lital Levy to call an urgent team meeting. Saban entered the conference room first, and when he asked Avraham, 'Where's her son? Did you arrest him?' Avraham had no doubt that Sharpstein had told him about the events of the morning. Avraham nodded and said to him, 'Soon,' because he was waiting for Eliyahu Ma'alul and Esty Vahaba, who arrived next and took seats around the table. Ma'alul noticed the facial composite that had been drawn with Diana Goldin's help and which Avraham had placed on the table next to the umbrella and asked, 'That's him? Did we catch our killer?' And Saban looked at the computerized drawing in amazement. He asked Avraham to get started, because he was short of time, and Avraham looked mainly at him when he began by saying, 'We have a new lead in the investigation.'

He was certain of so few facts, and to most of the questions posed to him in the meeting he didn't have answers, but the feeling that had accompanied him since the previous day, guiding him in the investigation this morning, was one of real certainty. Saban asked, 'So it's not the son?' And Avraham said, 'No. I believe Leah Yeger was murdered by a policeman, who set up a meeting with her for the purpose of an investigation.'

Saban straightened up in his chair and placed his phone on the table. And Avraham continued: 'Yesterday evening I received new testimony, which I haven't yet managed to tell you about, because this morning we interviewed Yeger's son. Another rape victim, Diana Goldin, said that a few days ago a man came to her home and introduced himself as a policeman working in the Ayalon district and questioned her about the rape she suffered. According to inquiries we have since made with all the departments in the district, no policeman was sent to her with this task. I believe this is what happened to Leah Yeger as well.'

Saban was flustered by what Avraham said. 'But what are you basing this on?' he asked. 'Just on the testimony of that neighbour who—' He suddenly went quiet, and Avraham took advantage of this to continue.

'We have the testimony of the neighbour who saw a policeman in the building after the murder. And today I found the victim's diary in her flat, with an entry for the time at which the murder took place. So we have two policemen that we cannot identify, at scenes tied to rape victims, at a distance of a few kilometres and separated by a few days. Diana Goldin wasn't assaulted by the police-man because he succeeded in deceiving her until the end, but I believe that Leah Yeger realized that he wasn't who he said he was and tried to call the police. He figured this out, and then a struggle took place between them, by the end of which she was murdered.'

Ma'alul pointed at the composite drawing. 'That's the man?' he asked, and Avraham nodded. Esty Vahaba also studied the composite and her gaze was serious.

'In my estimation,' Avraham went on, 'the policeman's methods are very sophisticated. He makes arrangements by telephone with the rape victims and confirms that they're not suspicious of him by means of two phone calls. This at least is what he did in Goldin's case. He offers to meet them at the station in order to neutralize any suspicion. I assume that if they are suspicious of him or ask too many questions on the phone about who he is exactly and the reason for the meeting, he cancels or doesn't show up. He comes to their home in uniform and asks the woman to describe the rape she experienced, ostensibly for reasons tied to the investigation or legal deliberations on the matter. At the meeting with Diana Goldin he took notes and also recorded everything she said to him on a mobile phone.'

Saban picked his own phone up when Avraham finished speaking, and then said, 'This sounds like a dangerous lead to me, Avi. And beyond that, even if we suppose that there's a connection between the incidents, how do you intend to find the suspect?'

The facial composite that was drawn with Diana Goldin's help was lying right there on the table. Avraham explained that the policeman had left an umbrella with her; thus they would have fingerprints that could be compared to prints from the murder scene. It would also be possible to compare the log of incoming phone calls to Leah Yeger with the list of calls made in recent weeks to Diana Goldin. Other than that, this weekend Diana Goldin would look at photographs of all the policemen in the district and, if need be, those of every policeman in the country.

'Why of policemen? Do you think he's really a cop?' Ma'alul asked, and Avraham said, 'I think so. Or an ex-policeman. Otherwise, he wouldn't have access to information about rape victims.' In addition, Avraham planned to try to identify the suspect from the footage of security cameras in the area around where the murder was carried out. To go over film after film, looking for the policeman who, according to the testimony of the neighbour hadn't got into a patrol car but had left the scene on foot. Until they found him.

'And then what?' Saban asked.

Avraham hadn't thought about this, but said to Saban that then it would be possible to publish the facial composite or a picture of the policeman in the media, and Ma'alul smiled at his words, but Saban did not.

'You're suggesting that we publish a photograph in the newspaper and say that the man shown is perhaps a policeman who perhaps harassed rape victims and perhaps murdered a woman, without being certain that this is correct? Did you fall on your head, Avi? This is just what the police need, with everything that's happening here already! For every policeman in the county to become a suspect in the harassment of rape victims and in a murder? You're out of your mind.'

After the meeting, when Avraham was left in his office with just Ma'alul, he understood that, maybe, he could be mistaken, but when he had returned from Leah Yeger's flat he didn't have an organized plan for continuing the investigation, only preliminary thoughts about the next steps. He didn't know enough about the policeman, other than that he was the man Leah Yeger had been waiting for. And he also hoped that the man wasn't a real police officer, but in that case he wasn't able to understand how he had in his possession information about the women who had been assaulted, because, even among police, access to rape files was limited to the detectives who dealt with the cases directly.

Saban had left the meeting room without saying another word and returned after speaking to someone on the phone. He said, 'We aren't publishing anything, Avi. No composite sketch. No photograph. We'll continue checking this angle, but we'll do it very, very discreetly, are you with me? And beyond that, we have another suspect who you actually released from custody. What do you intend to do with Yeger's son? From my perspective, he's the prime suspect.'

Avraham was just about to answer him when Esty Vahaba interrupted. 'Maybe it's possible to do this without publishing photos,' she said. 'We can speak to other rape victims and find out if they encountered the policeman or if a policeman contacted them. It could be that he didn't do this just twice.'

Saban opposed this suggestion as well, because he didn't want to provoke anxiety among rape victims and thought that if too many women were questioned it was liable to leak to the media, but there wasn't any other way, and Avraham insisted. He looked at Saban from his new place at the head of the table, the place where Ilana Lis had sat, and said quietly, 'That's a good idea, Esty. We'll look for a photo of him from the security cameras and, even if we don't find one, we can speak to the victims and show them the composite sketch. And Erez Yeger isn't going anywhere. We'll see to that. In any case, we'll question him again at the beginning of next week. But according to the findings, the assailant is not a relative, and I'm telling you he's not the murderer and that our primary lead as of now is the policeman who went down the stairs and disappeared.'

Avraham stayed in his office at the station until after midnight that day. Read the summary of Diana Goldin's testimony again and again, and examined the photographs from the scene under the strong light of the desk lamp. The window was open but he felt no need for a cigarette, and he didn't even put the unlit pipe in his mouth. Leah Yeger's picture remained before him on the table.

Marianka called him a few times during the day, but he answered her only at ten in the evening. She'd have liked him to come home early, but when he was detained she prepared the flat herself for her parents' visit and reminded him that at four thirty in the morning she and Avraham were supposed to be waiting for them at the airport, in the same arrivals hall where he had hidden from her a few months before. After speaking to her he stood for a long time by the window and watched the passing cars. He thought that, despite the confrontations with Sharpstein and Saban, he was steering his first murder investigation in the right direction, and that, if he would have liked to call Ilana Lis, this wouldn't be so she'd give him support but rather to swap ideas with her about the policeman's motives. When he'd been alone with Ma'alul earlier, Eli-yahu had said to him, 'That was a hell of a meeting, Avi,' and Avraham replied, 'You were right about what you said to me, you know? That I was dealing in bullshit and that I had someone to rely on.'

Ma'alul no longer averted his gaze, and there was a smile in his dark eyes. 'Forget it – I have,' he said. And perhaps because they were close again and because Avraham couldn't speak with Ilana, he said to Ma'alul, 'I wasn't stressed because of Saban, but because I didn't truly understand how to conduct a murder investigation. Until today.'

'Like any other investigation, Avi, no?'

'No. Not exactly.'

The report from the lab had helped, as had the statements gathered from all those interviewed, but the main thing had been to bring Leah Yeger back to life. For the last time that day Avraham saw her in his imagination, sitting next to the table in her kitchen when the knock came at the door. If she had told her son or daughter that a policeman was coming to question her in her flat, Avraham would now know with certainty that he wasn't mistaken, but her son had cut off relations with her and, apparently, she wasn't close enough to her daughter to tell her either. She made arrangements for the meeting and tidied up the flat because she didn't have many visits. And she wasn't suspicious of the policeman until he made some kind of a mistake. She had planned on telling him how she was attacked and perhaps was even happy about the visit because she wanted to talk. When she heard the knock she got up from her chair and hurried to the door, behind which stood the policeman, looking around to confirm that no one else had seen him. *What was he seeking from Diana Goldin and Leah Yeger?* This Avraham still didn't understand and couldn't even guess at, and he said to himself that he had to think more about *him*, and not just about her. Was *he* surprised when she opened the door and he saw her face? Or had he already looked at it in pictures from the investigation file?

He wanted to know everything. You understand? Every detail. From the beginning. That's what Diana Goldin had said.

Why, Leah, why didn't you tell anyone he was coming? Avraham whispered, as if to himself, and then tried again to concentrate on the policeman waiting behind that door. A few hours later, while he was with Marianka at the airport, this was the question still echoing inside him.

PART TWO: THE KILLER

9

When they returned from the airport with Bojan and Anika Milanich, Avraham didn't recognize his home. Throughout, tablecloths he didn't know they had were spread out, and vases he had never before seen, containing enormous bouquets of flowers. In the small office, which for three days would serve as her parents' bedroom, Marianka had placed a small basket filled with grapefruit.

Avraham's eyes were red because he hadn't slept, but as they all ate breakfast on the porch he could see Marianka's excitement. His mobile was sitting at his feet, on the floor, and he tried not to check it for new messages too frequently. Marianka had told her parents that he was in the middle of a murder investigation, and her mother pretended to be interested in the case, but he couldn't tell them much because he hadn't revealed most of the details even to Marianka. And every time he looked away or went to the kitchen to help her with the food, her parents whispered to each other in Slovenian.

Despite this, they did not succeed in hiding the point of their visit from him.

Bojan and Anika Milanich detested him, a fact of which he was already well aware.

When they had first met, during the summer that he

spent with Marianka in Brussels, they had been friendly, but when they heard about her plan to join him in Israel the friendliness had disappeared. She didn't tell him everything they had said, but Avraham felt their disgust with every look and at every meeting. She spoke to them on the phone once a week, usually on Sundays, and she told him that they had come to terms with her move, but he didn't believe it. When he asked, 'So how is it that they're coming here suddenly?' she said, 'To be with us; what do you mean? And also to get to know you.'

If this was the case, why were they sitting forlornly on the porch of his flat, barely saying a word?

Anika Milanich didn't touch the omelette that he and Marianka had prepared and just drank milky coffee. She was fifty-one years old but looked no more than forty. In Slovenia she had been a teacher at a music academy, and in Brussels she gave private piano lessons. Her favourite composer was Chopin, and the pieces that she loved to play more than anything were the mazurkas. When Avraham was invited to their house for the first time, she had asked him which mazurka was his favourite and he hadn't known what to say. She was tall and smartly dressed, but when no one was watching her smile twisted up into a grimace. Marianka told him once that one of her students at the academy had become a world-renowned pianist and that her mother had tried to set her up with him, even though he was gay. Bojan Milanich, holder of a black belt in karate and an instructor at a theological seminary, sat beside his wife and looked at the skies of Holon. He was a solid man with a rock-hard potbelly and broad shoulders, and Avraham was certain that he was willing to kill any man who approached Marianka with a *yuko gari* kick, even if it happened to be Glenn Gould. He was fifty-three years old, and even though everyone said that Marianka resembled him, Avraham insisted that he couldn't see it.

After breakfast Avraham did the dishes in order to let the three of them be together. He hoped that after this the tension would ease. They rode in his car to Tel Aviv, and walked the length of Rothschild Boulevard, from the National Theatre to the old neighbourhood of Neveh Tzedek, under a blue sky. Marianka showed them Tel Aviv as if it was her home, pointing at the buildings she liked, talking about the restaurants and the cafés and the sea, but Bojan walked quickly ahead of everyone with his gaze fixed on the ground, and Avraham saw how Marianka's face fell. They returned to Holon early, to have time to rest, and in the evening, when they walked from their flat to his parents', Marianka pointed out that this was the neighbourhood where Avraham had grown up. When Anika said, 'You must love this place, if you returned to live here,' Avraham answered, 'Yes,' and afterwards, 'No,' and then tried to say something else but was prevented by his lack of English. Holon wasn't elegant like Brussels or picturesque like Koper, the port city where Marianka had been born and which he had so far seen only in photo albums, but nevertheless it was his home.

His mother tried so hard to make the dinner festive. She wore the clothes that she had bought in the autumn for his promotion ceremony, and had made his father wear a white oxford shirt over his T-shirt, and the place was sparkling clean. The television had been turned off for the first time in years and all the lights were on, and even the wool blanket they always sat on so the sofa wouldn't get dirty had been removed. At first she invited everyone into the living room, but she was unable to bear the tension and urged them to move to the kitchen table because the chicken was ready. His father sat at the head of the table, his eyes staring at his empty plate and with a napkin wrapped around the collar of his shirt, but when Avraham looked at him he saw another man who wasn't sitting there. Avraham touched his father's shoulder, as he had begun doing in recent months, and then bent over and whispered in his ear, 'We have guests. Marianka's father and mother,' and a smile lit up his father's eyes as he nodded.

Marianka had warned her parents about his father's stroke and deteriorating condition, but despite this it seemed to Avraham that Bojan and Anika were looking at his father the way in which they had observed the streets and buildings on their way: with contempt and pity. His mother said that his father no longer understood or felt a thing, but Avraham knew she was mistaken. Did his father not see how beautiful Marianka was in her black dress? And the fear in her eyes that dinner too, like the breakfast on the porch and the walk through Tel Aviv, would be a failure? And did he not hear how she tried to start up a conversation every time silence descended over the table?

Avraham hoped his father didn't see the nauseated expressions that were pasted across the faces of Bojan and Anika while they ate. They answered the questions his mother asked in faltering English, about Slovenia and the move to Belgium, and afterwards about classical music and the principles of the Christian faith, the way you answer a child. In their home, dinners were entirely different, boisterous and with many guests, and at the end Anika would sit at the piano and Bojan would force Marianka to dance at least one mazurka with him, and Avraham thought that the bitterness he felt towards them was also tied to the fact that they were younger than his parents and full of life.

At meals in their house bottles of wine were opened and gulped down one after the other, whereas his mother brought to the table one bottle, white and bland, which had been opened a few months ago at a meal in honour of Avraham's birthday and kept in the refrigerator since. When he was helping to clear the plates after the main course his mother said to him in the kitchen, 'They don't like the food,' and Avraham said to her, 'What are you talking about? They said that everything is delicious.' Bojan and Anika had brought her a gift of a green tablecloth and a pair of candlesticks, and she asked him in a whisper, 'Do you think that they expect me to put them on the table?'

All that Friday Avraham felt that if he didn't find the policeman within a few days, he would never be caught. And that soon no one other than him would care who had murdered Leah Yeger.

In the weekend papers there wasn't a single item about the murder that had taken place only four days earlier, nor was there anything about the storm, which had been forgotten as if it never happened; most of the articles were only concerned with the coming elections. Like almost every Friday since the start of the winter, stones were thrown in the Arab neighbourhoods in Jerusalem, and district policemen reinforced the Jerusalem police in order to prevent disturbances after prayers at the mosques. In the station's log no unusual incidents were recorded that day other than a stabbing at a club in Bat Yam, and when Eliyahu Ma'alul and Esty Vahaba went in to watch footage from CCTV and police traffic cameras in the area where the murder occurred, they were almost alone at the station. Avraham called them at every available moment, even during the dinner at his parents', from the room that was once his, but they didn't have anything to tell him, and Ma'alul asked that he stop calling. Ma'alul had brought sandwiches and a flask of black coffee with him from home, and he and Vahaba watched the footage late into the night, but the policeman who went down the stairs and disappeared wasn't to be seen in any of it. Diana Goldin arrived at the station in the afternoon and went through photos of the district policemen with Vahaba, but didn't identify anyone.

And on Saturday as well, right through till the afternoon, there were no developments. Avraham had hoped that in the morning, while drinking his first coffee, he could go over his notes and continue thinking about the policeman, but Bojan and Anika got up before him and, since Marianka was still sleeping, he prepared coffee for the two of them as well and they drank it together in silence on the porch. Despite the disturbances, they insisted on travelling to Jerusalem to visit the holy sites. Ma'alul had announced in advance that he would remain home on Saturday, and Esty Vahaba didn't get to the station to continue watching the footage until nearly ten. Avraham called her twice, and they agreed that if she didn't find an image of the policeman she would begin, once Shabbat ended, reaching out to rape victims in the district with the computerized facial composite. But at noon she called.

They were standing in the square in front of the Church of the Holy Sepulchre when Avraham heard the ring from his coat pocket and then saw the phone number and asked Marianka and her parents to go in without him.

And even though at that point it wasn't yet a positive identification, because the picture still needed to be sent to Diana Goldin and shown to the neighbour, Vahaba was convinced. At 2.28 p.m., a short time after the murder, a policeman could be seen passing by the cameras of a Bank Hapoalim on Sokolov Street, not far from the scene. Avraham held the phone close to his ear because a tour guide was speaking in the square before a group of pilgrims from Poland. Three policemen were guarding the entrance to the church, but none of them recognized Avraham.

The policeman in the footage had been cautious and hadn't stopped at the kiosk or at a supermarket to buy a packet of cigarettes or to hide from the rain, as they had hoped. But for an instant he had passed in front of the bank's external security camera, facing the street, and had been recorded by it. And it was his bad luck that the bank had recently undergone a renovation and sophisticated, up-to-date cameras had been installed which caught his face in profile, but clearly; and when she saw it, Diana Goldin immediately confirmed that it was him.

A brown leather jacket covered his light blue shirt, so it was impossible to see if there was a rank on it. Avraham asked Vahaba to send the picture straightaway to all department heads in the district so that they could try to identify the policeman. He also asked her to show the picture to the neighbour from the second floor, but the man wasn't at home. Then he called Ma'alul to inform him that a picture had been found and that it was of excellent quality. Ma'alul promised that he'd join Vahaba in the evening and asked him, 'Are you coming in too?' And Avraham answered without hesitation that he would.

His fingers shook when he tried to enlarge the pictures Vahaba had sent to his phone to look at the sharp face.

The policeman was short and stocky, as Diana Goldin had described. In his right hand he held a small bag. Avraham searched for his eyes in the picture, as if he'd find answers in them, but the policeman wasn't looking at the camera lens. He didn't know how long Marianka and her parents spent in the church, but when they came out Marianka asked him, 'Why didn't you come in?' and then she realized that something had happened.

When he said to her that they'd need to return early to Holon she asked him, 'Now?'

His phone was back in his coat pocket, and he didn't take it out. And, anyway, it was impossible to do more with the picture than he had already done. If he'd had Saban's permission, he would have posted it right away on the police Facebook page or had it broadcast on the television news in order to enlist the public's help in the search. For a moment it occurred to him to post the picture without permission. After all, they only needed one person to recognize him.

Because of the despair in Marianka's eyes, Avraham

suggested that they get some hummus at a restaurant in the Old City, but Anika tasted one warm chickpea and left the entire serving on the plate. Avraham already knew that he'd be going straight out to the station when they got back, so he strove to be friendly and talkative. They had only one more day together and, for Marianka, he made an effort. He asked her father about his work at the theological seminary and when he had started doing karate and about the move to Brussels, but Bojan gave him short answers, as if against his will. He did eat all his hummus, as well as the portion that Anika left, but all the time it seemed as if he wanted to say something else.

Marianka kept quiet throughout the entire meal and, when they ordered coffee, Anika, of all people, turned to him and said, 'Are there developments in the murder case?' And Avraham said, 'Yes, it seems so.'

'So you must want to go back, right? I feel that you aren't with us.'

Bojan signalled to the waiter that they would like the bill, and Avraham looked at Marianka when he said, 'I have no choice,' and Anika said to him, 'Police never get a holiday.'

He tried to smile when he said to her, 'Sometimes they do.'

'I mean a time when you don't even think about your work. You certainly take your investigations everywhere.'

Avraham hoped that the waiter would come quickly with the bill, but he passed before them with five plates of hummus on his way to another table.

'Why do you love it so much?' Anika asked, and Avraham tried to understand what she meant.

She went on. 'Why did you decide to become a police detective? You certainly could have done other things.'

Avraham was still thinking how to answer when he heard Marianka say, 'Avi needs to be near pain,' and then saw her father nod, like a consultant who confirms the diagnosis of a junior doctor. This wasn't true, but Avraham knew that this was what Marianka thought, because they discussed it sometimes. He had tried to explain to her that since he was a boy he had dreamed of being a policeman because of his addiction to detective novels and his sense that he could prove that they were wrong and that the people convicted were innocent. No one knew that this was the reason, other than Marianka. Not Eliyahu Ma'alul and not Ilana Lis, and definitely not his parents, from whom he had hidden his dream to join the police until the day when he had been accepted into the force and informed them that he wouldn't be becoming a lawyer. When he said, 'I think I became a policeman to save people in danger,' Avraham sought out Marianka's eyes, but she was looking in a different direction, and on Bojan's face rose a forgiving smile, as if his answer was incorrect.

And actually he didn't have much to do in his office once he got there. After Shabbat ended, Vahaba began showing the policeman's picture to rape victims in the district, but Ma'alul still hadn't arrived. Avraham tried calling the neighbour from the second floor again but he still wasn't at home, and then he looked again and again at the footage in which the policeman could be seen passing by on the street. Perhaps because he was alone in his office and because he had watched the clip so many times, Avraham suddenly realized that in his head he was talking to the policeman in the second person, as if he was sitting across from him in the room. *How did you obtain details of the rape victims? And what did you want from them?* He wrote the questions in pen on a clean sheet of paper. When he sent Ilana Lis a brief text message – *Maybe we can meet anyway?* – she invited him to come to her home on Monday. And Benny Saban sounded as if he had just woken up when he called and asked Avraham, 'What picture are you talking about?'

He explained to Saban that a high-resolution image of the policeman had been found, and suggested that they post it on the police Facebook page or publish it in the media, and Saban said he would get back to him, and when he called Avraham after a few minutes he announced, in a tone even more aggressive than the one he had used in the meeting on Thursday, that there was no chance the picture would be published. Before hanging up, Saban asked him, 'You're off tomorrow anyway, no?' and Avraham said, 'Not sure yet. The guests are going tomorrow night, but in any event I'll be available all day. Everyone knows what they need to do, and they'll keep me up to speed, and if I need to, I'll come in.' Vahaba and Ma'alul were supposed to go through all the sexual-assault victims in the district until another woman who had been contacted by the policeman was found, and to report to Avraham after each interview was carried out. And they did call him every hour or two, but by Sunday evening they still had no news. None of the women they presented with the photograph recognized the man in the picture, and none of them had been questioned or received a request from a policeman she didn't know. Avraham spent these hours on visits to churches and monasteries with Bojan and Anika because he didn't want to leave Marianka alone. First in Nazareth and afterwards at the Sea of Galilee, in the place where Jesus was said to have walked on water. His phone didn't stop ringing, and Marianka stopped trying to draw everyone into conversation, so they wandered from site to site silent and expressionless, as if they belonged to a forlorn Trappist order, counting their remaining hours together. Towards evening, when they had returned to Tel Aviv and were sitting in a restaurant on the promenade, Avraham even thought about ignoring the ringing of his phone, but finally picked up and heard Ma'alul saying in an agitated voice, 'Avi, are you alone? Can you speak for a moment? It's very urgent.'

Marianka gave Avraham a look when he went out of the restaurant to the car park.

'What's going on? Is everything OK?'

'Definitely not, Avi. You have no idea what went on here today, when we weren't here.'

Through the glass windows of the restaurant Avraham saw that Bojan was speaking to Marianka, and she looked upset, exactly like Ma'alul sounded.

'What happened?'

'Sharpstein brought Yeger's son in for additional questioning. And arrested him. We'd just got back to the station and Saban informed us that we're not to continue showing the picture of the policeman to the victims, because Erez Yeger has been arrested and the investigation is now focused on him.'

Avraham was stunned. And remembered that Saban

had asked him yesterday if he was taking the day off, and hadn't tried to convince him to cancel it.

'What exactly did he arrest Erez Yeger for? We know that the assailant isn't a relative.'

He paced back and forth and absentmindedly put his hand in his coat pocket to take out a packet of cigarettes when Ma'alul said to him, 'That's the thing, Avi, he's not her son. I mean, not biologically. He's adopted, apparently. The daughter revealed this to Sharpstein during questioning early this morning, and he brought Yeger in as a precaution and arrested him immediately. His alibi doesn't hold water either, because he was released from his reserve duty a few hours before the murder and could have reached Holon. Didn't you know that he wasn't her son? And in the meantime he's refusing a to take a lie-detector test or have his DNA examined. He's engaged a lawyer and is exercising his right to remain silent.'

Avraham took the phone away from his ear. He recalled a thought that had passed through his head at the funeral when Erez Yeger had thrown himself on to his mother's grave mound: *He doesn't resemble her at all.*

'Avi, can I ask you something?' Ma'alul said, and Avraham answered, 'Yes.' He knew what Ma'alul wanted to ask even before he heard his words.

'I'm with you on this policeman, but isn't it possible we're mistaken?'

He didn't respond. Before Diana Goldin had entered his office he had indeed been able to imagine Erez Yeger standing on the other side of that door.

'I'm not saying that we'll stop checking out this angle,'

Ma'alul continued, 'but the son is a logical suspect, don't you think?'

But Leah Yeger wouldn't have written a meeting with her son on her calendar, nor in her diary, and there was also the testimony of the neighbour regarding the policeman who came down the stairs and the picture of this policeman had been found! And besides this, the neighbour didn't see anyone else leaving the scene of the murder. Ma'alul listened to him and then said, 'But maybe there's an explanation for that, you know?' And Avraham fell silent. 'Her son does his reserve duty at an air-force supply base, and it could be that the neighbour got confused between a police uniform and the uniform he was wearing, see?'

When Avraham got back to the restaurant Marianka looked strange to him.

Her eyes were red, as if she had been crying and had washed her face. And how was it that nothing Ma'alul had told him weakened his confidence? If he had been alone he would have got straight into his car and gone to the station, but it was almost ten and he didn't even leave Saban a message when he called him and didn't get an answer. Before they said goodbye Avraham told Ma'alul, 'Anything's possible, Eliyahu. And there's certainly a reason why the son lied. But I think they simply don't want the investigation to head in the direction of the policeman, don't you see? In any case, I ask that tomorrow you and Vahaba continue showing the photo to the remaining victims. And if we need to I'll find a way to publish it, with or without Saban agreeing.'

When none of them asked him why he had left the restaurant for such a long time, Avraham sensed that something had taken place. The waitress came to their table and Marianka didn't order anything for herself and then said, 'Do you want to share what you have to say with Avi as well? He deserves to hear what you think.' Both she and Anika looked at her father, and Bojan spread a napkin over his lap and began to speak.

At the start of his speech Avraham still wasn't listening attentively because he was thinking about the things he'd need to do at the station the next morning. But the words soon sharpened in his ears, and he couldn't believe what he was hearing. And even though Bojan's remarks were directed at Avraham, he looked only at Marianka while he spoke.

'As you can imagine, and as we already told Marianka, we didn't come here for nothing,' he began. 'We've missed her and were also happy to meet your parents and visit places that until now we had only read about, but the reason we're here is to try to convince Marianka to return home. We had misgivings before we came, but now we are certain that this is what she must do. We have no intention of hiding anything from you, and therefore we now say this to you as well.'

Next to Avraham's plate was a glass of red wine that he hadn't ordered, and he sipped from it and waited. Marianka sat next to him and played with her fork but didn't look at him. 'Why do you want to convince her to go back?' Avraham asked, and Bojan said, 'Because she made a mistake when she came here. We told her our opinion beforehand and we say it again now. She has nothing to do here. We all started building a new life for ourselves in Brussels. She had a good job with the police and a chance to advance, and here she is alone and far away from people who truly have her best interests at heart.' Bojan was silent for a moment and then looked at Marianka and carried on. 'We know that you won't admit this in front of us,' he said, 'but we feel that you are very miserable here. You're throwing your life away, and we think that you know this and we want to ask Avi too to understand and help you come to right decision. It is important for us to say that we are not opposed to the relationship between you, but we understand that there's no chance that Avi would ever leave his job and come to live with us in Brussels.'

Avraham didn't say a thing. Marianka raised her eyes from the table and looked at her mother when she quietly asked, 'Do you really think I'm miserable here?' And Bojan smiled. 'I look miserable to you?' she asked her mother again, but Anika didn't answer.

'Definitely. You are miserable because you're alone and far from the family and the life that you built for yourself and which we helped you to build,' Bojan said. 'And we see this even though you try to pretend. You're squandering your talents and your life in a place where you have no one. Avi has a job and a family and he can't take care of you. And you won't find work that is appropriate for you without knowing the language. And you aren't a Jew either.'

Avraham needed to interrupt and stop him then, but Marianka and her father were looking only at each other, as if he and Anika weren't sitting at the table, and Marianka said, 'But I *am* happy here, don't you see? I love Avi and we have a home. For the first time, I have my own place. It's true that I don't yet know what to do with myself, but I'll find something.'

'And if you don't find anything?' Anika suddenly asked, and Bojan signalled with his hand that he wanted to continue speaking and said, 'It is important to us that you hear these things, because no one else loves you enough to say them to you. And I don't know what you mean when you say that you love Avi, but you thought that you loved other men as well before him, right? And at some point those loves ended. In any case, our obligation as parents is to inform you that we won't support your life here. We won't be able to visit here again because that would be an expression of support for your choice. And it is important to us to emphasize that we have nothing against Avi – quite the opposite, we respect him, and because of that we hope that he will understand and help you to leave.'

He had to say something, if not for himself then at least for Marianka. Or maybe he just needed to take her hand and get them out of there. He tried to smile when he said, 'I understand your concern for Marianka, but I want you to know that she's in good hands. We're thinking about our shared future. For now we haven't made any decisions, and if it gets hard for Marianka we'll think together about what to do. I can promise you that I want only what's good for her.' Everyone was silent when he finished, as if he hadn't said a word.

Bojan kept looking only at Marianka. The waitress served the appetizers and, on the table, a short candle burned. 'I don't know if you're a believer, Avi,' Bojan said, 'but we are. We *all* are. And a day before we came here I saw from the window of my office a sight that was for me a sign that we are doing the right thing. On the street opposite the window there was a dove that had been run over, and then I saw another dove land next to it and begin to peck at its corpse. I tried to understand what I was seeing, until I realized that it was impossible to know if the second dove was kissing the first or saying goodbye to it or perhaps even eating its flesh. Do you understand what I mean?'

Avraham didn't, but Marianka did. And he couldn't help but recall the birds on the rug on which he found Leah Yeger's body. If the conversation had taken place at another time, and not minutes after Ma'alul had informed him that Saban and Sharpstein were trying to wrestle control of the investigation away from him, perhaps Avraham would have responded differently, especially when Marianka put down her wine glass and smiled at her father and said to him, 'You're an idiot, you know? I now finally understand how much of an idiot you are.'

'I'm trying to say to you that your good intentions don't change the situation, Avi,' Bojan continued, as if Marianka hadn't spoken. 'I believe that you want only what's good for Marianka, as you say, but she is the one who's been run over in the street now, and you're pecking at her flesh, even if it seems to you that those are kisses.'

Anika touched Bojan's hand, as if to signal to him that he had gone too far. Or perhaps she did this to show that she supported him. Marianka was the one who got up first and left the restaurant, and Avraham simply went after her. And only later on, when they returned to their flat, did he ask her, 'What the hell was that crazy fable about the dead birds?'

Marianka asked him to open the car door, and then she got inside and sat in the passenger seat and burst out laughing.

'Let's go,' she said to him, and when he asked what her parents would do she answered, 'Doesn't matter. Let them go back on foot.'

They stopped in a car park not far from there because Marianka wanted them to go down to the beach, and when they sat facing the dark water she said to him only, 'I'm sorry,' and he asked her, 'About what?'

'That you heard all that. I should have known that this was what would happen. You were right.'

So why did he feel that he needed to apologize to her? To apologize for bringing her to Holon and for not responding to her father and mainly for hiding from her everything he had been going through since the start of the investigation and for truly abandoning her. That night they hardly talked about her parents at all but about themselves instead, about her and about him, and Avraham managed to tell her everything he hadn't said in recent days. He told her about the conversation this evening with Ma'alul, and about Erez Yeger, who wasn't his mother's biological son, and about the fact that Leah Yeger was raped in her home by a man she knew, and about the policeman who he was sure asked to question her, for reasons he still didn't comprehend. When Marianka asked him why he hadn't shared all this with her before, Avraham told her the truth. That he had no idea. And then he added, 'Maybe to protect you from something,' and she said, 'To protect me? From what? And why do you think that I need protection?'

The next day, at four in the morning, beside the cab driver who was waiting to take Bojan and Anika to the airport, they said goodbye in the street, without hugging.

Avraham couldn't get back to sleep, and even though he would have liked to spend the day with Marianka, he went ahead and left for the station early. When Esty Vahaba called him towards noon he was in the car, on his way to Ilana Lis so that she could advise him on how to publish the picture of the policeman who went down the stairs and disappeared, but Vahaba said that she thought she had found a woman who perhaps knew something about the policeman.

He slowed down and asked her, 'What? He visited her too?' and Vahaba said, 'No, she didn't say that, but I could tell she was quite shocked when I showed her the picture. And I have a feeling that she didn't tell me everything she knows.'

That was the first time Avraham heard the name Bengtson.

10

The policewoman called Mali on Monday morning.

She was in a meeting with a new client when a number she didn't recognize came up on her mobile. She didn't answer, but the second time she said, "Excuse me," and stuck an earbud into her right ear. She had no doubt that it was her fault. She inserted the second earbud then heard the voice on the other end of the line. A woman asked to speak with Mazal Bengtson, and Mali said, 'Speaking.' And she was sure that the policewoman had tracked her down because of the phone call to A & E a few days before. She got up from her seat without apologizing to the client, and hid her mouth with her hand while she spoke. The policewoman asked if they could meet, and when Mali said she was at work, the policewoman asked her where she worked. She was sure that the policewoman knew, since the phone call to A & E had been made from the office, and so she said, 'In Holon. On Shenkar Street.'

'I can come to see you there,' the policewoman said. 'And this won't take more than five or ten minutes.'

Mali asked her colleague Yana if she could take over the meeting with her client and went to the ladies' toilets. A cleaner was mopping the floor and Mali waited for her to leave before entering one of the stalls and calling Kobi.

★

During those past few days the two of them had had so many opportunities to try to alter their fate, but they didn't.

Mali asked herself countless times what Kobi would have done had he been awake and answered the phone so she could tell him that a policewoman was on her way to question her about the accident. *Would he have told her the truth then?*

Throughout the weekend the two of them had hoped that everything was behind them, or at least tried to hope, and maybe that's why she was so unprepared for what happened. Kobi kept pretending that he was in a good mood, but she saw him taking those deep breaths, as if he was suffocating. The weather had improved, and on Saturday he suggested that they take the girls to the amusement park in Tel Aviv, as they had promised them back at the start of winter. Mali would have preferred that they stay home, but once Daniella and Noy got wind of the idea there was no chance that they'd relent. Kobi woke early and went up to the roof to work out. When she was making pancakes he came up to her from behind and wrapped his arms around her stomach and asked, 'Are you coming with us or staying here?'

Once they got there she couldn't tell him why she wasn't going on the rides, but perhaps hinted at it when she said that she was nauseous and had a headache and was scared she would throw up. There weren't queues for most of the rides, and Kobi took Daniella and Noy on the Devil's Tunnel, which was a let-down, and then on the roller coaster and the dodgems, and went with them again and again on the giant octopus, whose metal arms spun around high above the treetops. Mali looked at them from below. At the outbursts of horror and laughter on the girls' faces. How they held Kobi's hands. She took pictures of them with her phone, because Kobi asked her to. And over the weekend she did think about the woman that he had hit with his car. She was sorry she had called the hospital and hoped that they wouldn't call her back as they had promised, though on the other hand she wanted them to call to say that the woman had been released. It didn't occur to her even for a moment that Kobi had lied.

She didn't look at the pictures from that day at the park until much later, and then she was unable to stop looking at them. Especially at a picture she took of the three of them on the roller coaster: Daniella and Noy in Kobi's arms in a green car climbing towards the end of the track, a moment before the drop.

In the weeks to come Mali met the policewoman many times, but that morning she didn't know that her name was Esty Vahaba. She was very short and younger than Mali, and smoked a cigarette during their conversation. She asked Mali for an identification card and then crossed her thick legs and placed a plastic clipboard on her knees and sat bent forward while she filled out the forms. Vadim, the bank's security guard, watched them as they walked away from the bank and went to sit on a bench. The policewoman placed a paper cup on it and when later she drank from it coffee spilled on to her fingertips.

Mali watched the cars that passed by, as if Kobi might be in one of them, and recalled the policewoman who had questioned her in Eilat. She was older than Esty Vahaba and attractive, and she had stared at her computer screen while, over and over, she asked Mali questions about the wine she had drunk at the party and her relationship with Kobi and if she was one hundred per cent certain she hadn't invited a man up to her room. When Vahaba asked, 'You were assaulted a few years ago in Eilat, is that correct, Ms Bengtson?' Mali didn't understand why she was mentioning this and how it was connected to the hit-and-run. The policewoman's cigarette troubled her because of the pregnancy. But then Vahaba said, 'I ask that you keep secret the things I'm going to tell you, because we're talking about confidential information from an investigation in its earliest stages, and we're not sure about anything, OK?' And only after Mali nodded she continued: 'We suspect that there's a policeman, or a criminal who dresses as a policeman, who works in the area and harasses women who were victims of rape. What I want to check with you is, whether a man like this has contacted you or met with you?'

Mali immediately said, 'No,' and at first felt only relief. The policewoman put out her cigarette on the end of the bench, as if she sensed that the smoke was bothering her. 'Are you sure?' she asked, and Mali said to her, 'Yes.'

'Do you remember when you last gave evidence?'

It took her a while to answer, because she honestly didn't remember. And while she was trying to remember she realised the words that Vahaba had said: *a criminal who dresses as a policeman.*

'I don't remember exactly when. A while ago. Maybe a year.'

'And no one from the police has contacted you since? Maybe in the last few weeks? Not even by phone?'

'No.'

'And are you perhaps in contact with other women who have been assaulted, who you know have been recently reached out to in this way?'

Did Mali know then? In contrast to the woman who took her statement in Eilat, Esty Vahaba looked at her when she spoke. Her eyes were large and opened wide, as if unnaturally. On her forehead, above her left eye, was a scar. She paused before bending over the clipboard again and writing a few lines. She remained sitting in her place when she said to Mali, 'There is a gag order on this investigation, in order not to create panic among women who've been attacked, so I'm asking you again to keep the details I'm providing you with secret, OK? And if a man who introduces himself as a detective from the police contacts you and asks for a statement, or if you remember that this indeed has happened to you or hear of anyone that this has happened to, you'll inform me immediately, right? We're afraid that he's done this to a few women and that he'll do it again.'

Mali put the policewoman's card in her coat pocket without looking at it, and as she rose from the bench she felt something twisting and turning in the pit of her stomach. No one had contacted her. The things the policewoman had said, about the panic among women who had been attacked and about the fact that the policeman had done this a few times, were what caused Mali finally to understand with certainty.

'Do you know who this man is?' She shouldn't have asked, but she needed to know.

The policewoman still sat on the bench, as if it was hard for her to get up. She said, 'We don't know his name, but we have a good picture of him and we'll find him soon.' And Mali asked to see it.

Vahaba stared at her with her big eyes and then removed the photograph from a grey folder that was resting on her knees. And Mali looked at the photograph momentarily, for no more than a second, before everything went dark. She asked Vahaba, 'When was the picture taken?' since this was her final hope, but the policewoman said to her, 'Last week.'

Daniella and Noy were at nursery and school, and for the first few minutes Mali didn't know what she would do with them after she picked them up. At eleven she had another meeting, and she sat across from the customer as if nothing had happened. She explained to him why the bank was rejecting his mortgage application, and he raised his voice. How much time passed before she understood that *there had been no accident*? She imagined herself suddenly in the delivery room, without Kobi and without anyone else next to her. The spasms in the pit of her stomach turned to nausea, and when she went to the bathroom and tried to vomit they thought at the bank that the reason was her confrontation with the customer.

For the second time in a few days she needed to explain everything to herself from the beginning: the job interview and everything else that happened on the day of their anniversary, Kobi's absence on the following days and the message he'd left for his father and the car that wasn't in the car park. Now there was also perhaps an explanation for the umbrella and for Kobi desperately searching for it. And perhaps also for him watching the news and reading the newspapers. Kobi hadn't been lying when he said that the police were looking for him, but he had lied with regard to the reasons. And she never lied to him. Never. Even though there had been no accident, she still pictured the young woman he hit with his car lying bloody on the street and no one coming to help her.

When Kobi woke up he tried to call her because he could see that she had called him many times, but she didn't answer because she still didn't know what to say. He sent her a text message: *Everything OK?* And she answered him: *Yes, in a meeting.* Maybe that first lie gave her the idea? The policewoman's card was in her pocket, and Mali thought about calling her or her sister Gila, but by the time she had picked up Daniella and Noy from nursery and school she had already decided that she would return home and not say a thing to Kobi for now. The girls sat in the back and Mali looked at them in the mirror while she drove and asked Daniella why she was quiet. Noy was practising the song that they were preparing in class for the Purim party. When she saw Kobi's car in its parking space she remembered the Monday before. *This was the day when he was discovered, apparently.* The car hadn't been there when they returned home then, but she had smelled his aftershave in the lift and found that the door to the flat wasn't locked, and when they went inside she heard him showering. His clothes had been thrown on the bedroom floor, but there hadn't been a policeman's uniform.

Today when they came home the table was set and ravioli was cooking on the stove. When Kobi opened the door for them he said to her immediately, 'Why didn't you call me back after your meeting? I tried you a few times.' Mali said that she had had back-to-back meetings and that she had called in the morning because she was worried that she wouldn't manage to get the girls, but in the end it had worked out. Her eyes avoided his, but in a strange way she wasn't as frightened as she had been before the meeting with the policewoman, only confused. And she didn't touch her food. Noy told Kobi about the preparations for the Purim party at school, and Daniella remained quiet and, like Mali, didn't eat a thing. Mali felt that something inside her was also growing stronger or hardening, perhaps out of anger. After Eilat it was as if she had left her body, and even when she returned to Kobi it was a partial return; but during those hours at home, after the conversation with the policewoman, it was as if the broken parts had joined together again.

Kobi asked her, 'How was work?' and Mali said to him, 'Good.' Before, she wouldn't have been able to lie to him like this. When she went to the bathroom and knelt over the toilet she managed to throw up. Kobi hurried after her and waited outside the door, and when she came out he asked her, 'Are you throwing up?' She said that she had eaten something that had gone off at work and that she felt better now. Because she didn't want to be alone with him, she didn't go into the bedroom. She did homework with Noy and let Daniella watch television, and when

Daniella fell asleep on the sofa Mali sat down next to her and stroked her hair. At five Kobi asked her if she was feeling OK and if he could go to the gym, and she said yes. Maybe all she had to do was ask him, 'Why'd you go back to it?' and he would have told her. Only when she saw his car leaving the car park and driving off did she hurry to the bedroom and start looking. She looked for the uniform among his winter clothes and in the underwear drawer, and afterwards up above with his summer clothes and in the dressing-up box, but it wasn't in the bedroom or in the utility room on the roof, or even in his drawers, which she opened for the first time.

The nausea disappeared, and she didn't stop looking, even though she didn't know what she would do with the policeman's uniform if she found it.

The first time she had seen Kobi wearing it, Mali had been lying in their bed, trying to fall asleep.

Kobi had come into the bedroom and turned on the main light, and his eyes were red, as if he had been crying. She asked him, 'What is that?' and Kobi had sat down on the edge of the bed in silence and she had asked him again, 'Kobi, why are you wearing those clothes? You're scaring me.' And she had started to cry.

This had been a few weeks after Eilat.

The cut on her neck hadn't completely healed, or at least that's how it felt, even though no one other than her noticed it any more, and her wrists also still hurt sometimes, like they had the morning after. In the mirror she was still the other woman. And Kobi was the person who helped her sometimes remember who she was. He didn't explain why he was wearing the uniform and began speaking only after she stopped crying. But when he spoke she again burst into tears, and he had hugged her and she had stopped.

Everything hurt then, like flesh where the skin has been peeled off, and she had tried to tell herself that he was bleeding as well, and if she would only lay her hand on his wound it would pass. When he had asked her to come with him to the kitchen and sit across the table from him she had agreed, because she had no choice. On the table were his mobile and a pad of yellow paper and a pen, as if it was an interrogation room.

Towards evening Mali looked for the police uniform among the dirty clothes at the bottom of the laundry basket and even in the girls' rooms, although by now it was clear to her that she wouldn't find them. When she returned to the bedroom to search the box of sheets under the bed, she saw the picture of her and Kobi on the wall and wanted to shatter the glass and tear up the photograph. Nothing of what she would do next had yet occurred to her during those hours, but she did imagine herself again in the delivery room, without him, without knowing where he was, and afterwards there also appeared in her thoughts a picture of the four of them together in her car: she was driving and Daniella and Noy were sitting in the back seat, and next to them was the baby in its special car seat, but the passenger seat was empty.

At six thirty, when knocking could be heard at the door, she was on the roof. She thought that Kobi was early and had forgotten his key, and because she didn't want to see him she didn't go down right away; but Daniella called from downstairs, 'Mum, it's for you,' and when Mali came down the stairs she saw the policewoman who had questioned her in the morning and felt her knees go weak.

Behind Esty Vahaba stood another policeman, one whom Mali didn't yet know.

Only at the very end of questioning Mazal Bengtson, right at the last minute, did Avraham bring control of the investigation back into his own hands. Up until then, for a few hours, he sensed that he was again being hesitant, as he had been on the first day. He watched Sharpstein lead Erez Yeger into the interview room, and he didn't intervene when Sharpstein tried to get him to admit that he had murdered his mother. And he listened to the things Ilana Lis hurled at him without responding. Until almost the last moment he also sat in Mazal Bengtson's sparsely decorated living room, hardly involved in the conversation. Bengtson again said that no policeman had contacted her, and Esty Vahaba's feeling, that Bengtson hadn't told her everything during the first questioning, seemed unconvincing to him.

The flat was on the seventh floor of an old residential building. 8 Uri Zvi Greenberg Street.

The door was open when they entered the building a little before six thirty in the evening, and the stairwell remained dark even after they turned the light on. The narrow lift gave off an odour of cigarette smoke and animals, cats perhaps. And Avraham was forced to stand too close to Esty Vahaba. On the mirror were two stickers, one with the telephone number of a plumber and the second of a pest exterminator, and Avraham read them in order not to look at himself in the mirror and see what Ilana Lis had seen.

Vahaba knocked on the door twice before ringing the bell. A four- or five-year-old girl, with fair hair and blue eyes, opened the door for them and then called for her mother, who looked nothing like her. Mazal Bengtson was tall and dark, and her hair was black. Perhaps thirty-five years old. She wore a grey fleece and slippers, and to Avraham it seemed that they had interrupted her while she was cleaning. She didn't ask them why they had come, and this should have grabbed his attention, but his thoughts were still in Ilana's flat.

The girl who opened the door for them remained standing in the doorway to her room and stayed there throughout their conversation, as if to watch over the mother. Mazal Bengtson led them to the living room, offered them coffee or tea and went to the kitchen to boil water, as those being questioned sometimes do when policemen show up in their homes with no warning, in order to relieve the tension. That night, when he recalled their conversation, Avraham thought how little Mazal Bengtson resembled her daughters. Like Erez Yeger and the woman who wasn't his mother. He looked around him while they waited for her. The blinds in the window facing the street were closed, and the feeling in the almost empty living room was claustrophobic. In its centre were two black leather couches and a small glass table, and a flat-screen television hung on the wall opposite them. The rest of the walls were bare, except for one small photo that was hanging on one of the walls, as if by accident. The two of them sat on one of the couches, and Mazal Bengtson set their mugs of coffee on the glass table and sat across from them on a stool. Throughout most of the conversation Avraham gazed at the photograph of the deer skipping through dense forest, fleeing from the hunters' rifles or the camera. Under the photograph was a small bookshelf and on it were two rows of books, mostly in English, and this too should have attracted his attention, but at that time he didn't remember the English accent of the policeman who had questioned Diana Goldin, and even if he had remembered, he might not have made a connection. On the sofa a woven blanket was spread out, like at his parents' flat, and something about it and the bare walls caused him to think that they hadn't been living here for long or that it was a temporary refuge of sorts which they planned on leaving.

And actually, he didn't even want to be there. He came with Esty Vahaba because that was the only way to make progress on his angle of the investigation, and because he didn't know what to do when he returned to his office from the terrible visit with Ilana Lis.

Since that morning, everything had gone against him. He had hoped that Erez Yeger would agree to a lie-detector test and DNA examination in order to prove that he wasn't the assailant, but despite the advice that he received from his lawyer Yeger refused and didn't say another word to Sharpstein in the interview room. Nor did he explain why he had concealed the fact that he was adopted or the phone call with his mother on the day before the murder.

Through the interview-room window Avraham heard Sharpstein threaten the handcuffed Yeger that if he didn't agree to the tests the police would announce that a relative had been arrested on suspicion of involvement in the murder. Avraham thought that this was just an interrogation technique, but while he was eating lunch Ma'alul informed him over the phone that the website Ynet had posted an article saying that the police were close to solving the case.

It took the page time to open because the internet connection at the station was slow, and when Avraham read the piece he couldn't believe it.

The headline said: *Police Close to Solving Holon Murder*, and in the body of the article it was written that in less than a week the investigation team had succeeded in arresting a suspect in the murder of Leah Yeger, a member of the victim's family, and that in a few more days he would be charged and the gag order would be lifted.

Avraham immediately called Benny Saban, but he didn't answer. And when he hurried to his office he discovered that he wasn't at the station. When Vahaba came in to update him about the statements she had gathered from rape victims, it all seemed utterly pointless, since the investigation was nearing its end. Vahaba first saw the Ynet article in his office. She wasn't certain that additional questioning of Mazal Bengtson would yield any more information, but it seemed to her that Bengtson was the only one out of all the women she'd spoken to who perhaps knew more than she had let on. Bengtson's rape case had been handled by the Eilat district, and Vahaba explained to Avraham that she had taken the decision to speak also to women who weren't attacked in the district but lived there, and Avraham looked at her with admiration when he asked to read the file. 'But why would she be hiding something?' he asked, and Vahaba said, 'I have no idea. But she asked to see the photo and I'm sure she was surprised when she saw the policeman in the picture.'

Bengtson's fair-haired daughter, who was still standing in the doorway to her room, also looked at them with a frightened gaze when Avraham said to Mazal Bengtson, 'I am Police Superintendent Avraham, Head of the Investigations Division in Ayalon district. As my colleague here told you today, we are in the middle of a very sensitive investigation concerning a policeman, or a man who presents himself as a police detective, who gathers testimony from rape victims, and we came to share with you additional details from the investigation which might perhaps help you to recall if you recently met with this man.'

Mazal Bengtson's gaze passed back and forth between him and Vahaba, and neither did she stop sending fleeting glances in the direction of the girl standing by the door, but Avraham did not attribute much importance to this.

'May I ask you a few preliminary questions? I understand from Esty here that you were assaulted approximately three years ago, is that correct?'

'Yes.'

'In Eilat.'

'Yes. In a hotel.'

Avraham couldn't recall from the rape file that he had read in his office before coming whether Bengtson was married or divorced, and on the door he hadn't noticed any sign with names on it. He felt that she wanted them to leave so she could continue cleaning the flat. Perhaps she didn't want to return to the assault, which she certainly would have tried to forget, either. Avraham opened his notepad and searched through his pockets for a pen, and when he didn't find one he asked Vahaba for one. He then continued, 'You told Esty today that you don't remember the last time you gave a statement to the police. We have it documented that you were questioned in 2013. Is that correct?'

'It could be. If that's what's documented.'

'And do you recall who questioned you then?'

'Always the same policewoman.'

'Yifat Asayag from the Eilat police?'

'Yes.'

What was he supposed to ask her? And for what purpose? Did he think that she'd suddenly tell him that the policeman had been in her home and before he took off left her with a full name and a telephone number? He tried to get rid of the doubts that had plagued him ever since the meeting with Ilana Lis and to concentrate on the woman sitting in front of him, but even so it was as if he didn't see her. Mazal Bengtson was a good-looking woman, but he didn't register that because of the fleece she was wearing, or because of the gloomy living room, and only when he next met her would he notice. There was a ring on her wedding finger, and a second ring on the other hand. And Avraham remembered what he had read about the night when she was attacked in Eilat.

She had been alone there, attending a work conference. And the man who attacked her was never found.

Among the theories put forward by the investigation team was that her assailant had been a tourist who was staying at the hotel and had fled Israel that same night, or was a refugee who had only recently entered the country via the Sinai Desert. A different theory was that Bengtson had invited to her room a man whom she met at a party in the hotel but wasn't willing to admit this. What bothered the team was that no traces of the attacker were found on the clothes she had worn when being questioned that night, and only when they told her that did Bengtson say that after the attack she had taken off her pyjamas and put the clothes that she had worn to the party back on.

How old then was the daughter who watched them from the door? And did she know anything about all this? Despite his efforts to concentrate, Avraham's thoughts kept wandering back to his conversation with Ilana. He heard himself say to Bengtson, 'One of the details we have discovered is that the policeman makes phone contact with the victims and ensures over the course of a few conversations that they aren't suspicious of him before setting up an actual meeting. Perhaps you recall something like this? Someone who tried to set up a meeting with you?' Bengtson thought for a few seconds before saying no.

'This means that you're certain that, since 2013, no person introducing himself as a police detective has contacted you, not even by phone? Perhaps you want to see the photo again?'

It all seemed so unnecessary, or at least that was how he felt.

Avraham fell silent and grabbed his warm mug and looked at Esty Vahaba sitting next to him. When the girl came near to them on tiptoes, as if they wouldn't sense it, Bengtson said to her, 'Daniella, go back to your room, OK, sweetie? We'll be finished soon, right?' And Avraham nodded.

Only when Ilana opened the door for him earlier that afternoon had it occurred to Avraham that this was only the second time he had ever visited her home. And that she had never been to his flat.

The previous time had been during the shiva for her son, who had been killed on a training exercise. Avraham didn't come alone then but rather with a delegation of officers from the station, and they stayed less than an hour because the house was full of visitors. But he remembered everything. The well-lit living room, with its shelves full of books and strange *objets d'art*, dark clay masks and colourful pictures in which nothing was clearly depicted, and the wooden sculptures that Ilana and her husband had brought back from their travels around the world and which were scattered throughout the house. Even Ilana looked the same to him, at least at first glance. She wore a loose-fitting dress and a scarf had been wrapped over her long red hair, but her blue eyes looked at him in just the usual way, and at least at the start of their meeting Avraham felt they contained affection. They didn't hug, but shook hands. And when he asked, 'How are you?' Ilana said to him, 'You see, everything's OK. I'm still alive.'

Did Avraham only understand then how much he missed her? How much he longed for her presence at the meetings of the investigation team? He wanted to talk it all through with her, from the moment he left the murder scene, because almost since his first day with the police she had accompanied him on every case he had worked on. And in each one of the team meetings he had led since the murder he had thought about what she would do were she sitting in his place. There was complete silence in the flat, not even noises from outside could be heard, and he wanted to ask Ilana what she did all day before her husband returned from work, when she said, 'So I'm finally having some holiday. I'm taking advantage of the time to read books I never got to,' as if she really could hear his thoughts. On the giant wooden table in the dining room, next to a plate of dates, he saw the book *The Man Who Mistook His Wife for a Hat*, open and face down, and for some reason he thought that she had put it there for his benefit and that she hadn't actually been reading it before he arrived. Hadn't she told him once, many years ago, that she had read that book? He didn't know if or how to ask her about the disease and her treatment. When they sat at the table it seemed to him that he noticed in her pale face signs of her illness and that she wasn't telling him everything. She had grown thin, and when she led him to the living room she walked with difficulty. Finally, he asked, 'How do you feel?' and Ilana said, 'Excellent. The surgery was successful and I have two more rounds of treatment, and then I'll return to work.' But she didn't look to him like someone who could soon return to work. When she asked him, 'How are you?' he was struck by a strong desire to tell her about Marianka and her parents' visit and his father's deteriorating condition, and at the same time he felt the exhaustion of recent days building up in him, and thought that if he just lay down on the thick pillows scattered on the sofa, he'd fall fast asleep. He said, 'I'm fine.'

'And how is your girlfriend? Is she managing here?'

That's what it had been like ever since he had told Ilana about Marianka. She refused to call her by her name.

'Yes. Quite well, actually.'

'What is she doing? Is she working?'

'She's found work at a health club. Giving karate lessons. And she's looking for other work too.'

'Wasn't she a cop there?'

'Yes, she was. But she was also a karate instructor.'

Ilana said that you wouldn't know by looking at him that his girlfriend was a fitness instructor, and Avraham laughed. He was sure that she'd change her mind and wouldn't refuse to help him when he asked to share his troubles with her, and when she questioned him about working with Saban it seemed to him that he'd been right. 'What did you want to ask me about?' she asked, and Avraham said that everything had changed since the last time he called.

'We have a hell of a case. You must have heard,' he said, and Ilana was quiet for a moment before asking, 'Do you mean the murder of the old woman? I heard on the radio earlier that it's closed.'

'They've arrested the wrong man,' Avraham replied, and Ilana asked, 'Who did the arresting?'

'Saban. And Sharpstein was with him.'

'And why do you think it's the wrong man?'

'Because it's someone else. Not her son.'

Had he been mistaken when he'd felt that Ilana was listening to him with great interest? He updated her on the details of the investigation she wasn't familiar with, told her that Leah Yeger had previously been raped, and about the testimony of the neighbour and Diana Goldin and about the photograph they now had of the policeman. Ilana didn't interrupt him once. He was now the head of the investigations unit and Ilana was on leave, and they were at her home and not at the station, but it was exactly the way their conversations used to be, especially when Ilana left the living room and returned with an ashtray and a packet of Marlboro Lights. Avraham hesitated before saying to her, 'No, thank you. I gave up,' and she looked at him, surprised.

'Are you sure? Is it because of the athletic girlfriend?'

He felt better when he'd finished talking, and when Ilana asked him, 'So how can I help you with this?' he said, 'I don't know. You tell me. I want to convince Saban to publish the photo of the policeman, but I don't know how. He's scared of the damage it's liable to cause and, as you can imagine, it's the last thing the police need right now, but I have no other way to get to the killer. Do you have any idea how I should approach Saban? Or maybe I could speak to someone above him?'

Ilana exhaled the smoke too close to him. And said, 'I think that in this matter Saban's right. To publish a photo-graph like that, when you know so little about the suspect and his involvement, would be irresponsible. And I also agree with him about the harm it will do. Understand, Avi, you're seeing just this investigation, but whoever's above you has to see the bigger picture. There are other investigations as well as this, and the police have other tasks as well as solving this murder. That's exactly the responsibility of a district commander.'

'But I have no other way to get to the policeman, Ilana. And I'm sure I'm not mistaken and that it's him, and once we know who he is we'll be able to confirm it with the evidence at the scene. Do you at least agree that everything points to him?'

Ilana set the cigarette down in the ashtray and Avraham almost reached out his hand to it.

'How could I know?' she said. 'I haven't seen the investigation materials and I haven't read the testimony and I have no way of helping you with this. I have no idea how trustworthy your witnesses are and, most importantly I haven't questioned her son. It sounds to me as if you could be right, but I'm sure you'll succeed in catching him even without publishing a picture in the newspapers. I trust you.'

Avraham placed the bag that he'd put by his feet on the table and said, 'I have everything here, Ilana. All the paperwork is here.' It was forbidden to remove files from the station, but he'd had to bring it. Ilana put out the cigarette and asked him suddenly, 'Avi, what do you really want?'

There was anger in her gaze, and he didn't understand why.

'You know you're not allowed to share the paperwork with me because I have no official position in the police right now, and I'm happy about that. And I asked you not to involve me in any investigations. It's not good for me, and it won't give me peace of mind, trust me. I want to detach myself from all this. And you don't need me.'

'I'm not trying to give you peace of mind, Ilana,' he said. 'And I'm telling you that I do need your help. Saban is only concerned about how he and the force look, and his superiors also, apparently, don't like it that I'm searching for a cop.'

Ilana interrupted. 'I've known you for long enough to think that you're doing this because you think that if you include me I'll feel better. But let me decide what's right for me, OK? And don't "help" me, Avi. Not like this, at least.'

That wasn't the reason he was there, and he told her again that he was in real need of her help.

'I told you, I can't help you.'

'I think that you can.'

'How?'

'Help me work out how to get to him. If not with the photograph, then in some other way. And also about his motives. Why would a policeman do a thing like that?'

For a moment Ilana looked interested. Avraham recognized that flash in her eyes when a certain detail in an investigation sparked her imagination. This was exactly like before she had got ill, in her old office at that Ayalon district station or in the new one at the Tel Aviv district headquarters. Her and him and a cigarette burning in an ashtray between them and smoke exhaled towards an open window. The intimacy between two detectives who know that, thanks to the cooperation between them, an endless number of past cases have been solved. 'You don't have a motive?' Ilana asked.

'I have theories.'

'Such as?'

'Revenge, perhaps. He wants to get back at the police for something. If he's still a policeman, it could be that he's frustrated. Maybe it's someone who was fired from the service.'

Ilana said, 'Could be,' and went to the kitchen to empty the ashtray, and Avraham thought this was a sign that she'd look at the paperwork, but when she returned the intimacy had faded and Ilana again refused to discuss the case. He pressed her again, until she suddenly asked him, 'Do you want to know what I really think?' and lit another cigarette.

He said that he did.

'I think that Saban is right.'

'Right about what?'

'This photo, as I told you, cannot be published. Full stop. And investigations into the son can progress at the same time as you look into the matter of the policeman; I don't see why not. Do you remember what we always said? That you have to listen to all the possible stories simultaneously? That the most severe mistake we make is to lock into just one story *because it suits us* and not listen to the other stories?'

He heard the hint in what she was saying, even if she hid it in different words.

'You think I locked into the story *because it suits me*?'

'That's not what I said, Avi. I said that—'

'But that's what you think?'

'I told you that I think you've got the right angle. But that it wouldn't hurt to check other angles at the same time.'

'Why do you think that this story suits me?'

Ilana was silent. She put out her cigarette, even though

she had only just started smoking it. When he asked her again she snapped angrily, 'Maybe because you resemble this cop a little, no?'

He thought that she was joking, but in her eyes there was something else which he didn't recognize when she continued speaking. 'Don't get all insulted, please. I mean that cops will do anything in order to catch people who break the law and put them in jail. That's our goal; do you agree with me? Something else is guiding you, just like with this cop. He's not questioning the women in order to catch their assailants, right? He does it for other reasons. For *his own* reasons. And you're like that too. I'm not sure that I understand what's guiding you, Avi, what you're looking for exactly, and the truth is that I always thought that this is what prevents you from being the exceptional detective you could be. But maybe it's not too late for you to change.'

On Avraham's way back to the station, with the things Ilana had said to him going round and round inside his head, he understood that she hadn't meant to hurt him and had simply let out the rage that had built up in her for weeks at the disease that had spread throughout her body and about leaving the work she loved so much, and that she wouldn't dare to admit even to herself that she wouldn't be returning to. And he also remembered what Marianka had said to her parents, about Avraham being a policeman because he needed to be close to pain. But when he first heard Ilana's words he had frozen and didn't respond, and then he rose and put the paperwork back into the file. Ilana said, 'So you are insulted? But you wanted to hear the truth,' and Avraham said quietly, 'That's not the reason the story *suits me*, Ilana. The story suits me because it's the only possible story according to the evidence and because all the other stories aren't reasonable. But thanks for the help.' He didn't wait for her to walk him out, and as he went towards the door he heard her call out from behind him, 'Did you come so I'd give my blessing to whatever you said, Avi?' And he tried to smile when he turned around and said to her, 'I didn't come for that, Ilana. I came to see how you were doing.'

He had no more questions for Mazal Bengtson, and he waited for Esty to finish questioning her as well so that he could go back home. Vahaba bent over towards the glass table and said to Bengtson almost in a whisper, perhaps so her daughter wouldn't hear, 'I want to be completely honest with you, Mazal. There's a reason that we're here, having already spoken to you this morning. I felt after our conversation that perhaps you were scared to say that you did meet with this man. That perhaps it's unpleasant for you to admit this. And I wanted to tell you that you have nothing to be ashamed of and that you have nothing to fear if that is what happened. You're not the only one who has fallen into his trap and agreed to give him a statement. There's no way you could have known that he's not an on-duty policeman if that's how he presented himself. But if you know something, then you do have a way to help us to prevent him from reaching other women.'

Bengtson listened and again said that she hadn't met the policeman, and that if she had she wouldn't hesitate to say so. And Esty Vahaba sighed and said, 'But if you remember something, we're here.'

This was the end of the interview, and if it hadn't been for the phone call from Ma'alul, Avraham wouldn't have seen a thing. His phone rang and he got up and walked away from them, in the direction of the entrance, and listened to Ma'alul, who said to him, 'Avi, I have some good news for you. I was with the neighbour and I showed him the policeman's photograph, and he says it's for sure the man he saw. He's certain that he didn't see Erez Yeger, but rather the man in the photograph. Do you hear me?' And Avraham didn't respond to him because, while he'd been listening, he'd spotted the picture through the open doorway.

For a moment he considered going in straightaway, but he didn't.

From where he stood he could see only part of the naked body, along with her face. He said to Ma'alul, 'Excellent, Eliyahu, but I'm here in the middle of something. I'll call you in a bit,' and then he approached Bengtson and Vahaba, who got up from their seats, and he asked where the bathroom was. Afterwards, when Avraham tried to explain to himself why he did it, he thought that what had drawn his attention was the contrast between the woman they had spoken to in the living room and the one he saw in the picture. Mazal Bengtson pointed towards the white door at the end of the hallway and Avraham waited in the bathroom with the light on until he heard her walking away and then he silently opened the door and slipped out.

The next room along was dark, and he passed by it on his way to the bedroom, which was lit, even though no one was in it. If she had noticed him, Avraham would have explained that he was looking for a towel to dry his hands.

The picture that he had glimpsed from the hallway was hanging over a double bed, and at first he saw in it only the woman who had sat before him without managing to grab his attention. But then he noticed the man whose arms were wrapped around her breasts.

12

The thought of turning him in crossed Mali's mind as soon as the police left.

While they were there, she couldn't say anything, partly because of the girls, but mainly because Kobi could have come back at any moment. Daniella had stayed by the door, even though Mali had asked her to wait in her room, and Mali watched her daughter and the door, scared that Kobi would return and see the police and that they in turn would see and recognize him. This, and not their questions, was what gave rise to her fear, maybe because she felt that she would be answering them soon enough anyway. She didn't believe that they had come back because of something in the previous conversation; she was sure they knew more about Kobi than they had let on. And the strange thing was that in the meantime she had carried on lying. She had already lied to Kobi earlier that day when she hid the policewoman's visit to the bank from him, and she continued to lie that evening when she didn't tell him that the police had been to their home. And that night she lied to Gila, just as she had lied to the two police officers who had shown her the picture of Kobi in uniform. She had been such a terrible liar since they had been girls, and all of Gila's efforts to teach her how to do it without blushing or bursting into tears had failed, but this time she didn't fall apart and, despite the lies, she felt for the first time in a long while that she was doing what she needed to do. As if the lies were necessary in order finally to speak the truth.

She found it easiest to lie to the detective who had accompanied Vahaba to their apartment. He didn't even look at her while she was speaking and didn't seem to be listening to her answers, but instead stared at the photo Kobi had taken during a hunting trip he had organized with his father, as if he could see something in it that others didn't see. Mali thought that the detective's face was familiar – maybe he had gone to school with her or served with her in the army – but she was unable to recall where they might have met.

He was the one who spoke at the beginning of the conversation. He again asked when the last time she had been questioned was and if anyone had tried to contact her since, but indifferently, as if he wasn't interested in her responses, and Mali managed to answer without her voice shaking. She attributed his indifference to the fact that they already knew all about Kobi, and she didn't understand why they didn't ask her directly: *Is your husband the man who dressed up as an officer?* What would she have said if they had?

Afterwards, the detective was silent and looked like he'd lost interest in her, and the one who addressed her was mainly Esty Vahaba. Even though she wasn't high-ranking like the detective, there was something calming and trustworthy about her, and Mali felt an inexplicable intimacy with her, which grew in the weeks that followed. And something Vahaba said at the very end of their conversation played an important part in the decision Mali made: *You do have a way to help us to prevent him from reaching other women*, she had said, and this thought remained with Mali.

That evening she felt that she was doing it mainly for Kobi's sake. To save him. And also for their sake, for the sake of Daniella and Noy and the baby, whom she felt in her belly during the conversation with the police, as if it could hear and was frightened like her, or felt what she was going through and was trying to calm her from inside. But the thought of the women Kobi had sat across from and forced to relive their ordeal also pursued her in the coming hours. She remembered the woman she had seen in her imagination lying injured in the street, and then recalled the night when Kobi had come back to their flat wearing the uniform.

Mali had asked him then, 'Why are you wearing those clothes?' and Kobi had sat down on their bed with his back to her and hidden his head in his hands. Eventually, he had said, 'I can't take it any more,' and she had asked, 'But where were you?' And he told her.

Neither of them slept at all that night.

She had told him everything he wanted to know, just so that he would stop and not do it again to any more women. His mobile phone sat on the dining-room table, and Kobi spread out the stack of papers next to him and she sat down across from him and refused to stop, even when he suggested that she give up because she was sobbing. Daniella woke up once during that night and came to them in the kitchen, because of Mali's crying, and Mali took her back to bed, stayed next to her until she fell asleep and continued to cry without a sound. Kobi promised her then that, if she told him everything, he would never do it again.

He returned home a few minutes after the police had left, and since he didn't ask about them she thought she had been lucky, and it didn't occur to her that perhaps he had seen the squad car parked in front of the building and waited for the police to leave. She had forgotten to clear away the mugs of coffee that she made from on the table in the living room, but Mali thought that she managed to get rid of them without him noticing. His face was damp and his stubble scratched when he kissed her on the cheek. And when he discovered that the girls hadn't eaten dinner, he offered to cook something for the three of them after his shower. He placed the bag of sweat-drenched workout clothes on the floor in the corner of the bedroom, and it remained there like that, soaking in the smell of his sweat, until she opened it three days later. Mali took advantage of his being in the shower to get dressed, and when he came out she was by the door and said that she'd try not to get back too late. Kobi looked surprised and asked where she was going, and she answered him while looking for her keys in her handbag so that their gazes wouldn't meet. She avoided looking at him, simply because she was scared he'd see. Daniella and Noy were waiting in the kitchen for their dinner and Mali kissed them before leaving, and suddenly she thought they might tell him that the police had been there. But she couldn't say anything with him there. When she looked in the mirror in the lift, she thought she should go to the police that very evening. The face she saw in the mirror was again her face, as if it had been brought back from a faraway time, and she looked at it until she felt in the soles of her feet the thud of the lift stopping. And while she was on her way she decided that, rather than tell Gila everything, she'd tell her about the hit-and-run, as if it had truly happened.

Gila had no hesitation. Mali had know that this was how it would be, and perhaps that was why she had decided to ask her for advice.

In her text, Mali wrote only: *I have to meet you this evening. Even if you're not free,* and when she sat down across from her in the café Gila immediately asked her, 'What's happened? You scared me like crazy,' and Mali said that a few days earlier Kobi had hit a pedestrian with his car and fled and had then asked her to help him hide the accident from the police, but today two cops had come to their place, suspecting Kobi. When Gila spoke, Mali was aware of the gulf separating them, and how the events of the past few years had increased it. Gila was full of life that evening, even more so than usual, and perhaps that was partly Schadenfreude. Even in appearance they no longer resembled each other. Gila ordered another cappuccino and afterwards asked Mali to step out to smoke a cigarette, and said in a loud voice, even though there were people in the street, 'You have to tell them. I don't see any question about it. If you want, I'll do it. Do you understand that if you keep cooperating with him they could accuse you of obstruction of justice? And what would you do with the girls then? Ask Mum to take care of them?'

Mali had been oblivious of this until then, and the prospect of Daniella and Noy in her parents' house frightened her. Suddenly, she again saw herself alone in the delivery room; the baby was almost out, and she was shrieking, but no one else was there, and she understood that, even if she wasn't accused of anything, she would be alone, at least for a few months, for the pregnancy and after the birth, and this was the only time that day when she couldn't choke back the anger that rose up in her. She didn't answer when Gila asked, 'You told him that he has to confess and he said that he wasn't ready?' or when she said, 'I don't understand you, Mali. How much do you think you have to suffer because of him? Do you want Dad to say something to him? Or should I speak to him?'

A sharp pain shot through her abdomen, as if someone was repeatedly stabbing her there. She tried to erase the picture of the birth by replacing it with the other vision that had appeared to her that morning, in which she was driving a car and the girls sat in the back with the baby and the seat next to her was empty. 'Do you know what happened to the woman he hit?' Gila asked, and it took Mali a minute to understand who she meant.

'Was she killed? Was she seriously injured?'

'Of course not,' Mali said, panic-stricken. Then she lowered her voice and added, 'I don't know what happened to her. I searched but didn't find out anything.'

'So make him go to the police, and tell him that, if he doesn't, you'll go instead. And explain to him that if he turns himself in, that'll help him afterwards. Don't the two of you get that?'

But Mali didn't go to the station that night.

It was late, and she didn't want Kobi to get suspicious.

And despite this she hung around in the car under their building, because she was hoping that Kobi would be asleep when she got back, until a neighbour passed by and saw her. Was this what she thought that night? That if she presented herself to the police and explained to Esty Vahaba what had happened, then they would understand and be lenient? Kobi would never willingly turn himself in. For a few weeks, or even for a few months if they were unlucky and the punishment was severe, she would return home of an evening and Kobi wouldn't be there. She would always enter a dark flat and grope for the switch to turn on the light. She would lock the door and would need to get used to sleeping alone at night, despite the heavy hand. The bed she would get into would be empty, and in it she wouldn't find that familiar body – one that had hardened but still held the memory of the softness Kobi had had when they met.

He wasn't asleep when Mali opened the door.

All the lights in the flat were on, and she heard Kobi get up from the bed. His eyes were soft when he said to her, 'You're back late,' and she tried to smile when she answered, 'That's how it always is with Gila, you know.' All this was so hard, harder even than speaking the truth and recognizing it, but what she had started was already impossible to stop. Kobi asked, 'Do you want me to warm you up something?' and Mali said that she had eaten. And when he tried to hug her she said that she had a headache, and he asked her, 'Is everything OK? Did something happen at work?' And Mali shook her head. The flat was silent, Daniella and Noy were sleeping, and this was another opportunity, almost the last, to tell him about the baby and the police and to beg him to turn himself in. They didn't speak much in bed, other than about Harry. She remembered that Kobi had said that tomorrow everyone would need to say goodbye to him because there was no point in waiting any longer.

She forced her eyes shut and felt Kobi continuing to look at her in the weak light given off by the reading lamp. And despite her efforts, like every time she squeezed her eyes closed, she felt the hand coming from out of the darkness and trying to crush her throat, and for a moment she had trouble breathing, but this time she succeeded in fighting against it. Was this what it would be like every night until Kobi was released and came back? He placed a hand on her hair and caressed her, and she said, 'Not now,' and even though she was lying with her back to him she could feel his eyes still on her.

The next day, while the three of them ate breakfast in the kitchen, Daniella asked, 'Mummy, why did they come here yesterday? The people from the police?' But Kobi was still sleeping and didn't hear.

Noy asked, 'What people?' and Daniella said, 'The man and the woman who talked with Mum yesterday,' and Mali didn't even remember what explanation she gave them and how they switched to talking about the costume that she was going to buy Noy for Purim.

That afternoon Mali went from the bank to the police station. She turned off her mobile so that Kobi wouldn't be able to call while she was there. In the morning she had told him that her mother would collect the girls from nursery and school, and Kobi had said, 'Why your mum? I can get them myself.' She walked quickly down Feichman

Street, as if she had another destination, and passed the police station without looking at it. Three officers sat on the stairs leading to the station, smoking.

She still didn't know what exactly she'd say, even though, throughout the day, between meetings and even during them, she had been rehearsing the sentences she woke up with that morning. *I came so that you'd help my husband. He's the man who dressed up as an officer, but he didn't mean to hurt anyone.* She planned to ask to speak to Esty Vahaba because she felt that she'd understand. *It's my fault he did this and he didn't mean any harm. And he needs help. We have two small girls, and we'll soon have a baby.*

She turned right and began walking away from the station, but in the distance there was nothing to calm her and the buses that drove by shook the street. Maybe the reason she wasn't at peace with what she wanted to say was because it wasn't really her fault. Also the picture of her giving birth alone kept on hurting, she and the baby crying in the room without anyone to hear, and the thoughts about the darkness that would greet her each time she opened the door.

This was the last evening.

Mali remembered that darkness fell after six and that she carried on walking further and further away from the station. She walked slowly, and only when someone walked too close to her did she increase her pace. But she wasn't afraid, and when she reached the park near the old public library and heard the voices of high-school students nearby, she sat down on a bench. The lamps in the park weren't on, and the only light came from the street.

One of the girls came up to her and asked if Mali had a

cigarette for her, and only then did Mali realize that in this very park, years ago, she had kissed Kobi for the first time. She had stolen a cigarette from Gila for him and was scared to smoke it, even though she wanted to try so badly, but after he had smoked it she surprised herself by leaning towards him and kissing him to know how it tasted, and because Kobi wouldn't have made the first move. She left the park and returned to the car and drove to the shopping centre to buy Noy a *Frozen* costume, as if the lives of the four of them would continue as usual, and when she returned home she again had to lie to Kobi when he asked why her phone had been off. The girls were already asleep, and that was good, because she didn't have to speak to them. Kobi told her that in the afternoon they had all said goodbye to Harry in the garden. He had carried him in his arms in the lift, and they had taken a last walk in the apartment building's garden, and afterwards let him eat salami, and he took a picture of Noy alone with him on the roof because Daniella had refused. They didn't cry, because Kobi had explained to them that he was taking Harry to a hospital for an operation, but he said that Harry was old and might not return.

Lying in order to finally tell the truth. And to save him.

Kobi didn't touch her at all that evening. Even though they passed right by one another, it was as if they were in different, separate spaces, each one preparing themselves for what was soon to come. She got into bed alone as she would need to get used to, and in the silence that was in the flat she heard him from the living room, speaking to his father.

He said in English, 'Dad? It's me, Jacob,' and afterwards

she heard him say, 'No, I'm not coming. I just wanted to assure you everything's OK. You don't have anything to worry about. I'm sorry about the message I left you. Everything worked out, so don't worry about me, OK? And how are you, Dad? You feeling OK?'

Something in his English was so natural, and she could recall the tobacco that was on his lips back then, as if the English brought back something of its taste, and after the taste came the memory of the public park and of the morning in January 1991 when he had waited for her and her father.

'Kobi? It's Mali from class. The war started.'

His sleepy voice when he said to her, with the accent he had then, *'In the middle of the night?'*

Suddenly, she wasn't sure she'd be able to go to the police station the following morning, but she did go. Kobi was in their bed when she awoke, a bit before six, and he didn't notice her getting up. She opened the blinds in the living room and saw that rain was falling and so put the girls' jackets on the sofa in the living room so they wouldn't forget them, next to their Purim costumes. When Daniella again said she wouldn't dress up, Mali didn't insist. Noy asked if they'd go to the Purim party at school and Mali said yes, because she really hoped then that it wouldn't take more than two or three hours.

13

For the first few minutes Avraham didn't mention the picture he'd seen in the bedroom, despite his excitement. He got into the squad car parked on the street and they drove off in silence. The coming hours and what he had to do in them rolled around in his thoughts, and he forgot that he wasn't alone. Only when Esty Vahaba said to him, 'So what do you say?' he remembered that she was there and answered her without taking his eyes off the road: 'It's her husband.'

Vahaba looked at him. 'Whose husband?'

'Mazal Bengtson's husband. That's the policeman.'

When they stopped at the lights he saw the surprise on Vahaba's face and told her about the photograph hanging over the bed. He had paused, taking it in for a moment, and then regained his composure and walked softly back to the small bathroom and flushed and turned off the light before closing the door behind him. Mazal Bengtson and Vahaba had been waiting for him in the living room. And the girl who had stood by the door to her room throughout the questioning wasn't there any more. He had wanted to stay and continue the investigation, but had preferred not to arouse suspicion; he needed to put his thoughts in order before deciding how to proceed. He had said to Mazal Bengtson, 'Thank you very much for your help,' and her gaze had avoided his when she answered, 'It was nothing. Sorry I couldn't be of more help.' On the letterbox for Flat 13 there was no name, but Avraham had taken a letter from the national insurance out of it and on the envelope had seen his name for the first time: *Yaakov Bengtson*.

The man he was looking for.

The man who had set up an appointment with Leah Yeger and knocked on the door to her flat, wearing a uniform. Who had strangled her and left her on the rug in the living room, and was then seen going downstairs, and had disappeared.

He wasn't a cop.

That night, after the emergency team meeting, Avraham couldn't stop thinking about Bengtson, even though at that time he knew very little about him. Marianka was sleeping, and Avraham walked silently through the flat and turned on a light in the kitchen. On the table was a small basket of fruit, and the fridge was full of food, which they had bought and cooked for Anika and Bojan's visit, but he defrosted a frozen roll in the microwave, as in the days when the fridge was empty. He prepared a cheese sandwich and made black coffee, despite the late hour, and sat on the porch to eat with Mazal Bengtson's assault file. He again read about how she had been attacked in Eilat by a man who was never caught.

It had happened shortly after one a.m.

In a room on the seventh floor of the Royal Club hotel in Eilat.

What had amazed Avraham during the team meeting that he arranged on returning to the station with Vahaba was that no one other than him raised the question of the motive, whereas that was the only thing he could think about. Before then, when he had assumed that the assailant was a policeman or a man who had been fired from the ranks of the police, he thought that the motive could have been frustration or revenge. But Bengtson wasn't a policeman. And why had his wife lied? Avraham had no doubt that there was a connection between her unsolved rape and the crimes committed by her husband.

Absent-mindedly, he again found himself conversing with Bengtson, as if they were sitting across from one another in the interview room.

Is this what you did? You searched for whoever attacked your wife? Did you believe you could catch him alone? Or perhaps you were trying to prove something to the police, who were unsuccessful in catching the rapist? He didn't think much about Mazal Bengtson that night, and in retrospect he should have been thinking about both of them, or about the connection between them, a connection that he was far from understanding even when everything was over.

Ma'alul was on the bus on his way home when Avraham and Esty Vahaba returned to Feichman Street, and Avraham asked him to get off at the next stop, take a taxi and return to the police station. Saban was called away from talks on another case. And Avraham informed Marianka that he'd be late because of developments in the murder case and heard the disappointment in her voice when she asked, 'So when will you get back?'

He didn't know. And he didn't ask Lital Levy to summon Sharpstein to the team meeting, but no one commented on his absence. When everyone had taken a seat around the table, Avraham's thoughts went back to his visit to Ilana Lis that morning. When he left her flat he had been debating whether or not to go home and leave control of the investigation to Saban and Sharpstein, but he now sat at the head of the table, his powers returned, and waited for silence to fall over the room. Saban as usual set his mobile on the table and was just starting to tap at it when Avraham said, 'That's it, we've located the policeman,' and then paused to note Ma'alul's response and facial expression. In the centre of the table was a bowl of clementines left over from a previous meeting, and Ma'alul was reaching out his hand to take one when Avraham began speaking. Saban paused and waited for him to continue.

'Beyond that, I think we've also figured out his connection to women who were rape victims,' Avraham said. 'We're talking about a man whose wife was assaulted a few years ago in Eilat. Her name is Mazal Bengtson, a resident of Holon, and her attacker was never caught. Her husband, Yaakov Bengtson, is the man we're looking for. And he isn't a cop.'

Avraham said the last sentence mainly for Saban. The eyes of the district commander lit up when he asked him, 'How do you know?' And Avraham said, 'We were there just now. The credit goes to Esty, who spoke to the wife this morning as part of the questioning she was conducting of rape victims and felt that she was hiding information. She suggested that I join her for another round of questioning at their home, and I saw his picture there. Afterwards, we made an inquiry with HR. We don't, and have never had, a policeman by the name of Yaakov Bengtson.'

Ma'alul peeled the clementine and placed two segments in front of Lital Levy, who was sitting next to him. When the cleaning woman entered without knocking and asked if it was possible to clean the room, Avraham signalled that now wasn't convenient. All this wasn't as celebratory as one might think the meeting in which the solution to his first murder case was presented would be, but this didn't bother him. When Saban asked, 'And you're absolutely certain that this is the man from the photograph?' Avraham nodded.

In the photograph in the bedroom Bengtson wasn't dressed, but it was impossible to mistake his face – especially the eyes. Both photographs were black and white and in each of them Yaakov Bengtson was shot in profile and his pale eyes were identifiable. Avraham was sorry that he hadn't photographed the picture with his phone in order to show them, but he hadn't thought about this when he was there. Saban put his phone into his trouser pocket and asked, 'But you showed her the picture, no?' and Vahaba answered yes for him.

'And what – she didn't identify him?'

'She said she didn't know him,' Vahaba answered. 'But understand that she was the one who requested that I show her the photograph we found on the security tape when I questioned her this morning. And when I showed it to her, it seemed to me that she knew something. That's what made me suspicious.'

'So do we assume that his wife knows and that she is cooperating with him? Or protecting him?' Ma'alul asked, and Avraham didn't answer, because this was one of the things he still didn't know. This question continued to bother him that night too, on the porch, during the phantom conversation he conducted with Yaakov Bengtson, and even then he didn't have an answer to it.

Did you tell your wife that you were continuing to track down the man who raped her? That you dressed up as an officer and questioned women, and that you killed one of them because she realized that you're not a cop?

'I have no idea. I assume that she identified him and lied. This at least has to be our working hypothesis,' Avraham said, and when Ma'alul asked, 'Just a moment, Avi. Did you also tell her that he's suspected of murder?' Avraham looked at Vahaba, because he didn't know what she had told Bengtson in the morning. Vahaba said, 'What do you think? Of course I didn't tell her.' And Avraham exhaled in relief.

Ma'alul and Saban thought that Bengtson should be called in for questioning that night, but Avraham wanted to know more about him before they met. The questions that he wanted to ask were only just beginning to take shape, and the right questions were the key to the right answers.

Saban said, 'Nice work, Avi. And you too, Esty. And you see that it was possible to find him without publishing the photo in the papers and embarrassing every police officer in the land? In any case, I think we should question him quickly but at the same time not abandon the angle of the son. Is that acceptable to you? What do you intend to do now, Avi? Do you want to bring him in?'

Avraham shook his head.

His working hypothesis was that Bengtson knew that

the police were on his trail. Vahaba had presented the security photograph to his wife that morning and revealed many details of the investigation, even if she had said nothing about the murder. If Mazal Bengtson shared that information with her husband, he'd know that they were on to him and would definitely be ready for this when he was called in for questioning. Therefore, it would be better for now to put him, in fact the two of them, under surveillance, and wait.

'Wait for what?' Saban asked, and Avraham said immediately, 'Wait until we've gathered firmer information and evidence, and until we know more about who he is and why he did what he did.'

This was the plan of action that he had formulated since seeing the photograph. Later he would think that perhaps he had made a mistake, but in any case, it was impossible to summon Yaakov Bengtson in for questioning without being prepared. Avraham asked Ma'alul to compile a profile of him using all the information he could manage to collect. He wanted to clarify whether or not Bengtson had a prior record and if his DNA and fingerprints were in the criminal forensics database and, if so, to have them compared to the samples taken from the murder scene. He wanted to know where Bengtson worked and what car he had, and if it had been caught on camera in the area on the day the murder took place. He even asked Ma'alul to find out if Bengtson had a Facebook account and what kinds of thing he posted there. Ma'alul wrote this down in his notebook and said to him, 'No problem, Avi. You'll get it by noon tomorrow.' Esty Vahaba was asked to gather additional information on Mazal Bengtson.

When Saban sighed and asked him, 'Do you need anything from me?' Avraham hesitated for a moment before answering, 'Yes. Erez Yeger, the son,' and Saban looked at him in amazement. 'You want to release him? You're sure that's not premature? You made progress today, but you still don't know if this Bengtson, or whatever he's called, was involved in the murder. Only that apparently, he dresses up like a cop, the son of a bitch.'

That wasn't correct, and that wasn't what Avraham wanted. He did know that Bengtson was involved in the murder, even if he still didn't know everything. He knew that Bengtson was the man who had been seen in Leah Yeger's building, and he knew that he was the man who had set up a meeting with her. 'No, I want the opposite,' he said to Saban. 'I want to detain Yeger for another forty-eight hours and to make another announcement to the newspapers about prolonging his detention and the additional progress we're making in our investigation.'

His objective was to confuse Bengtson.

A week had passed since the murder, and Yaakov Bengtson had had time to cover up the evidence, certainly if he knew that the police were on his trail. And to Avraham it seemed that Bengtson knew just what he was doing. He had removed from the scene everything he thought would incriminate him, and the chance that they'd succeed in finding the uniform that he had worn that day or the mobile on which he had recorded the conversations with the women was tiny. Avraham had to try to give him the impression that the investigation was advancing in a different direction, despite the visit to his home, and in the meantime understand who he was. Only then would there be a chance that Bengtson would unwittingly lead them to the evidence, for instance the uniform he was wearing during the murder or where he had disposed of Leah Yeger's handbag and calendar, or that he would unintentionally say something to someone. He had to lull him into a false sense of security, so that he would sleep at night, while they were awake, ready for any move he'd make.

Saban listened to his plan, and when he saw that Ma'alul was nodding as well he approved it.

And perhaps if Avraham had summoned Bengtson for questioning straightaway he would have received answers to the questions he continued to ask him without a sound, on the porch, in the dark.

Do you also wait for the morning to come in order to act?

At around two he went to bed, lying down next to Marianka's thin body, and she moved away from him in her sleep. All this was so strange: he was in the flat where he had resided for many years, in the bed on which he had placed his heavy body at the end of the working day for more than ten years, and nevertheless the feeling was different. He stared into the darkness and listened to the humming of the fridge in the kitchen, but he couldn't drop off. Marianka turned to him and, without opening her eyes, said something he couldn't hear, in a language he didn't understand. A little later he poured himself a cold glass of water and returned to the porch because it was obvious he wasn't going to fall asleep.

Ma'alul emailed him the report the next day at noon.

And from the first line it was clear that the pieces of the

puzzle were falling into place. *Yaakov (Jacob) Bengtson was born in Australia in 1976*, Ma'alul wrote, and this explained the accent that Diana Goldin had mentioned. *He arrived in Israel in 1990, received citizenship because his mother had Israeli citizenship, was drafted into the army in 1995, served in the Nachal Infantry Brigade and was discharged in 1998 with the rank of first sergeant.* He had no criminal record. His first visit to a police station was when he made a complaint against an employer who had allegedly harassed him, but the case was dropped for lack of public interest. The second and last was when he gave a statement to the Eilat police about the rape of his wife.

Avraham asked Lital Levy not to put through any calls other than those from Ma'alul and Vahaba. He read the report in his room, twice, while eating lunch. He didn't hear from Saban throughout that day, and the conversation with Ilana had been forgotten, because everything had happened so quickly since then, and exactly as he had hoped. In the margin of the report that he had printed out Avraham began noting down questions in advance of Bengtson's interrogation, some of them ones that he had thought of the night before and some that came to mind while he was reading it. And the more he read about Bengtson, the more Avraham felt how much he longed to sit across from him in the interview room. Since the morning there had been a policeman and a volunteer from the district detective staff stationed in front of 8 Uri Zvi Greenberg Street, but Yaakov Bengtson hadn't left the building. His wife, by contrast, had dropped off her daughters and continued in her car, a Suzuki Alto, to a branch of the Israel Discount Bank on Shenkar Street.

When Ma'alul called Avraham and asked, 'So, did you read it?' he asked him, 'Tell me, do you have any idea if he has a valid Australian passport?' and Ma'alul promised to find out. What especially caught Avraham's attention was the fact that Bengtson had tried a few times to get work in the security services and had been rejected, generally because he hadn't passed the psychological evaluations. *In 1999,* Ma'alul had written, *Bengtson passed an examination with the Shin Bet national security agency as well as the evaluations, and was accepted to an agents training course with the prime minister's office, but he was released a few weeks after the start of the course, because he was unsuitable. In 2002 he tried to get accepted for police work, but was rejected on the basis of the first round of psychological evaluations.*

He wasn't a policeman but *wanted to be.*

When Avraham read that Bengtson's last place of work had been a security company that guarded building sites near the Green Line, and that he had been fired from this job following a conflict with his supervisors, he wrote a question in the margin of the report: *He's not working somewhere else now?*

Ma'alul didn't have a definite answer for this when they spoke in the afternoon.

'And do we know why he didn't pass the psychological evaluations?'

'Unsuitability. I asked them to send the reports to me, but it's not yet known whether they keep them and, even if they do, they'll have to find them in the archive. But listen, Avi, I spoke to two of his former employers and both of them tell me that he's very borderline. Or unstable. One of them is the man Bengtson filed a complaint against. He has a tendency towards confrontations and outbursts, and it was impossible to know when he would come to work and in what mood. You don't want us to bring him in yet?'

He thought that it wasn't yet time. They first needed evidence that would tie Bengtson directly to the murder, in addition to the testimony of the neighbour who had seen him on the stairs, and it seemed to Avraham then that they had time to get it. Ma'alul said, 'Are you sure, Avi? So he doesn't do a runner to Australia.' But there was no chance of that, because he was under surveillance.

'What about his car?' Avraham asked. 'Have you started looking for photos of the vehicle in the area of the murder scene?'

'Not yet. I'll start now.'

'And Facebook?'

'He has quite an active page, but in recent days he hasn't posted anything. Which could also say something, no? Other than that, there's nothing special there. Pictures of his daughters and clips of Thai boxing.'

'Nothing against the police?'

After the conversation with Vahaba, who called him a little before three, Avraham felt that they were even closer to him.

Mazal Bengtson had worked at the Israel Discount Bank for sixteen years and was considered an exceptional employee. Vahaba couldn't go to the branch where she worked and take statements from her co-workers, for fear of causing suspicion, but she spoke discreetly with Mazal Bengtson's immediate supervisor and he told her that she had been absent from work one day last week, that she hadn't requested extended time off and that, to the best of his knowledge, she wasn't planning a trip. Vahaba also phoned the detective from the Eilat police who was responsible for the rape case, and the detective told her something that possibly had a connection with regard to both members of the Bengtson couple and the police. As Avraham read in the file, during the rape investigation they examined the possibility that Bengtson had been assaulted by a man she knew at the party and had invited to her room, even though she refused to admit this. The detective had no evidence that such an invitation had been issued, but a few things gave rise to the suspicion – the fact that Bengtson was apparently drunk on the evening of the assault, the time that passed between her leaving her room and the reporting of the assault, and the clothes that she afterwards claimed she had changed into. Similarly, the investigation had looked into the possibility that it had been the husband, Kobi Bengtson, who assaulted the complainant, and he was asked to prove where he was at the time of the rape. His alibi convinced the detective and the possibility was dismissed. According to their investigation, during the assault Bengtson was with the couple's daughters in their flat in Holon.

Did you think that the police didn't seriously investigate your wife's assault? Is this your problem? Or were you hurt by the insinuation that she invited the rapist to her room?

Avraham didn't put down the pen during the conversation with Vahaba either. And while he listened to her he thought that she was the only person on the staff to whom this investigation was as important as it was to him. Vahaba was the one who, on a Saturday, had found Bengtson's picture in the security footage and the one who felt, as she took a statement from his wife, that the woman knew more than she was letting on. Without her, it was possible that they wouldn't have found Bengtson and would be just as far from the murderer as they had been on the day the murder took place. And, in retrospect, her feelings about Mazal Bengtson had also been correct. Before they hung up Vahaba said to him, 'You don't think it's possible that she's not cooperating with him? That she's concealing the investigation and that it would be worthwhile trying to speak to her?' But Avraham didn't think so. He thought that this wasn't logical, because they knew Mazal Bengtson had lied to them. And, in the afternoon, when Vahaba called again and there was excitement in her voice when she said to Avraham, 'Mazal Bengtson might be on her way to the station,' he didn't believe she'd turn him in. The two of them waited on the phone while Bengtson parked her car not far from the police station and walked in the direction of Feichman Street. But she passed the station without entering, and then continued walking somewhere else.

'She wants to tell us something, Avi. I'm sure of it. She's just scared of him. Maybe she even knows that he's a murderer. Are you sure that you don't want me to bring her in now? I'm telling you, she'll talk to me.'

He asked to think about it before deciding, but just then Ma'alul entered his office, without knocking, his eyes sparkling and a smile across his face. Avraham asked him, 'What's happened?' and Ma'alul said, 'We have him, Avi. We're on to him.' And of all the things he could have said, this was the one thing Avraham hadn't thought of.

'Bengtson got a ticket,' Ma'alul said, sitting down across from him, and Avraham asked, 'What do you mean?'

'A parking ticket, Avi. A stupid parking ticket. On the day of the murder. About two hours afterwards. Guess where.'

He could have guessed, but asked all the same, and Ma'alul placed a sheet of paper on his desk and said to him, 'On Krauze. Do you get it? From now on, every time we say, "With God's help," we will also add, "and with the help of the city's traffic wardens."'

The arrest warrant and the search warrant of the Bengtson family's apartment were issued that evening, a little after nine o'clock. Avraham was at home and told Marianka how everything was turning out as they'd hoped, and what their plan was for the next day. A team of detectives was supposed to arrive at the flat in the morning, while Mazal Bengtson was at work and the couple's daughters were at school and nursery, conduct a preliminary search there, confiscate electronic equipment and bring Bengtson to the station. The investigation file, and in it the list of questions Avraham had prepared, were already there, in his office.

The first question was very direct: *Can you tell me what happened when you arrived last Monday at Leah Yeger's flat?*

'Do you think he'll confess?' Marianka asked, and Avraham said, 'I don't know. I still don't have any idea who this man is.' On the table in the interview room he planned to spread around pictures of Leah Yeger's body from the murder scene, and next to them he planned to place the umbrella that Bengtson had left at Diana Goldin's flat as well as the pictures of him wearing police uniform from the security footage. In the middle would be the picture of Leah Yeger that had been taken when she was still alive. The camera in the interview room would start working, and Avraham would wait silently, allowing Bengtson to look at the pictures, the umbrella, to digest his situation, to understand that he was trapped. Only afterwards would he begin asking him questions, without exposing the information they had in their possession about the parking ticket and the neighbour who saw him in the building.

And in the morning, he and Marianka even managed to eat breakfast together. Marianka asked him, 'Are you ready?' And Avraham nodded while sipping his coffee. He even said that perhaps they'd be able to go out to eat that evening, if he got home early. Through the small window in the kitchen rain clouds could be seen, but that wasn't the only reason that he wore the heavy blue coat which he'd left at the murder scene. This was the last day of his first murder investigation, which had begun a week and two days earlier, and he wore the same coat as on the day it opened. He wanted to sit across from Bengtson and look at him up close as he examined the pictures spread across the table, but he also thought about the next case, which perhaps wouldn't be a murder case and about the fact that he'd take another day off and spend it with Marianka. Because of the rain he had planned to go to the station on foot, but at seven thirty his phone rang.

Lital Levy sounded upset. 'Avi, are you on your way? Because it looks like we need to change our plan.'

He asked, 'What happened?' and looked at Marianka, who set down her cup of coffee.

'His wife set off alone, without the girls. This means that he'll, presumably, take them to school and it's not clear whether or not he'll return to the flat after that. Apart from which, his wife appears to be on her way to us.'

He quickly drove to the station, and even though he arrived within five minutes, Mazal Bengtson was there before him. Lital called him again as he pulled into the car park and said, 'She's already inside. Where are you? She told Ezra that she wants to speak with Vahaba, and she's waiting for her at reception. What do you want me to tell her?'

He didn't know then why Mazal Bengtson had decided to come to the station, or whether she was protecting her husband or was there without him knowing. Did Avraham already sense that something in the connection between the two of them would disrupt his plans? He thought he would question Mazal Bengtson in his office, but then changed his mind, because of the cameras. And he didn't know exactly what he'd ask her because he'd been preparing to question her husband, not her.

When Avraham entered the building he saw her standing at the reception desk.

He took a deep breath before he approached and pretended to notice her as if by accident. And then he asked, 'Are you looking for me?'

14

In the days that followed, all the rage that was inside Mali was directed at him, not at Kobi. She saw Avraham in a dream slowly walking out of a room that resembled the room at the hotel in Eilat, and then heard an explosive sound that woke her in a fright from her sleep. Her fist was clenched and damp, because she was the one who had held the gun and shot the policeman in his back. The time was 3.21 a.m. The girls were in their beds, and her father, who insisted on sleeping over with them, was curled up on the couch in the living room. By then Mali knew his name, but at the start of that morning, at the police station, she didn't remember what he was called or whether he had introduced himself when he had questioned her two days earlier.

But she remembered his heavy steps on the stairs and the coat he wore, a blue winter parka. When he suggested that she come up to his office, she assumed that she'd wait there for Esty Vahaba. And he actually didn't need her to tell him a thing, because he knew more than her and used her in order to confirm what he had discovered and then entice Kobi into turning himself in. To her it seemed that she was finally taking responsibility for their past and their future, but she didn't understand what, in truth, was happening at the station that day until it was already too late.

★

Other than the rage, what stayed with Mali from that morning were sights that devoured one another and fragmented sentences, and most of all so very many minor details. Had the rain not got stronger, it's possible she would have stopped in front of the stairs leading to the police station and maybe even left, but the rain sent her hurrying inside, and she found herself standing across from the policeman at the entrance, unprepared, even though she had thought of nothing but this for the last two days. At that moment the day still had logical outlines of time and place which she thought she'd be able to control, like a girl who plays with the hand of a clock: the time was eight o'clock, and Mali believed that she'd be no more than a few hours at the police station and would manage to get to the Purim party at the school. She planned to ask Esty Vahaba to invite Kobi in for questioning in the afternoon or tomorrow, and then to be there with him and explain what he would be unable to, or wait outside the room so he wouldn't be there alone.

Her hair was wet, and she wiped water from her forehead. Ahead of her in the line stood a man whose car had been stolen in the night and Mali hoped that dealing with his complaint would take for ever. She looked out through the glass door. Maybe the rain had stopped and she could escape into the street. And outside it was still Holon then, cars and buses stood in a traffic jam which the rain had caused on Feichman Street, and she wasn't yet lost in the labyrinth of massive forests that surrounded her afterwards.

The desk sergeant asked the man to wait until the duty detective became available to take his complaint, and then he asked how he could help her. The business card that Esty Vahaba had given her was in her jacket pocket, and Mali took it out and asked to speak with her, and the desk sergeant said, 'I don't know if she's here. Did you arrange to meet with her today?' And she didn't notice Avraham until she heard his voice. He approached her from behind and asked if she was looking for him, and Mali told him that she was waiting for Esty Vahaba. It seemed to her that he was surprised to see her there, beside the desk, but she didn't suspect a thing.

She did remember that when they sat in Avraham's office his first question was, 'How can I help you, Ms Bengtson?'

Before this he took off his blue coat and hung it on the door and offered her coffee. He waited for her to sit down and then left and closed the door behind him, and Mali placed her bag on the desk as if she had only come for a moment. Of all the details, why did she remember those so well? Instead of remembering what shirt Kobi was wearing that day and how his face had looked sunk into a pillow when she gazed at him that morning. Thick folders were arranged in a high pile on Avraham's desk, and it didn't occur to Mali that in one of them were documents from a murder investigation in which Kobi was the prime suspect. Next to them was a wooden frame, and in it was a picture she couldn't see.

When Avraham returned, with a coffee mug in his hand, he asked Mali to come with him, and they left his office and went into another room, further down the corridor. A small room with a table with a computer on it and two chairs; on one of its walls, above the table, hung a camera.

It took her a while to understand that he wanted to begin questioning her and didn't intend to wait for Vahaba. She knew that she'd be able to insist, because since she had decided to turn Kobi in, the woman she saw in the mirror was herself and not the woman of recent years. Avraham asked for her identity card and filled out the details, first on the computer and afterwards on a paper form, by hand. There was no expression on his face, and this strengthened her sense that he didn't know why she was there. When Avraham finished registering the information he raised his head from the page and for the first time looked at her directly and asked how he could help her. And she said to him, without her voice shaking, 'Esty Vahaba hasn't arrived? Because I'd prefer to speak with her.'

Vahaba was on her way to the station and would join them in a few minutes, he said. And then he asked, 'In the meantime do you want to tell me what it is you need to speak to her about?'

Mali didn't mean to answer him and wasn't afraid, not even when Avraham asked her, 'Did you come to talk to us about the policeman?'

When he got up and left the interview room for the first time, Mali thought he had given up, but after a short time he returned and placed a folder on the table and removed from it the picture of Kobi. 'Do you want to have another look at the picture we showed you and tell me if you recognize this man?' he asked. She didn't look. When he said to her, 'Ms Bengtson, I asked you to look at the picture,' he had already raised his voice. 'Do you or do you not recognize the man in the picture?'

She began to speak because she suddenly saw Kobi.

Exactly as then, in room 723 in the Royal Club Hotel in Eilat. Kobi looked at her over Avraham's shoulder and smiled his smile, which was almost the only thing about him that hadn't changed, and this was what caused her to answer. She said, 'I came because of my husband, Kobi,' and Avraham brought the photograph closer to her and said, 'You're not answering the question, Ms Bengtson. Do you or do you not recognize the man in the picture?'

This was another sign that she missed, like so many others. She didn't say to Avraham that the man in the photograph was Kobi, but his next question was: 'Ms Bengtson, do you confirm that that's your husband?'

There was no longer a man behind Avraham. Kobi had disappeared, leaving her alone.

Avraham gripped the pen in his hand and wrote something and then sighed and asked her, 'Does your husband know that you're here now, Mazal?' and Mali said, without expecting to, 'Please call me Mali, if you can,' and Avraham looked at her for a moment in silence as if he was thinking about it. And then he just said again, 'Ms Bengtson, I'm trying to understand if you're here voluntarily.'

During those hours Avraham often left the interview room, and Mali thought that this was because he wasn't ready for what he discovered, or because he was waiting for Esty Vahaba, as she had demanded. But it was exactly the opposite. Vahaba was outside, waiting for Avraham's approval to join them, and Avraham was leaving Mali in the room alone in order to continue spinning the web in which she was trapped, not realizing that Kobi had entered it as well.

But this allowed her to think.

Without her wanting it, she was again in the room where everything had begun. She heard the sound of the water flowing into the bathtub. The television playing. The only sentence she succeeded in saying then: *I have two little girls*. The interview room at the Holon police station was almost identical in every way to the room in Eilat where she had sat and answered the policewoman's questions about the clothes she changed into and the party that was held at the hotel before the assault. But now she was different. Daniella and Noy were at nursery and school, one without a costume and the other dressed as a princess. And she thought a lot about Kobi. About his appearance in the room and about the fact that he wouldn't be with her in the delivery room. About the months that they would be apart. When she imagined herself driving in the car with the girls and the baby, were they on their way to visit him in the place where he'd be? It was clear to her that Kobi would be angry when he discovered what she had done, but she hoped that he'd come to understand. He would see that he would have been caught regardless and that her confession helped the police to understand him. She planned to tell him about the pregnancy and to ask him to cooperate with the police, so that even if he was punished he'd get out not long after the baby was born and they could simply leave Israel and go to Australia.

The door opened again, and Esty Vahaba stood there. Avraham entered after her with a chair, but from that moment he allowed Vahaba to ask the questions and was barely involved. And Vahaba's voice calmed Mali, at least for a while.

'Hello, Mazal. How are you?' Vahaba asked.

She was terrible – but at the same time better than she had been for years.

'I'm happy that you came, Mazal, you know? I had a feeling that you would, and I think you did the right thing.'

Mali imagined the camera was recording her, and at that moment this gave her strength. When Vahaba asked, 'Do you understand that your husband is suspected of impersonating an officer and of harassing rape victims, as we discussed?' Mali nodded.

'Did you say anything to him about our conversation? And tell me honestly, because it's important.'

'I didn't tell him anything.'

'Does he know you're here now?'

'No. I told you. But I won't hide from him that I was here.'

This was correct, because her fear of Kobi had also disappeared at the moment she made the decision. And in its place were only sadness and longing.

'So why are you here now? Why didn't you tell us about him when we were with you the day before yesterday?'

'Because I was afraid that he'd come home. And I also wasn't sure that he did it. And I've come to explain to you what happened.'

'What do you mean, you weren't sure that he did it?'

'I wasn't sure that it was him.'

'And how do you know now?'

Avraham didn't stop looking at her, but his gaze didn't frighten her. It was as if she had finally succeeded in getting up from the bed in room 723 without waiting, shutting off the television that was on and turning off the tap.

'Do you mean that you knew he was impersonating an officer even before we showed you the picture?'

'I knew, yes. But not that he was doing it now.'

'I don't understand what you're telling me, Mazal. Explain to me, please, and make it simple and straightforward.'

'I knew that Kobi did it once,' she said, and her voice was clear and didn't shake.

Vahaba asked, 'When was this once?'

'A few weeks after what happened to me in Eilat. More than two years ago. He did it only one time.'

'And how did you know about this, Mazal? Did he tell you himself?'

Mali didn't answer straightaway, because the questions were getting closer and closer to what was hard for her to say, even though she was no longer afraid.

'Mazal, you said that you came so that we would understand him,' Vahaba continued, 'and I'm trying to understand the two of you. Look me in the eyes, please. I know what happened to you in Eilat. And also that your assailant wasn't caught, is that correct? Did your husband try to catch the rapist?'

Mali shook her head, because that wasn't the reason. Kobi never mentioned the man who attacked her.

'So what did he want, Mazal? Was he trying to prove something to those investigating your rape? To get back at the police?'

These were the things that were still hard for Mali to speak about, the things that had made her unsure if she'd even be able to enter the station and turn him in. She asked Vahaba, 'To get back at them for what?'

Suddenly, Avraham interrupted the conversation and said, 'So what the hell was he trying to do? Why would someone dress up as a police officer and harass women who went through something like that?'And then he removed another photograph, of a young woman, from the folder. 'Do you know this woman?' he asked, and it seemed to Mali that her face looked familiar. 'Let me tell you who she is. Her name is Diana. She was raped in 2012. Like you, no? Do you want to know what your husband did? He contacted her and introduced himself as a police officer and set up a meeting with her. In her flat. And forced her to describe the rape she experienced in great detail, and also recorded her. And then he assaulted her. Do you understand this, Ms Bengtson? Can you imagine what she went through? What your husband did to this woman?'

What shook her and brought the fear back to her were the things that Avraham said about the assault. She looked at Esty Vahaba in order to understand if Avraham was lying before she said to the two of them, 'He wouldn't have hurt her. You don't know Kobi.'

'How do you know? Did he tell you everything he did, Ms Bengtson? I'm telling you he did assault her. Cruelly, even. Did he forget to tell you that? Do you want to see pictures of what he did to her? Or perhaps he did tell you and you're collaborating with him?'

Because of the young woman's face in the photo, she recalled the hit-and-run incident that Kobi had made up and the woman she had imagined lying injured in the street. *Had he been trying to hint to her that he had hurt someone? Maybe unintentionally.* She didn't believe this, but nevertheless the fear returned, and she recalled the first night he had put on the uniform. And that was the moment when the story burst out. Mali closed her eyes, and Avraham spoke to her from out of the darkness. 'I'll ask this one last time, Ms Bengtson. Before I accuse you of being an accomplice and obstructing justice. Tell me, please, how you knew what your husband was doing and what exactly he told you.' But she still didn't answer him. When he came right up to her she opened her eyes, because he was too close as he said, 'Why aren't you talking to me, Ms Bengtson?' And Mali whispered, 'Because he did the same thing to me.'

Silence descended on the room, and Vahaba asked, 'What do you mean, he did the same thing to you?' And Mali again said, 'He did the same thing to me,' before she again lost control of herself.

The hours that came after this were even foggier in her memory.

She remembered that Avraham brought a cup of water up close to her and then mumbled something to Vahaba and left, and she remained in the room with the policewoman, unable to stop crying. Afterwards she told Vahaba everything, not about herself but rather about the woman who wasn't her, whose face first appeared in the mirror of the hotel lift, and how only now she had managed to erase her from all the mirrors. She also remembered the phone call in which she had asked Kobi to come to the police station, even though she wanted to forget it, and then running on the stairs of the station. Later in their conversation Vahaba even tried to give her a hint as to what Kobi was truly suspected of, but Mali didn't understand that hint either. Vahaba waited for her to drink and stroked her hair and asked her, 'Do you want to tell me what he did to you?'And when her crying quietened Mali spoke about the woman who wasn't her who was raped in Eilat, and about her husband who arrived at the hospital the next morning and in the months to come didn't leave her for a moment. The woman had two small girls and her husband quit his job and stayed at home with her and took care of their daughters by himself and she wouldn't have got through this period without him. Throughout this time he didn't ask her a thing and only waited patiently for her to recover. And actually it was when it seemed that she was getting stronger, thanks to him, and when she decided to return to work and he stayed home because he hadn't found another job, that their hell began. One evening, after the girls had gone to bed, the husband asked his wife, 'Why can't you tell me what happened there?'And when she asked him, 'Where?' he said to her, 'There, in Eilat.'

'I don't know. Why do you want to talk about it?'

She hadn't known how bad things would get, and had she known, she would have responded differently. 'You told the police everything, no?' the husband asked, and the woman who wasn't her was silent because she didn't know what to say.

When he insisted that he had to know what had happened, she said to him, 'Enough, Kobi, please,' but the husband wouldn't let up. 'Imagine that you're with the police again,' he asked, and she said only, 'I don't want to.'

That was the beginning.

And the end as well.

The camera fixed on the wall filmed her, and Vahaba wrote while she spoke, and it seemed to Mali that when she finished talking everything would be behind her. She'd be able to go, leave the woman she was talking about in the station and not see her again. Vahaba put down the pen and asked, 'And what happened after this, Mali? Did you know that he did the same thing to other women as well?'

'Do you mean back then? I explained to you, he did it only one time,' she said. 'And he told me that same night. He didn't want to do it – do you understand? I know you don't believe me, but you'd have to know Kobi to get it. I had a support group of victims and he found the list and went to a woman whose details were on there. I didn't even ask him who. He told me that night and swore that he wouldn't do it again. I told him everything that had happened to me that night in Eilat so that he'd stop.'

Something in the words she spoke drew Vahaba's attention, and only in retrospect did Mali understand what. She asked, 'Do you still have that list at home?' and Mali said, 'I don't know. I haven't thought about it in a long time.'

'Do you think you could find it?'

'Maybe.'

'Have you seen it recently?'

'No.'

'Maybe Kobi has it?'

Was Vahaba trying to hint to her what Kobi was truly suspected of when she asked her, 'Do you remember if in your group there was a woman by the name of Leah

Yeger?' A knock came at the door and Vahaba left, and when she came back into the room Avraham was with her, and some time after this, maybe an hour or maybe more, came the phone call.

The two of them were treating her differently now, and Avraham spoke to her in a soft voice and Mali truly thought that everything was behind her, because she had told them all she knew, but when she asked him if she could go, Avraham said to her quietly, 'Not yet.'

He asked, 'Do you know where your husband is now?' and she explained that Kobi was supposed to be at the vet's and that afterwards the two of them needed to meet at Noy's school for a Purim party and then take the girls home, and Vahaba asked if she could call someone else and ask them to pick up the girls.

'But why? Do you want to arrest him now? You can't wait until tomorrow or later on?'

There were so many terrible moments that day, but that was the worst. She had thought that she was helping Kobi and she had lied to him so many times that week, and even the last lie was supposed to be for his benefit. To lie in order to tell the truth. In order to save him.

'Will you arrest him at home? Isn't it possible to wait until he isn't at home?' she asked, and the two of them were silent.

'Don't arrest him at home, I beg you. We won't be able to go on living there. We have two small girls. Can't you get him to come to the station?' And Vahaba asked her, 'How? Without telling him he's a suspect?'

And this too she'd never be able to forget, that the idea had been hers.

'I'll tell him to come and meet me here. I'll tell him that there have been developments in the rape investigation and that you asked me to come in.'

They looked at each other, and Avraham left the room, and when he returned he held out her phone to her. Vahaba sat next to her while she called, but Kobi didn't answer, and she tried him again, and again he didn't answer, and Avraham walked away from them and said, 'We'll give it a few minutes and call again,' but the phone rang before she could try. They looked at the phone and she nodded, and Avraham signalled to her to answer.

'Hi, Mali, did you call me?'

She heard children in the background and was sure she could heard barking as well, and therefore she asked him, 'Are you still at the vet's?' and Kobi said, 'No, not any more. I'm on the way home. I couldn't do it in the end.'

She lied to him in order to tell the truth, in order to save the two of them, when she said in a steady voice that she was on the way to the police station on Feichman Street. That they had called the bank and asked her to go there urgently, because there was a development in the rape investigation, without explaining what. 'Can you meet me there? Do you know where it is?'

There was a moment of silence before Kobi asked, 'And what about Noy?' and Mali said, 'I spoke to my mum. She'll go the party instead of us and will take the two of them back to her place.'

And those were the last sentences.

Did he know where she was calling from? Or did it take him time to understand? He asked, 'Are you already there?' and Mali said to him, without her voice shaking,

'No, not yet. I'll be there in two minutes,' and Kobi again was silent before saying to her, 'I'm coming right away.'

Afterwards, she only remembered herself running. Not like at the hotel, where she barely managed to walk down the hallway to the lift.

She was sure that Kobi would arrive in a few minutes, and the police left, taking her phone with them, but a long time passed before they returned. Vahaba set a bottle of water on the table, and when Mali asked her if Kobi had arrived she said, 'Not yet,' and Mali wasn't sure Vahaba hadn't lied. She didn't feel movement in her belly even though she placed her two hands on it after Vahaba left and she tried to feel something inside her, and then remembered Australia, because it was clear to her that, when everything was over, they'd go there. For a moment the two of them were in their twenties again. They walked beside each other among the eucalyptus trees that were so tall that they could both hide from the rain in a cave-like hollow in one of the trunks. They walked and ahead of them were two large dogs, their feet not making a sound when they padded across the forest floor, which was covered in wet brown and yellow leaves. Kobi tried to show her something at the top of one of the trees, a bird perhaps, but Mali couldn't see anything there.

Did all that really happen then? Did she really think about Australia while she was waiting for him or only after she heard the shot?

The interview-room door was open and the corridor was long and empty and she didn't know which way she should run, but when she saw policemen hurrying down a flight of stairs she set off in the same direction and didn't feel her legs moving, even though she hadn't run in so many years. It was easy, as if she hadn't ever stopped running, and she was fast, as if she could still catch the assailant who had left the room. On the second floor many people were running, down the stairs, mainly policemen in uniform, but in the commotion no one noticed her. Vahaba wasn't among them, and nor was Avraham.

Afterwards, her running came to a stop and her memory was cut off all at once. As if life had ended. A sense of time and place was lost to her for a few hours, and from out of the darkness other times and voices appeared. She ran out of the room at the hotel and would never return to it. On the forest ground lay a policeman in uniform. From another, even earlier time, words could be heard in the voice that was once her voice: *Kobi, can you hear? The war started. Do you hear me at all?*

15

Avraham was sure that he heard the shot first, as if it had been fired right next to his ears an instant before it could be heard throughout the station. And even though there were policemen who reached Bengtson before him, because he was waiting for him in his office on the third floor, Avraham was the first to identify the man lying on the floor in the station entrance. Dressed in uniform. David Ezra, the desk sergeant, was trying to staunch the wound in Bengtson's neck with a bloody hand, and people were screaming, 'Policeman shot!' as Avraham pushed his way through them. Had he known it was Bengtson when he heard the shot through the open window? And how did he immediately recognize that it was him on the station floor? The gun lay next to him. Ezra was bent over him, his knees in the expanding puddle of blood. When Avraham leaned over them Ezra looked at him in shock and Avraham said only, 'He's not a cop.' His shoes were in the red pool when he placed his right hand next to Ezra's, and he felt the blood and the pieces of wet flesh between his fingers. The gunshot wound in Bengtson's neck was black and giving off smoke and his head was twisted on the floor in a strange position, almost torn from the body, and Avraham tried to massage his chest and called out loud, or so it seemed to him at least, 'Can anyone do CPR?'

Bengtson's legs struck against the floor again and again. And, like Leah Yeger's eyes, his eyes weren't closed all the way.

The ambulance left for Wolfson Hospital within less than three minutes, and Ma'alul called Avraham from there to tell him that Bengtson was alive when they arrived. And this filled him with hope. On the way to the hospital Ma'alul had searched Bengtson's clothes for a suicide note or a confession, but didn't find anything. At first Avraham didn't understand why, but Ma'alul said to him, 'Trust me that this is the thing we need to find right now. Can you search his car and their flat?' In those moments Avraham found himself unable himself to think of the right thing to do. He went out to the street to digest it all.

Because of the ticket that Bengtson had received, he knew the make of his car and the registration, and it took him a few minutes of searching for the blue Toyota in the streets around the station until he found it parked on Gol-omob Street. One of the rear windows was slightly open, like Bengtson's pale eyes before he was taken away, and Avraham threaded his hand inside and opened the back door. When he sat down in the driver's seat and looked out through the windscreen, he suddenly thought that this was the closest that he'd get to Bengtson, and the thought made him tremble. It couldn't end like that. He asked himself if Bengtson had known when he left his car and walked to the station that he wouldn't be returning and, if so, why had he bothered parking and locking the doors?

The rain grew stronger and Avraham returned to the station dripping wet. Only when he encountered Ezra standing outside smoking, his shirt spotted with blood, did he see that his own trousers and the blue sweater he was wearing were also covered in Bengtson's blood, which had been absorbed by the fabric, been soaked in the rain and had now turned brown. Someone brought Ezra tea in a polystyrene cup, and Avraham saw through the glass door that the forensics team was working around the large puddle of blood. The gun was still lying on the floor in the place where Bengtson had let it drop from his hand.

'So he's not a cop?' Ezra asked without looking at him, and Avraham shook his head.

'No.'

'Why was he wearing a uniform?'

They stood under the awning at the entrance while the rain continued. The tumult in the station was considerable, and Avraham needed to go inside and put an end to the Chinese whispers that were spreading, that a criminal had shot a policeman who tried to arrest him or that an armed terrorist had infiltrated the station and fired a gun, but he stayed outside for a moment longer to calm down and think.

'So who is he then?' Ezra asked. They stood right beside one another so as not to get wet, and the steam rising from Ezra's cup of tea reached Avraham as well. 'He was suspected of murder,' he said. 'Did you manage to speak with him before he fired the shot?'

'Speak about what? He entered and immediately pulled out the gun. I didn't see him at all before then. By the time I saw him he was already on the ground.'

'And he didn't say anything to anyone? He didn't scream anything?'

'Not a word.'

Ezra tossed away his cigarette butt, pulled a packet out of his trouser pocket and lit another one, and when he brought it to his mouth Avraham noticed that he had already washed his hands. He, by contrast, didn't wash his hands until the afternoon and not only because he didn't have time.

Fifteen minutes after he got back to the station he was already being pressed to provide explanations, and he realized that Ma'alul was right. The only thing that interested his supervisors was verifying that Bengtson was the murderer. They didn't want to know if he would live and perhaps even hoped that they'd be able to announce from the hospital that he had died on the operating table. They questioned Avraham only about the evidence.

The Tel Aviv district commander, Doron Mizrahi, arrived at the station with the district spokesman, and they conducted a preliminary inquiry in Benny Saban's office. The main entrance to the station was closed, and the reception was indefinitely shut down. The police commissioner demanded an immediate report on the incident and the minister of internal security was also told, even though he was on a trip to Berlin. First it was necessary to repudiate the rumours that the man who was shot was a policeman, as well as those about a terrorist infiltrating the station. In Saban's office there weren't enough chairs and Avraham stood the entire time, but this didn't bother him.

'Can you explain to us what happened? Saban told me that he's a suspect of yours,' Mizrahi said, and Avraham tried to explain, to himself as well.

Everything was supposed to have happened differently.

He had planned to question Bengtson that morning.

The investigation file was ready and the evidence was arranged in order, and the questions that he had prepared last night on the porch and the previous day in his office were written down on a piece of paper. *Can you tell me what happened when you arrived last Monday at Leah Yeger's flat? When did she become aware that you're not a policeman? As soon as she opened the door? Or only when you sat at the table and began speaking?*

He hadn't expected Bengtson to answer his questions straightaway, but he had thought that, once he understood that they had enough evidence to place him near the murder scene, he'd break. He'd planned to show Bengtson the photograph in which he was seen in a police uniform, and to place his umbrella on the table. Bengtson would crack – this had been clear to Avraham when he'd prepared himself last night for the interrogation – and he only feared that at the last moment he'd manage to flee the country with his Australian passport, and therefore a detective team had been stationed outside the building where he lived and was prepared to immediately implement the arrest and search warrants issued by the court.

Doron Mizrahi spoke to Avraham quietly. Avraham didn't know him, since he was new to the position and had arrived from Jerusalem, and had only heard that he was thought of as an officer who liked getting down to details and being involved in operations conducted under him, especially white-collar investigations. Saban looked on with concern when the man presented Avraham with his questions, but he didn't appear agitated and made no accusations. He jotted a few things in a notebook while

Avraham spoke. The district spokesman, who sat next to him, typed non-stop on a laptop without interrupting the conversation.

'Can you tell me what you know about the gunman and to what extent you're certain that he's involved in the murder of this woman? And how on earth did he enter the station with a weapon?' he asked, and Benny Saban said quickly, 'We are absolutely sure of this,' even before Avraham had started to answer.

At the beginning of the day Avraham had honestly thought he knew all he needed to know about Bengtson. That he understood why he dressed up as a policeman and questioned rape victims and what had happened at Leah Yeger's flat the week before. Afterwards, it became clear that he didn't know everything. Although he had proof that Bengtson was in the building at the time of the murder, he was still missing a last piece of evidence that he had been in the apartment itself, and this he would obtain easily from Bengtson's DNA and fingerprints. He had also been convinced that Bengtson would admit to it during questioning and believed that a search of his home would turn up the handbag that he had taken from Yeger's flat in order to disguise the murder as a robbery or the mobile phone on which he recorded her speaking, or the calendar he took from her kitchen. But since then, things had changed. Mazal Bengtson had apparently been frightened by the questioning two days earlier, and decided to turn in her husband without knowing that he was suspected of murder. And the announcement that she was on the way to the station disrupted his plans. He instructed the detective team to delay executing the arrest and search warrants until he heard what she had to say, and he received her in his office without knowing why she had come or what to ask her, and the uncertainty made him anxious because he had been so prepared. Despite this, while questioning Mazal Bengtson he still had a sense that everything was under control and that the changes to their plans were even working in their favour, and he didn't think he was wrong when he hid from her what they truly suspected her husband of having done. She came to the station voluntarily and said that her husband dressed up as a policeman and questioned rape victims. And she even explained, without understanding its significance, how Bengtson obtained addresses and telephone numbers of rape victims from a list of women who participated in a support group that she had in her possession, and Avraham felt that the decision to postpone the execution of the arrest warrant and listen to her was the right thing to do.

But there was also one moment during her interview in which Avraham's confidence was shaken, and he didn't share it with Doron Mizrahi. Perhaps he should have realized that nothing would play out as he'd expected, because from the start of this investigation almost everything had happened by chance. This was when they were trying to understand how Mazal Bengtson knew that her husband was dressing up as a police officer, and asked her about this over and over until she broke and said, '*Because he did the same thing to me.*' Avraham halted the questioning and left the interview room, not only because she had burst into tears but also because, suddenly, he wasn't sure that he understood Bengtson or his motives. And after she told Vahaba what had happened in their home, he understood even less. Mazal Bengtson again said, '*You don't know Kobi; he did the same thing to me,*' and Avraham looked at her through the glass window of the interview room and thought that perhaps she was right. And also that he should not under any circumstances have brought her into the interview room and interrogated her after what she had been through. Then she had suggested that she get Bengtson to come to the station. Avraham explained to the Mizrahi and to Saban that he had hesitated at this point, but then accepted her suggestion because he thought that this way Bengtson would be apprehended unprepared. He would be brought to the interview room, ostensibly on other grounds, and only there would discover that he had entered into a trap. Mazal Bengtson had begged that they not arrest her husband at home, and her plea had also influenced his decision.

Saban looked askance at Mizrahi when he lit a cigarette, since smoking in his office was forbidden. He handed him a coffee mug for the ash and got up to open a window, and Mizrahi straightened in his chair and placed his notepad on the table.

'How much time passed, from the moment you called him until he arrived?' he asked, and Avraham said, 'It took him some time to get here.'

They waited over an hour for Bengtson, and already by then it was clear that something was wrong. He didn't come straight to the station, and the detective team trailing him informed them that the suspect had gone to his home. For a moment Avraham considered instructing the detectives to go up to the flat and carry out the arrest and search, but the temptation to surprise him unprepared in the interview room was too great, and there was also the promise Avraham had made to the wife. When Bengtson got into his car and drove in the direction of the station, the detective team told them that he was on his way but didn't inform them that he was wearing a uniform. And Avraham had been relieved. He had asked Lital Levy to make him another black coffee and again arranged the papers on his desk and then called Ma'alul, who said, 'It's nice when the fish jumps into the net by himself, no?'

Had Bengtson noticed that he was under surveillance? Or did he know that his wife planned on turning him in and that she had laid a trap for him? In contrast to Mizrahi and Saban, these were the only questions that interested Avraham, and to get answers, the doctors would need to save Bengtson's life. He peeked at his phone, but Ma'alul hadn't yet sent him a text from the hospital. And it was impossible to call him in the middle of being questioned by Mizrahi, which was going on and on.

'How did he have a gun, do we know?' he asked, and Avraham said, 'He was a security guard.'

'And you didn't take into account that he'd be carrying a weapon when you called him to the station?'

'According to the information that we received, he is not presently employed by any security company.'

'And do we know what the connection was between him and the victim? What's her name – Leah?'

'There was no connection. As I said, her name was apparently on a list of victims from his wife's support group. And he apparently set up a meeting with her, as he did in earlier instances with other victims, with the aim of questioning them. And apparently she figured out that he was impersonating an officer.'

Doron Mizrahi placed his burning cigarette in the mug, and Saban looked at him anxiously. 'There are too many "apparently"s in your answer,' the commander said. 'I don't like that. It's enough of a mess if a murder suspect enters a police station with a weapon and shoots himself in front of civilians and police, but it's an even bigger mess if he's wrongly suspected. So let's get his DNA now, and thank God we aren't wanting for pieces of him down there, and we'll compare them as quickly as possible to the DNA found at the scene. And have you sent someone to his home to look for her handbag or that list of victims?'

'I'll go there myself,' Avraham said.

'And please prepare a report about what happened, because we need to brief the police commissioner and the minister and put out a formal announcement. In the meantime, there's a gag order, but we must publish something by tomorrow morning. And please emphasize in your report that the two of them arrived at the station voluntarily. The husband, and the wife as well. And that the evidence points unambiguously to the fact that this man who committed suicide is the killer.'

Saban said, 'No problem, Doron. There will be a full report by tonight, right, Avi?' When Mizrahi interrupted and asked, 'And what's happening with the wife? Did she see him shoot himself? Is she still at the station?' Avraham looked at Saban because he didn't know what to answer.

He hadn't seen Mazal Bengtson since the shooting. Only when he left Saban's office did he see her through the glass window of the interview room, folded up in Vahaba's arms. For a moment he debated going in, but in the end he only knocked on the window.

'Did she see him?' he asked Vahaba, repeating the question Mizrahi had asked him.

'You didn't hear her scream? I managed to stop her two metres before she reached him.' Vahaba's eyes were red.

'And does she understand what happened? Did you tell her why we were looking for him?' he asked, and Vahaba said, 'Yes. Did I have any choice? She says that she murdered him. That because of her he's dead. And she wants to go to the hospital. Can I take her there?'

What could he say to her? That he too wanted to go the hospital? Vahaba noticed the blood that had turned brown between his fingers, and perhaps that was why she asked him, 'And how are you?' And even though he knew that this wasn't what she had asked, Avraham said, 'I'm heading out to their flat. Can you ask her for the key?'

That was the closest Avraham would get to Bengtson that day. He had been asked to find a suicide note or a handbag or a list of rape victims that would prove Bengtson murdered Leah Yeger, but he searched for something else, exactly as Ilana had accused him of doing, but he admitted this to himself only a few days later.

He opened the door with Mazal Bengtson's key. The same smell was in the lift as he had noticed in Bengtson's car, a smell of wet clothes and dog hair. The windows in the living room were closed, and he turned on a light. And he remembered the girl who had stood by the door while he questioned her mother.

There were only electricity and property tax bills on the dining-room table, and in the sink were two bowls with the remains of cornflakes and a bit of milk. Avraham turned over the bills, and on the back of one of them read a handwritten note: *I'll be back in the morning. Sorry about everything. Tomorrow I'll explain to you what happened.* This wasn't Bengtson's suicide note. But when had he written it? And what had he needed to explain? In this flat no one had been murdered, but nevertheless Avraham felt as if once again he was walking through a murder scene. The silence was exactly the same silence. Quiet rooms that no one would live in any time soon.

As on his previous visit, two days before this, it seemed to him that no one lived there, as if the place wasn't a home or as if the tenants were preparing to leave for good. In the living room were the two sofas and the blanket, and the television. On one of the sofas was a princess costume that had been looked as if it had been forgotten when the tenants rushed to leave. And the picture of the hunted deer on the bare wall that reminded him immediately of the other picture. And it wasn't possible, but he had a feeling that he wasn't in the apartment by himself. The stairs that he hadn't climbed on his previous visit led him to a small room with a window that opened on to the roof. A washing machine and a plastic basket full of clothes – but the handbag wasn't there either. Nor on the table or in the chest of drawers which would have to be thoroughly searched.

He went out on to the roof and looked down over the cement railing, and he was able to imagine Bengtson looking from here down at the detectives' car parked in the street. Heavy clouds touched the roofs but the rain had stopped.

He already understood that he wouldn't be asking Bengtson the questions that he wanted to ask. *Why did you do it? Did you think you'd catch your wife's rapist?* He called Ma'alul and Vahaba, but there wasn't any news from the hospital.

Or perhaps you wanted to take revenge? But on whom?

The only room that he still hadn't gone into was the bedroom. And when he turned on the light he saw the white dog. It lay at the foot of the bed and didn't move from its place even when it noticed Avraham, just stretched its head and turned its watery eyes on him and then placed its head on the floor again. Even though he tried with all his might not to see it, Avraham's eyes met the picture hanging on the wall. He averted his gaze from the two bodies, while in his ears he heard again Mazal Bengtson's confession to Vahaba in the interview room, which he had observed through the glass window.

This was where Bengtson had worn the uniform for the first time.

It was as if all the things that Avraham had seen and the evidence that he had heard were crowded into this room: Leah Yeger's body was sprawled out next to the white dog, and next to her knelt her son, who had collapsed on her grave, and Mazal Bengtson was lying in the bed recovering from the rape, and her husband, who took care of her with devotion, entered the room dressed in a policeman's uniform and asked her to tell him exactly what had happened.

Every detail. From the beginning.

Avraham took a step into the room to convince himself that none of this was really there and to search the drawers next to the bed as well, and the white dog again stretched its head and looked at him, and his knees buckled and he had to leave.

He called Marianka from the office and told her that he'd be home tomorrow morning. She asked him if the killer had been arrested, and Avraham only said, 'Yes,' and didn't elaborate. The station was reopened to the public, and behind the reception desk stood a different policeman, not David Ezra. Police officers approached Avraham and asked him how he was doing, and no one blamed him for anything. Lital Levy checked whether he had eaten and had a sandwich sent up to him from the cafeteria, and before he took a bite of it he washed his hands in the bathroom.

Had Mazal Bengtson not been at the hospital with Vahaba, perhaps he would have gone there, but he had a report to write, and when Saban called to remind him that Doron Mizrahi was waiting, Avraham promised that he'd get started on it. Vahaba told him that the girls were with their grandparents and still didn't know a thing about what had happened, and that Mazal Bengtson wasn't at the hospital alone but with her twin sister.

When Ma'alul entered his office after five, Avraham still hadn't started writing the report. On the computer screen the video of the interview with Mazal Bengtson was paused, but he hadn't dared to watch it. In the document that he had opened only three lines were written, which soon cut off: *In my role as head of Leah Yeger's murder investigation staff, this morning I received Mazal Bengtson, the wife of the murder suspect, Yaakov Bengtson, who arrived at the station voluntarily and without advance notice in order to deliver—*

'You OK?' Ma'alul asked, and Avraham nodded.

'You sure?'

'Yeah.'

'I spoke to Saban, and it looks to me as if everything will work out, Avi. They think that we should have guessed that Bengtson had a gun but, assuming that he's the murderer, no one's going to come after us with too many complaints.'

When Ma'alul asked him, 'What else do you need to do, Chief? Can I help you with anything or should I go home?' Avraham was filled with a desire for him to stay so they could both watch the video of Mazal Bengtson's interview and the footage from the security camera at the station entrance in which Yaakov Bengtson could be seen shooting himself in the neck and then Avraham bending over him with David Ezra and stopping up his wound. And so they could write the report for Doron Mizrahi together. He said to Ma'alul, 'Sure, you can go,' and Ma'alul's dark eyes had a smile in them when he said to him, 'You sure?'

They watched it together. The gun was in Bengtson's hand when he opened the station door, but it was impossible to tell that he wasn't a cop. As Ezra had said, he didn't say anything, just pointed the barrel at his neck and pulled the trigger even before the door had closed. Avraham was in the puddle of blood and doing chest compressions. The shout that he remembered calling out wasn't picked up by the camera's video.

They noted down the exact times according to the footage and then switched to watching the interview with Mazal Bengtson, and when Ma'alul asked why, Avraham explained that he had to detail in the report how Bengtson had voluntarily offered to get her husband to come to the station. But once they started they were soon watching it for other reasons. Ma'alul was transfixed, even when Avraham was seen drawing near to Bengtson and raising his voice, when Avraham couldn't watch. He wouldn't question either of them again, nor would he get answers to his questions. Everything that was possible to know was to be seen and heard in the video being screened before them.

The rest of the conversation between Vahaba and Mazal Bengtson, which Avraham had watched that morning from behind the one-way glass, did not resemble the interview with him at all. Vahaba remained in the room without him, placed her hand on Mazal Bengtson's hair and stroked it while she spoke. She asked her, 'Mazal, do you want to tell me what he did to you?' And when Bengtson answered, it was in a whisper, and on the tape it was hard to catch everything she said.

'You don't know Kobi – he didn't want to cause any harm. He couldn't bear it any more.'

'So what did he do?'

'You have to know him to understand. I simply didn't want to revisit it. I didn't want to tell him. I just wanted to forget it all.'

'And he insisted?'

'Yes.'

'How did he insist? Was he violent with you?'

'He kept repeating it: "Tell me what happened."'

'Did he threaten you?'

'No.'

'Did he beat you, Mali? You can tell me the truth.'

'No, you don't know Kobi. He's not a violent person.'

'So why did he want to know?'

'. . .'

'Why did he want to know, Mali?'

'I don't know.'

'You didn't ask him?'

'It was hard for him not having a job, and he couldn't find one. He was ashamed that he wasn't supporting the family and that I was the only one working.'

'But how are they connected to each other?'

'They're connected. He couldn't stand himself any more.'

'But why did he want you to tell him about what happened in Eilat? Did he want to prove to the police that he could find whoever assaulted you?'

'No. He didn't try to find him.'

'So, what then?'

'He came home wearing the uniform. I asked him why, and he told me that he had been questioning a woman who had been raped.'

'Do you remember her name?'

'No.'

'Did he tell you what her name was?'

'I didn't ask him.'

'And when was this?'

'A few weeks after Eilat.'

'And what did he tell you? What did he do to this woman?'

'Like I told you. He went to her place and questioned her.'

'How did he know about her?'

'I didn't ask him. I think from the list I got from the support group.'

'And did he record her? Did he let you hear the recording?'

'Record with what?'

'What did you say to him about this?'

'You don't understand how he was. He cried all the time. He didn't want . . . you don't know Kobi; he wasn't supposed to be like that. Something happened to him. I don't understand what, but he had no choice. He wanted to be other things. And I think he wanted you to catch him. Maybe that's why he's gone back to doing it again now.'

'Why do you think he wanted us to catch him?'

'Because he was suffering.'

'Suffering from what?'

'From himself. From everything that happened.'

'And did you tell him yourself? So that he wouldn't do it to anyone else?'

'Yes.'

'What?'

'Everything. What happened in Eilat. My rape.'

'What?'

'Everything. How I went back to the room and he came

in while I was asleep, or was already on the balcony. How he put his hand on my neck, and the knife.'

'And Kobi didn't do it any more? Did that stop him?'

'He saw that it was hard for me, so he let me stop, but after a few days he put the uniform back on and asked again.'

'For the same story?'

'Yes. But with more details about how exactly he did it and how long it lasted.'

'And how many times did this happen? Once?'

'No, for maybe a month. Eventually, he saw that I couldn't take it any more so he stopped.'

'And why did you agree to tell him?'

'. . .'

'Did you agree because you didn't want him to do the same thing to other women?'

'Yes. What could I do?'

'You could have gone to the police about him, Mali. You didn't have to go along with it.'

'But I didn't want anything to happen to Kobi. I didn't want there . . .'

'What?'

'You don't know him; he wouldn't have been able to stand it. He's not strong and he was . . .'

Avraham and Ma'alul watched the video in silence and didn't discuss it at all that day. And when Ma'alul left Avraham's office in the evening, the report still wasn't complete. He saw Ma'alul out of the station and thanked him for staying with him, and when Eliyahu walked away in the direction of the bus station, Avraham asked for a cigarette from a man who was standing in front of the police station and smoked it. Its taste was potent and it scorched his throat, and when he put it out he walked to a kiosk nearby and bought two packs of Time, like he used to do.

The rain had stopped completely, but the streets still glistened with water.

He finished the report alone late at night and sent it to Saban some time after four in the morning. He noted that *Yaakov (Kobi) Bengtson murdered Leah Yeger on Monday 23 February at approximately 2 p.m.*, because that was what needed to be written, but he already understood that the murder began a long time before then, in a different room in a different flat, without any one sensing what had begun.

A few hours after this Vahaba called and informed him that Bengtson had died in hospital.

16

Yaakov Bengtson's mobile was found in his trouser pocket, and Vahaba brought it from the hospital the next morning. It was registered as evidence and passed to the Advanced Computing Unit, and a short time later the voice file Bengtson had recorded in the moments preceding the murder was sent to them by email. Avraham first listened to the recording in Saban's office, in the company of Ma'alul and Vahaba. He hadn't slept all night and hadn't showered since the shooting, and throughout that whole morning he barely said a word. In his pockets were a lighter and a packet of Time cigarettes, and every hour he went out to smoke on the stairs leading to the station.

And it was exactly as he had thought.

Bengtson began recording only once they had sat down at the kitchen table in Leah Yeger's flat, so Avraham couldn't hear the knocking on the door that he had imagined from the moment he entered the scene, nor the first sentences they said to each other, but the exchange that led to the struggle and murder were clear. Bengtson asked Leah Yeger to say her full name and her identity card number, and then said, 'Tell me please about the rape,' and she said, 'What do I need to tell?'

Bengtson's accent was more noticeable in the recording

than Avraham had expected. He now knew that it was an Australian accent, and that this was also the source of his strange last name. Bengtson had been born in Perth to an Israeli mother and an Australian father, and had arrived in Israel at the age of fourteen.

There was hoarseness in Leah Yeger's low voice, perhaps traces of the flu. What especially surprised Avraham was her confidence and courage.

Saban was glad the recording had been found, because it confirmed beyond any doubt, and prior even to lab tests, that Bengtson was the killer. Vahaba, who like Avraham hadn't slept all night, rested her elbows on the table and covered her mouth with her hands. Ma'alul looked at Avraham when Bengtson said on the recording, 'Tell me everything you remember. From the beginning. Where it happened, how it started. When you sensed that the rapist was there.'

The same questions that Diana Goldin had been asked.

Only Leah Yeger had said to him, 'What do you mean, "there"? I invited him to my home. He'd been my husband's partner.' And Bengtson said, 'Right, I mean, when did you feel that you were in danger?'

Leah Yeger was silent. Avraham wanted her to continue speaking, because when her voice was heard in the room it was as if he had succeeded in bringing her back to life. She said to Bengtson, 'But what you do you need this for? You know this.' The words in Bengtson's mouth shook when he said to her, 'For the process of our inquiry it's important that you tell us everything from the beginning.'

When Esty Vahaba's name came up suddenly in the recorded conversation, Saban and Ma'alul looked at her.

Leah Yeger had said to Bengtson that she would like to speak with the policewoman who took her statement, and he explained to her that he didn't have her phone number. 'I think I have it,' Yeger said. 'Her name is Esty.' From the creak of the chair it seemed she had got up, and Bengtson said, 'If you prefer to do this with the policewoman, then we can postpone it to another day,' and Yeger's response was not recorded by the device. The creaking of another chair indicated that perhaps Bengtson too had got up from his seat. A few seconds after this the recording was stopped, and the rest Avraham had to complete by himself on the basis of what he knew. And imagined.

Her fear. And his.

The quickening heartbeats of the two of them once they understood.

They didn't know one another, but nevertheless they were imprisoned there together with no way to escape. Everything could have happened differently, but the two of them had no such luck.

Saban asked, 'Can you explain why he didn't even erase this from his phone?' and Avraham remembered that Mazal Bengtson had said that her husband had wanted to be caught. Was that why he had left his umbrella in Diana Goldin's flat? And despite this taken a risk and repeated the same offence a few days later? And did Leah Yeger lock the door with the key so that Bengtson wouldn't flee? From the confidence in her voice, Avraham thought this was a possibility. Maybe she didn't lock the door and only walked quickly to the study to look there for Esty Vahaba's phone number, maybe in the diary that Avraham had found in the room, but didn't find it because in the end she called emergency services instead. When she went to the study Bengtson presumably tried to leave, but if Yeger did indeed lock the door, as Avraham imagined she had, he discovered that he was trapped there. So he followed her to the study. In Avraham's imagination Leah Yeger was holding the phone receiver but put it down when she saw Bengtson approaching. Did she hide the diary under the papers on the desk because she understood what was about to happen and wanted to leave a sign for him?

2.23. 2 p.m.

Bengtson pulled on the cord, tearing it from the outlet on the wall because he understood who she was calling, and that was when she knew.

But, even then, everything could have gone differently. He could have admitted that he wasn't a policeman and asked her to let him leave. And she could have opened the door for him.

'*Can you give me the key? I'd like to leave.*'

'*Tell me who you are.*'

These sentences weren't recorded and Avraham could hear them only in his mind.

Saban called Doron Mizrahi to let him know that he could breathe easy.

'*Please give me the key so that I can leave. I am a police detective.*'

'*What are you doing here? What do you want from me?*'

This was the beginning of the struggle which the downstairs neighbour had heard going on above him.

Buses passed by, and at the building site workers were lifting metal beams up to the top floor when Avraham next went out to smoke. The gunshot echoed in his head, drowning out everything else, and it was impossible to erase the images. Mazal Bengtson's distorted face in the interview room when she broke down. The empty flat that he had wandered around in without looking for anything in particular. The sight of the street from the roof and the sense that Bengtson had stood there before him and noticed the police car and the trap they had set for him. And David Ezra, crouching on his knees in the widening puddle of blood.

When Vahaba returned from the hospital before dawn, Avraham saw in her face not just exhaustion but sadness as well. When he went to Saban's office, he found them watching the video of the suicide and of the interview that preceded it. Vahaba was stroking Mazal Bengtson's hair on the screen as she said, *'You have to know him to understand. I simply didn't want to revisit it. I didn't want to tell him. I just wanted to forget it all.'*

'And he insisted?'

Avraham couldn't bring himself to watch it. Ma'alul suggested that they stop the video, but Saban insisted that they continue.

'Why did he want to know, Mali?'

'I don't know.'

'You didn't ask him?'

'It was hard for him not having a job, and he couldn't find any work. He was ashamed that he wasn't supporting the family and that I was the only one working.'

'But how are they connected to each other?'

Avraham got up from his seat, but before he left he heard Saban asking Vahaba if she understood what

Bengtson was explaining to her, and Vahaba answered that she thought so.

'Because I don't understand,' Saban said. 'Do you think that it turned him on? That that's what it was about? That it excited him sexually to talk to these women?' And Vahaba said no. She had spent the night with Mazal Bengtson outside the operating theatre where the doctors were fighting to save her husband's life, and Mazal Bengtson had insisted that if Kobi had found work he wouldn't have done what he did. When her husband died she just repeated, 'I murdered him,' and Vahaba tried to convince her that she had had no way of knowing or preventing what had happened. Other than Vahaba, there was only Bengtson's twin sister, who had arrived at the hospital in the evening and remained.

As Avraham left the room, he heard Saban saying, 'Her explanation seems like nonsense to me, Esty. I'm sure it was also a matter of sexual stimulation,' and his words blended with Mazal Bengtson's voice when she said to Esty Vahaba, *'You don't know Kobi, he wasn't supposed to be like that. Something happened to him. I don't understand what, but he had no choice. He wanted to be other things.'*

He remained at the station until the afternoon, even though he had nothing to do there and was exhausted. Leah Yeger's picture lay on his desk before him, as if the case wasn't closed, and next to it materials from the investigation, arranged in order, and the piece of paper with the questions he had written, planning to put them to Bengtson. *Can you tell me what happened when you arrived last Monday at Leah Yeger's flat?* He had to move on to other cases, the ones that he had been neglecting during his first murder inquiry. After all, the killer had been caught and shot himself, and there were no more questions to ask. Late in the morning there was even an article published on the news sites about the fact that the criminal who had shot himself the previous day at Holon police station was Leah Yeger's killer. There were no other names in the article because the court had only partially removed the gag order. And for some reason it was written that the killer's mobile phone had been found by the investigating team in the flat where the killer had resided, and that the voice file in which Yeger was recorded minutes before her death had been successfully restored by the Advanced Computing Unit of the Israeli Police, despite the killer having erased it from the device.

When Avraham went to Jaffa he discovered that most of the streets in Holon's city centre were blocked off because of the Purim carnival, and he recalled the costume he had seen on the sofa in the living room of the empty flat. He sat in a traffic jam for more than quarter of an hour while the floats with clowns and princesses and soldiers passed by on the main street. A boy aged five or six, wearing a black Batman outfit and a mask, was standing by Avraham's car window with his mother and little sister and didn't stop crying. And when he reached Abu Kabir detention centre they told him that Sharpstein had already released Leah Yeger's son from custody, so there had been no point in his coming.

On the way home, he called Erez Yeger from the car. He apologized for the fact that he had been arrested during the investigation, but he really wanted to say something else to him, perhaps that his mother was a brave woman, and that he too would always carry something like a fracture inside him, that sometimes, with the passing of the seasons, would ache faintly. He spoke to almost no one that day, until the evening, when everything burst out of him when he was with Marianka, but he tried to prolong the conversation with Yeger, even though the son, like him, said very little. Before they hung up Avraham asked him, without planning to, 'Are you still not ready to tell me why you hid your adoption and the phone call with your mother from us? That could have spared you the days in custody.' Yeger didn't answer.

There was no reason to ask these questions, because the investigation was over. Yeger was in his car heading north and Avraham needed to return to his flat, to take off the clothes he'd been wearing since yesterday and shower, and then sink into sleep and not think any more.

'You also don't want to explain why you haven't been in touch with her since she was assaulted?' he nevertheless asked, but he wasn't expecting an answer. Erez Yeger said, 'Because she had relations with him before.'

'With whom?'

'With David Danon, the so-called rapist.'

Avraham stopped his car at the side of the road because he was stunned by the answer. He turned off the engine.

'He didn't rape her. They were having an affair even before my father died.'

But this wasn't true! And the police investigation had proved it. This was the rapist's and his relatives' line of defence, and her son believed them and not his mother. And even if it was true that they had an affair, on the day he came to her to talk about the taxi, David Danon had raped Leah Yeger.

Avraham was silent and Yeger was as well, and only then did Avraham understand. He felt his heartbeat quicken, lit a cigarette and said, 'She called to ask you to come to her, right?' This was what Yeger had hidden and wasn't ready to admit even at the price of being arrested. He wasn't hiding from them that he was in her flat on the day when the murder occurred, as Sharpstein had thought, but rather that *he could have been there because his mother had asked him to come and he hadn't*. Had she wanted her son to be present at the meeting set up with the policeman so he'd believe her? He asked him again, 'She asked you to come to her, Erez?' And Yeger immediately said, 'That's not correct,' and then added, 'She didn't say anything to me about a meeting with a policeman, I swear to you,' but Avraham didn't believe him. And he didn't tell Yeger the things that he had planned to say about his mother's bravery.

Not until that evening, talking to Marianka, did everything he hadn't yet said, and which had been seething within him since the shot was heard burst forth.

Marianka wasn't in the flat when he got back, and this was a relief. He took off his trousers and blue sweater and put them in the full laundry basket. He stood for a long time under the flow of hot water in the shower. When he woke up from his sleep, it was dark outside and Marianka was home, but she didn't ask him anything, and when Avraham suggested that they go and eat out, she got dressed and waited in the living room until he had finished a coffee. They went to Tel Aviv, but there were children dressed up in the streets and the restaurants were decorated with colourful lights for Purim, and since they hadn't reserved a place, they couldn't get a table anywhere, and that was just as well, because at some of them they were greeted by waitresses with moustaches drawn on their faces. So they returned to Holon and sat in a café in Weitzman Square. His pasta in cream sauce was the first thing Avraham had put in his mouth since the day before, and he ate it quickly.

'Can you tell me what happened now?' Marianka asked him once he had finished, and he answered, 'Tell you what?'

'Why you feel so bad. So guilty. You caught the killer, no?'

He looked at her in surprise because he hadn't told her he felt that way. From time to time fireworks could be heard in the square, and revellers in fancy dress on their way to parties passed by the window. And he told her everything. How he had treated Mazal Bengtson harshly in the interview room and how he had hidden the truth about her husband from her. He hadn't said a word even when she offered to phone and invite him to the police station, and in fact had used her to trap her husband. And even though he had been trying to blur his guilt in his thinking, it deepened like the bloodstain on the blue sweater. He reminded himself over and over that Mazal Bengtson had told Vahaba that her husband wanted to be caught because he couldn't bear to suffer any more, and that he didn't even erase the incriminating file from his phone. Yaakov Bengtson watched the squad car parked in front of his building from the roof of his flat, of this Avraham was almost certain, and nevertheless he decided to go to the police station. And since watching Mazal Bengtson's interview again this morning, Avraham hadn't been able to stop thinking about something else: the fact that the man who raped Mazal Bengtson had put his hand on her neck and then placed the knife up against it and cut her – and that Yaakov Bengtson had shot himself in the neck as well.

Marianka interrupted him. 'So what are you guilty of, Avi?' she asked. 'He alone decided to shoot himself, no? Apparently, because he preferred not to deal with the consequences of what he had done. And you just did your job. You're a cop.'

Did she not understand that it wasn't supposed to end like this?

This was his first murder investigation, and it had ended with a man shooting himself in the entrance to the police station and dying in the hospital with his wife certain that it was her fault he had died. He only wanted to sit across from Bengtson in the interview room on the second floor of the station and try to understand.

Marianka didn't touch the salad the waitress set before her. And didn't drink the wine.

'But you're taking responsibility for things that you didn't do,' she said. 'You caught him, you didn't—' and Avraham didn't allow her to finish the sentence, because the things she was saying were so wrong. Other than them there were only an older couple and two waitresses in the café, one of whom looked at Avraham when he raised his voice. 'If I had revealed to her that her husband was suspected of murder, she wouldn't have turned him in, Marianka,' he said. 'Or she wouldn't have brought him to the station. Don't you understand? Do you not understand why he shot himself? He was sure that his wife had turned him in, that he had been betrayed by her, that he was left with nobody else in the world to trust, but she *didn't turn him in*, because she didn't know what he was suspected of. And even if he had committed suicide regardless, once he understood he was caught, at least it wouldn't have been *because of her*. Do you know what she said? That she killed him. That it was her fault he died.'

This was the thing that hadn't let go of Avraham since yesterday and which wasn't bothering anyone else. Not Doron Mizrahi, and not Benny Saban, and not even Ma'alul. And Marianka wasn't convinced either. She asked, 'Why are you certain that she didn't know what her husband really did?'And Avraham looked at her without understanding and said, 'What do you mean, why? Because we didn't reveal it to her. Because *I* didn't reveal to her that he was wanted for murder.'

'And she can't have understood this without you having told her? And turned him in for precisely that reason?'

Avraham shook his head, and Marianka insisted, and he didn't understand why until afterwards. She was really talking about herself and about him. And only when she told him this explicitly did he think that perhaps she was right and feel that he had to question Mazal Bengtson immediately to clarify what she had truly suspected her husband of when she entered the station to turn him in. But he didn't do this. In the weeks to come, after he heard from Vahaba that Mazal Bengtson had left her parents' home and returned to her flat, he went to her street a few times and waited in front of the building in his car, with the window closed. Maybe if she had noticed him and approached, maybe he would have asked her, even though Marianka and Vahaba both begged him not to.

Marianka said, 'You really think that you, who didn't know him, who never once spoke to him, you knew that he was a murderer, while his wife, who lived with him and who definitely saw him on the day he carried out the murder, and the next day, and who went through with him what she told you she went through, had no idea? She didn't see what he was going through and didn't see his gun or know that he would kill himself?' It was as if that gunshot could be heard again in his office. Marianka's eyes burned as she spoke, and Avraham was no longer so sure, even though he said, 'I'm sure you're wrong. Why would she bring him to the station for us, if it was like that? If she knew that she was pinning a murder on him. She thought that he had committed a minor misdemeanour and that he would be questioned and released within a few hours. And that they'd return home together. She told us this explicitly.'

'You're truly asking why?' Marianka asked.

'Yes. Why would she do this?'

'Maybe because she wanted it to be over. For the nightmare of their lives together to end.'

When they got back home Avraham called Vahaba and it seemed to him that he had woken her. He asked her if she knew where Mazal Bengtson was, and she told him that she was with her parents. He still wasn't sure that

Marianka was right, but her words appealed to him. If she was right it would be easier for him to clean the stain that clung to the blue sweater, but this wasn't the only reason he believed her.

The man who had assaulted Mazal Bengtson was never caught, and perhaps, he thought, she couldn't bear the possibility that another assailant would escape without punishment. That another woman would be, like her, the victim of someone who would never be found. For a moment he thought to himself that the case wasn't closed and that he had more to understand, and later that week he was tempted to go to the shiva being held at Mazal Bengtson's parents' home, or to the funeral. It took place at the civil cemetery in Herzliya, because Bengtson refused to have her husband buried in the plot reserved for people who had killed themselves. Vahaba told him that at the funeral there were no more than twenty people, and that Bengtson's father didn't come from Australia because of his poor health. The girls Avraham had seen in the apartment weren't brought to the cemetery either, and Vahaba didn't know what their mother had told them.

When the waitress approached their table and informed them that the café was closing, Avraham took out his wallet, but Marianka asked, 'Can you sit for another moment?' and he set it down on the table.

'I want to tell you something about us,' she said, and he listened, even though at first he was thinking only about Bengtson. 'I know that you were busy and that you were stressed and that my parents' visit was hard for you, but you're doing exactly the same thing with me. Exactly the same thing.'

He didn't understand what she meant, and he waited.

'Like what you're doing with the woman you questioned, Avi. You take responsibility for my decisions as if I'm a little girl, and blame yourself, and don't believe that I understand perfectly well what I'm doing and that I'm making decisions for myself.'

He looked at her as if he hadn't seen her for a long time. And tried to place his hand on her's but she wouldn't let him.

'From the moment I came, you have felt guilty that I'm here, as if I didn't decide to come to you. And then you close yourself off and withdraw and hide from me everything tied to your work, because you feel guilty that I left everything and you have a job and I don't yet know what to do with myself.'

He said that wasn't true, and Marianka continued anyway.

'But I'm here because I want to be here now. It was my decision. This is a chapter in *my life*, Avi, not just in yours. And you didn't force me to do anything. I know how to decide for myself what's best for me, do you understand?'

The things that Ilana Lis had said to him in their meeting rose up in his memory, and he tried to ignore them.

'I brought myself here, Avi, and if it doesn't work out for me, I won't stay. And maybe that's what's hard for you to accept and that's what you're trying to cover up when it seems to you that everything is your fault and your responsibility.'

When he asked, 'So it's not hard for you here?' he felt how much he had wanted to ask her this before, on each day that had passed since she arrived, not only since the murder investigation began. She said to him, 'Yes, it's hard for me.

Of course it's hard for me. It's hard because I'm a stranger here and don't know the language and because I miss things, but it's mainly hard with you. It's hard for me that you're quiet and hide what you're going through from me. And that you feel you need to shut the door and hide from me in order to eat. And that you've started smoking again and didn't tell me. I didn't come here to live alone, but to try to live with you.'

Her two hands were on the table, and when he placed his hands on them this time she didn't pull them away. He didn't understand how she knew that he had started smoking again. And Marianka said, 'You don't need to be a detective for that, Avi. There wasn't just a blood stain on your sweater.'

Avraham asked her, 'So if it gets too hard for you, will you really go?' and she said, 'Probably. Even though I don't know where.'

'Can I join you?'

'If you're not in the middle of an investigation.'

Outside the café the chairs were already stacked up in a pile, but Avraham wasn't yet ready to leave. Marianka suggested that they smoke a cigarette in the square.

'It's true that I don't want to think that I'm just a chapter in your life,' he said to her when they were sitting on a bench, and Marianka asked him, 'Why? What's so bad about that?'

'Because I want to be the whole book. Right up to the happy ending. Or until the bitter end.'

'And you might be. But that's what's beautiful about books, no? That you can't know in advance how they'll end.'

'In a detective novel you always know,' he said.

The guilty one is caught. The innocent continue with their lives.

'But our lives aren't a detective novel, Avi,' she told him. 'And besides, as you explained to me, it's always possible to prove that the detective is wrong, so maybe even a detective novel doesn't really end. Remember you told me that the day we met? On our first walk together in Brussels? Would you have believed it if I'd said to you then that a year later we'd be living together?'

He recalled this conversation at the café a few weeks later, the last time that he waited in front of the building where Mazal and Yaakov Bengtson lived, on the last day of March.

He had seen Mazal Bengtson a few more times before then, mainly when she went out alone to run in the evenings, but he didn't dare approach her and didn't know exactly what to ask. That day, Esty Vahaba told him that Bengtson had returned to work and asked her father to go back home and leave her alone with the girls. Avraham thought that this would be a chance to go up and knock on her door without any advance notice. He parked his car and waited in front of the building for almost half an hour, and as he had done a few times in the weeks that had passed, he took advantage of the time to call Ilana Lis, and this time someone actually answered. But it was her husband, who informed him that Ilana wouldn't be able to talk any time soon, and when he asked Avraham if he wanted to leave a message, he said it wasn't necessary.

The time was six o'clock and it was still light because the days were getting longer.

And just as he started the car, intending to drive off, he saw her. Mazal Bengtson exited the stairwell with the two girls and crossed the street with them, not very far from him. One of the girls held the leash of the white dog he had seen back then in the apartment. Did they notice him? And was he wrong when it seemed to him that her stomach curved out under the short shirt she was wearing? He turned off the car engine and then remembered the things that Marianka had said to him in the café, and waited for them to walk away before switching it back on and driving away.

His thoughts and imagination were occupied by cases that he had neglected during the murder investigation and cases that had been opened since then, but the picture of Leah Yeger was still on his desk, among them, for a few more days in April. And the heavy blue coat that he had worn on the day the investigation began and on the morning when he greeted Mazal Bengtson at the station still hung unworn on back of his door, because the storm was a receding memory and spring flooded his office with light.

EPILOGUE

After he fell asleep she left the bedroom and went to the study to call her parents. She hoped that her mother would answer, but when she heard her father's voice she was glad. For a few seconds they were silent, and then Marianka said to him, 'I called to apologize. That we said goodbye like that.' And he said, 'That's OK. We forgive you. And we've tried calling you a few times since then.' When she asked him if she had woken him and he said no, she suddenly felt how much she missed listening to herself speak their language, her language, and how life in English drew strange words out of her mouth.

'I'm sorry if we were—' he said, and she cut him off and said to him, 'Yes. I know. You were.'

There was in her a flood of love and anger and longing that had been dammed up in the last wordless days, and the conversation with Avi in the café freed her all at once. She didn't know if her father was able to hear this in her voice, because he was never able to hear anything. He said, 'But I truly don't understand what's keeping you there, Marianka. He—' and Marianka again interrupted him. 'Nothing's keeping me here. And if something's keeping me, it's not him. And what do you know about him? Did you make any effort to get to know him when you were here? From the first moment that you heard about him you were frightened that he would take me from you, like you were always afraid when I met someone.'

She was speaking much too loudly, but Avi was sound asleep. He had fallen asleep immediately after getting into bed, and she could still hear his deep breaths, which as the night progressed, would turn into snoring. Her father was silent and this made her happy because it meant that he was listening, but it also saddened her because she hoped that they would talk some more. She apologized for interrupting, and he said that they were thinking about what was best for her, and he didn't once say that he simply missed her. When he asked if the murder investigation had ended and she said yes, her father said, 'So perhaps now you two will come to visit us?' And when she went out to the street afterwards she thought about the two of them in Brussels, perhaps walking in the falling snow, because there the winter wasn't over. She sat for a moment or two at the computer in the study, considering writing an email, maybe a letter to Avi, or even a detective story – why not? – but she was too worked up to write, and for the first time she went out alone at night, as she had done when she had been a girl in Koper and afterwards in Brussels.

The blast of cold that she was expecting when she went outside didn't come. The dry, dusty air cast a strange foreignness upon her. The streets of Holon were empty and most of the buildings dark, and Marianka didn't in fact know where she was going. Nor if all this wasn't a mistake – or the start of an adventure.